'One of the most hypnotically gripping books I've read in a long, long time. Masterfully written and utterly unputdownable'
Tess Gerritsen

'The very definition of a page-turner – the sort of book that causes you to lose half a day without even noticing'
Elizabeth Haynes

'Utterly gripping, fast paced and scarily believable'
Lesley Pearse

'Gripping, intriguing and unputdownable. I loved it!'
Katie Fforde

'Fiendishly addictive'
Guardian

'A pacy psychological thriller that perfectly captures the voice of a stressed-out working mum'
Sunday Mirror

'Cracking dialogue, compelling characters and a page-turning plot . . . She writes with a singular voice and a fierce passion that roars off the page, while also displaying a visceral understanding of the betrayals and humiliations of domestic life'
Daily Mail

Also by Paula Daly

Just What Kind of Mother Are You?
Keep Your Friends Close
No Remorse (digital short)
The Mistake I Made
The Trophy Child

Open Your Eyes

Paula Daly

CORGI BOOKS

TRANSWORLD PUBLISHERS
61–63 Uxbridge Road, London W5 5SA
www.penguin.co.uk

Transworld is part of the Penguin Random House group of companies
whose addresses can be found at global.penguinrandomhouse.com

First published in Great Britain in 2018 by Corgi Books
an imprint of Transworld Publishers

A CIP catalogue record for this book
is available from the British Library.

ISBN 9780552174237

Typeset in 11.5/14 pt Minion by Jouve (UK), Milton Keynes
Printed and bound in Great Britain by Clays Ltd, Elcograf S.p.A.

1 3 5 7 9 10 8 6 4 2

For Patrick

Dear Ms Jane Campbell,

Thank you for sending us your novel, which we have now read and considered. We are sorry to say though that your novel is not something this agency could feel 100 per cent confident of being able to handle successfully. However, there are as many opinions as there are agents and publishers, so we wish you all success in finding suitable representation elsewhere. Due to the large number of submissions we receive, we're afraid we're unable to respond individually to your query, or to provide feedback on your work.

Sincerely yours,
Phoebe Claystone
Literary Agent

1

Another year of my life . . . wasted. All that work. All that time I'd devoted when I could have been doing something else. Something more productive.

Hell, I could probably have learned Mandarin by now.

I was at a literary festival once. Nick Hornby was speaking. He was promoting his latest novel and a middle-aged woman in the audience stood and asked, voice quaking, how one kept writing in the face of constant rejection. It was very brave of her, I remember thinking at the time. Nick cleared his throat and I'm pretty sure we all expected him to tell her that she must *keep going*, that persistence really was key, and that all the great novelists faced rejection at some point or other. We thought he'd say that the only difference between a published novelist and an unpublished novelist was that the former persevered for longer.

But he didn't.

He asked how long the woman had been writing without success. Sheepishly, she replied, 'Around ten years.' And he told her that she might want to move on to other pursuits. Something less difficult, he said. Save yourself all the heartache and get back to enjoying life, he said.

There was a collective gasp from the audience. We were stunned.

Often these events are filled with would-be writers, hoping that the genius of the speaker will somehow float through the air, above the heads of our fellow audience members, choosing to inhabit *us*. If only we work hard enough, concentrate for long enough, if only we want it so much more than the person in the next chair, it *will* happen. Yet here was Nick Hornby telling us that hard work and yearning were not always enough. That if it wasn't happening then maybe we should give up.

That was ten years ago. At the time I'd been writing for a few months – short stories and whatnot; I felt certain I could be the next big thing. All I needed was an idea. An idea for a novel that could propel me through four hundred pages. Through one hundred thousand words. Through months of toil and frustration.

And in the end, one came. And then another. And another. I now had six unpublished novels on my computer, and it was looking as if no one was interested in novel number seven.

I had been rejected so many times that I had even developed a method of coping, a method to get through the hurt as quickly as possible, so that I might get straight back to work and begin the process of constructing a new novel all over again. The secret was to *feel* the pain. To give myself permission to cry as much as was needed and allow at least two full days of mourning when I didn't try to look on the bright side of things. When I didn't try to smile. Only then would the grief and humiliation begin to fade.

Why did I want to be published so much?

I had no idea.

All I knew was that the hunger, the longing to be a

published author, wouldn't go away. Even when I was presented with the evidence. Presented with evidence in the form of rejection after rejection, that I should, as Nick Hornby said, move on to other pursuits.

'It's the marketplace,' Leon said. 'It's the weak pound. Brexit. Jane, you know all of this.' Leon looked at me and could see I was upset. He softened his voice. 'You know how hard it is to break into publishing right now,' he said. 'The small houses are almost bankrupt. They can't take chances on new authors the way they used to. They can't give them the time they need to develop a career. It's not your fault they don't want your work . . . but I don't get why it has to hit you so hard every time.'

Leon was an author.

A successful author.

He wrote a series of gritty crime novels set in Liverpool featuring a tough-guy, vigilante detective named DS Clement. Think Dirty Harry, but black, and with a Scouse accent.

DS Clement liked to take the law into his own hands, acting as judge, jury and executioner. Though he always left a little room in his life for romance, as Leon's readers were, as is generally the norm, mostly women.

Leon closed the email from the literary agent. 'You need to take a break,' he said. 'A complete break. The whole thing's making you unhappy. It's all you think about . . . and besides,' he said, gesturing to the kids, 'they need you.'

'They need you as well, Leon.'

Leon sighed. 'They're growing up with a mother who's distracted.' He tapped his temple twice with his index finger. 'Your head is always elsewhere, baby. You imagine life would be so much better *if only* . . .'

'Find me a mother who's *not* like that, Leon,' I snapped. 'Find me a mother who doesn't think her life would be better *if only.* That's how mothers of small children get through their days.'

'Yes,' he said, beginning to lose patience now, 'but probably for good reason. Either they've got six kids, or they're bringing them up single-handedly. Or else they have a shitty job.'

I didn't have a shitty job. I taught creative writing. For a few hours a week.

Leon sighed again. 'Jane, you have none of those problems. Why can't you just accept that this is—'

'You don't have any of those problems either, and yet I don't exactly see you falling over yourself to "be present" with your children, Leon. Every time they need you, you're slinking out of the room, hoping I won't notice. Every time I ask you to do something you don't hear me, or you give some vague response that I'm supposed to interpret as *the writer of the house is thinking.* What about me? What about my career?'

'What about your career?'

'Don't do that,' I warned.

'Don't do what?'

'Don't do what you always do when we have this argument. Belittle my attempts. Make out like what I do is some kind of charming hobby. Whereas your work, of course, takes precedence. Your work is so bloody important because it—'

'Jane,' he said levelly. 'The reality is my work pays the bills. What exactly do you want me to do?'

'Oh, fuck off.'

It was actually Leon's birthday.

We had to be at his mother's house in half an hour for a special birthday lunch.

'I'm forty-six years old,' he'd said earlier that morning when we were lying in bed. 'Why am I, a grown man, going to my mother's house on my birthday?'

'Because she wants to see the kids and she wants to make you something nice to eat.'

'Surely by the time a person's reached forty-six they've earned the right to do whatever they please on their birthday? Every year it seems we end up doing the exact thing I least want to do.'

'Next year I'll make an excuse. What would you like to do instead?'

'Stay in bed,' he'd said, shooting me a hopeful look. 'Read. Watch TV. Open a bottle of wine. Have good afternoon sex with my wife. She might dress up a little. Something slutty. Any one of those things would make me a happy man. Just one of those things—'

'The kids are four and a half and nearly three, Leon. You can say goodbye to that dream birthday of yours for at least another five years.'

'Remind me why we had them again?' he'd said, smiling.

'Because our lives were empty and meaningless without children. Remember?'

'No.' He'd started to laugh. 'I don't remember ever feeling that way.'

We bundled the children into the back of the car. It was mid-August and Liverpool was hot as hell. We lived on the edge of the city, L17, close to Sefton Park. The house was Victorian, three-storey, semi-detached, on a leafy street. Lark Lane was just around the corner with its independent grocers, decent takeaways, Keith's Wine Bar. It was our dream house. Parking was a bit of an issue as the Victorians didn't exactly plan these streets with two- and three-car households in mind, but other than that we were exactly where we wanted to be. We shared the street with Liverpool's well-heeled: a barrister next door (Cilla Black's nephew), retired headmaster opposite, the owners of a luxury car dealership diagonally across to the left. There was a student house a little further along the street, but now, at this time of year, it was empty.

We'd been in the house for eighteen months. It was bought with the advance for Leon's fourth novel, back when he sold the rights to Germany. Germans read *a lot*, by the way. Making it big there can be akin to a recording artist breaking into America. Leon hadn't made it big yet though. He was still what publishers referred to as a midlist author. Still building his brand.

Those really big sellers? The authors you see on the *Sunday Times* Rich List? Forbes? Well you could fit those people into a small minibus. They're freaks. Oddities. Phenomena.

The general public has the misconception that anyone who writes a book is automatically a multimillionaire, but the reality is, most novelists earn less than a thousand pounds per year for their trouble. Or in my case, nothing at all. The few hours I spent teaching creative writing was the closest I got to making any money from the craft.

We always argued when we went to see Leon's mother. There wasn't anything particularly wrong with Gloria Campbell per se. As mothers-in-law went she was pretty standard issue; it was just that neither of us wanted to give up our afternoons to make the half-hour trip to Formby, when we could have been doing nothing instead. We didn't voice this to each other though. Instead, we'd partake in a constant, low-level bickering, our dread at making the trip coming out as snide remarks to one another. Dread, too, at visiting the red squirrel sanctuary for the hundredth time, dread at wading through another mountain of curry goat, rice and peas, a batch of which Gloria always had on the go.

Leon's father, Michael, had been born on Upper Parliament Street in the late forties to a Jamaican father. And here's a fun fact: there are more Campbells per head in Jamaica than there are in Scotland.

I'd always assumed when I saw the Frasers, Campbells and Stewarts lining up at the start of the hundred metres, ready to represent the Jamaican athletics team, that the array of Scottish names was a legacy of slavery, when slaves had been issued with the same names as their owners. Not so. In fact, it was Oliver Cromwell who, in the 1600s, by banishing Scottish convicts to the West Indies, became responsible for the proliferation of the Campbell name.

Leon's grandfather came over from Jamaica to Liverpool in 1948, encouraged by the British government to help fill the labour shortage caused by the war. He was put to work on the dock road. And that's how I ended up with two kids, Jack and Martha, who had a curious, but beautiful, combination of features: skin the colour of butterscotch, red afro hair and pale blue eyes. My neighbour, Erica, said they belonged in a Benetton ad.

The hair and eyes were from me, of course. I'm your typical redhead. My white skin burns on a cloudy day on a north-facing slope, and you can see the blue blood of my veins through the skin of my neck. Sometimes, I think I would do better living beneath ground.

But recent research says we age better. So there.

'Did you tell her we couldn't stay long?' asked Leon now. We were in the car. Leon turned the ignition. It was stifling hot but the air con took a while to kick in so we had the windows down.

'She's made a cake.'

'My mother always makes a cake. She likes making cakes. It's her thing.'

I shrugged in a helpless way.

'Shit, we've not shut the garage . . . Did she mention the squirrels?' he asked.

'Not this time,' I lied.

The squirrels were Gloria's preferred activity with the kids. Their sanctuary at Freshfield was just over a mile from her home and she derived great pleasure from the small reds, instructing her grandchildren on their merits, while at the same time maligning their evil grey cousins: 'Vermin! Imposters! No better than rats!'

'I don't want to get stuck there all day,' Leon said. 'Will you drive home later?'

I pulled a face.

'What?' he said.

'I hate driving through town at teatime.'

'That means I can't have a drink.'

'So, have a drink when you get home.'

'I don't want a drink when I get home,' he said. 'Fuck . . . if I'm stuck at my mother's on my birthday, I'm definitely having a beer.'

'You say this as though I arranged it. Like I called your

mother up specifically and said, "Leon would like nothing more than to spend his entire birthday with you, Gloria." And please stop swearing in front of the kids.'

'They have their headphones in.'

'They can still hear you.'

Leon turned in his seat. 'Martha, d'you want to skip Nanna's house and go straight to Disney?' When Martha didn't so much as lift her head, he said, 'We could leave right now, call at McDonald's, eat as much as you like. Eat till you explode. What about you, Jack?' he said. 'Disney, right this second. What do you say?'

Jack removed one of his earbuds. 'What, Daddy? I can't hear you.'

'It's pardon, son.'

Leon turned back to me, eyes shining, vindicated.

He held my gaze as he began playing with the hem of my dress. 'Your legs are looking good, baby . . . What about if we sacked going to my mother's altogether? We could get the paddling pool out for the kids . . . lie in the back garden . . . I could get a grip of you in that bikini. The blue spotted one. The one that shows off the curves of your arse so nicely.'

He lifted my dress a little. 'You know,' he went on, 'we could probably go at it right here and the kids wouldn't even notice.'

Playfully, I slapped his hand away. 'Sooner we get there, sooner we'll be back.'

'Jane,' he said, his tone mock-serious. 'I'm getting older. Every day I don't get to make love to you is another day wasted.' He leaned across and kissed me. He remained there, his mouth on mine, until, involuntarily, I reached for him.

I always reached for him.

'I'm so in love with you, Jane Campbell,' he whispered.

When eventually we pulled apart, the heat inside the car forcing us to, Leon must have caught sight of something in the rear-view mirror. He closed his eyes for an extended moment, as if in irritation.

'Great,' he said under his breath. Just as I became aware of a presence at the driver's-side door.

It was Lawrence from the house opposite.

'A word, if you don't mind, Leon?' Lawrence said.

'Actually, we're on our way out. It's my birthday and my mother's holding a party. We're really keen to get going as fast as possible, Lawrence, because—'

'Shan't take a minute.'

Lawrence and Rose Williams were in their seventies, originally from Mold in North Wales, and had lived on the street for thirty years. He'd been the headmaster at an independent over the water in Birkenhead, and Rose had taught physics at the same establishment. They had one oddball son, were keen gardeners, and got very hot under the collar if people didn't park in their proper places.

I turned to Lawrence and smiled. 'Morning!' I said cheerfully, too cheerfully perhaps, embarrassed he'd caught us in the midst of kissing, but Lawrence didn't hear me. This happened often of late. He seemed to have something on his mind.

Last summer, we'd taken a cottage for two weeks on the Jurassic Coast in Dorset. And it was so idyllic, the weather so kind to us, that we extended our stay by another week when the people renting the cottage after us pulled out. Atypically, Leon was on a writing roll, and when that happened he could work just about anywhere. Mornings, I'd get the kids out from under his feet, spending my time paddling in the sea with them, making things in the sand behind a striped windbreaker. Afternoons, we napped or took turns pushing Martha in the pram if she was being fractious. In the evenings, we cooked. And once the children were asleep, we drank, watched an arty film, and got quite giddy in the bedroom. It was parenting perfection. The only time I could remember feeling absolutely at peace with my situation as the mother of two small people who had arrived in our lives and completely taken over.

We returned home tanned, healthy, and really rather pleased with ourselves. We'd managed to make a success out of our first proper holiday together and we felt bolstered. We were in love with each other and in love with our beautiful babies and we came back excitable and happy, ready to pick up our lives in Liverpool. What we found when we got there was a very angry Lawrence Williams, waiting for us.

It seemed we'd made the staggeringly grave error of leaving my car on Lawrence's side of the street for Three Whole Weeks while we were away. What we should have done, according to Lawrence, was to leave my car in our *own* driveway, the single space usually occupied by Leon's car. This would have shown proper consideration to the other residents and of course would have been *the right thing to do.*

We apologized. We didn't see what the big deal was but we were new to the area and didn't want any acrimony. We pretended we were sorry. We sent flowers to Rose, who was rather distressed after having been forced to look at my car for almost a month, and we did our utmost to placate them.

Unfortunately, though, their displeasure ran too deep. And since last summer we'd committed a number of other transgressions, quite innocently, which had caused further insult and indignation in the Williamses' household. Lawrence and Rose had taken to speaking Welsh to one another now whenever one of us was within earshot – which made Leon's blood boil. So, in response, Leon would address me in French. Loudly.

This was amusing. But since I knew not one word of French, aside from the standard greetings, it was really rather pointless all the same.

'Hello, Jane,' Lawrence said, as if I'd not spoken seconds earlier and so I had to say 'Good morning, Lawrence' in return all over again. He was a tall guy, thin and rangy, with a broad forehead. When expressing certain emotions, the corners of his lips would pucker, which could give the impression of him having a mean little mouth. He was twitchy and clearly upset about something today.

On account of his height, Lawrence had to dip over to his right slightly to get a good look at the children in the back seat. I saw his eyes narrow at the sight of their headphones and tablets but he fought the urge to comment, saying instead to Leon, 'It's the cat, I'm afraid. It's taken to . . .' and pausing, checking the children were quite deaf to his words. 'It's taken to crapping in the raised beds again.'

'Can we do this later?' Leon said.

'No. We're going to sort this out now. It won't wait.' Lawrence cleared his throat. 'How would you feel plunging your hands into cat faeces daily, Leon? Rose's near sick with the stress. It's disgusting stuff and if you can't control your animal then we're going to have to—'

‘What, Lawrence?’ Leon snapped. ‘What will you have to do?’

Lawrence straightened his spine and took a step away from the car. ‘You’re being combative,’ he said gravely. ‘We’ve talked about this, Leon. I won’t deal with you when you’re being like this. It can be threatening.’

I stared straight ahead.

Leon could be combative. And he was six foot two inches tall with a shaved head and packed a lot of muscle, so yes, he could appear threatening.

‘So, don’t deal with me, then,’ Leon said. ‘I’ve already told you, Lawrence, cats are above the law. Look it up. If I had a dog and it was shitting in your garden you could have me prosecuted. But a cat, no. No one controls a cat. But you know all this. You know this and yet you continue to come around here and—’

‘Good that you should bring that up, because I *have* looked it up. Well, Rose did actually and she’s found a solution. A collar . . . Very reasonable. It has very good reviews and it might just put an end to this crisis.’

‘A collar,’ Leon said, flatly.

‘You’d need to set up the boundary wire around your property. And if the cat should try to stray across the said boundary, it would receive a small shock.’

‘An electric shock?’

‘Essentially, yes. But you’re making it sound far worse than it is. It won’t harm the animal, and, if you think about it, it will actually be safer. You won’t have to worry about it colliding with a car if it’s unable to cross the road.’

I had to kind of agree with Lawrence on this one. I loved our rescue tortoiseshell – Bonita. Loved her tiny, bird-like bones. Loved her to the extent that I found myself gritting my teeth whenever I picked her up, to stop myself from squeezing the life from her. I kissed her little head too hard and spoke to her in a ridiculous baby voice, calling her things like 'Little Lady' and 'Principessa'. But when she began crapping in my potted plants, a few months ago, I did rather lose patience. It felt like a personal affront. *Why must you punish me so when I give you everything you need?*

In desperation, I went online. I needed to put a stop to it before I lost my temper with Bonita. All the cat experts said the same thing: the cats don't do it in your potted plants to pain you, to get at you in some way, it's just that the soft soil proves so *irresistible* to their little paws that they simply can't help it.

That made me feel a whole lot better.

The site advised covering the surface of each pot with gravel, which I duly did, and the problem was solved instantly. Except now it seemed as if Bonita had found some equally irresistible, freshly tilled soil in which to do her business: Rose's garden. And Rose's garden was Rose's medicine, Lawrence was keen on saying. Ever since she began suffering badly from migraines a few years ago, the garden was the only thing that brought relief.

'I'm not leaving until we have this resolved,' Lawrence said, putting his hands into his pockets and puffing his chest out a little.

'Then you can wait there all day, Lawrence, because we're leaving.' Leon revved the engine loudly. Then he turned to me. 'Run inside and get me four cans from the fridge. I'll need a beer when we get to my mother's and she'll only have that rubbish from Lidl she gets in for Derek from next door.'

I got out of the car and headed to the front door, avoiding eye contact with Lawrence. I didn't do confrontation.

Of course, I did it very well inside my own head. And in my writing I was marvellous: yelling at people, coming back with all manner of witty retorts. Saying the kinds of things you wished you could say in the moment but knew you never would.

In real life, I panicked. I tended to colour up and I'd get a tinnitus-like ringing inside my ears. So I avoided confrontation. And if I had the choice I let Leon fight our battles.

'Shut the garage door on your way back out, Jane,' Leon yelled as I put the key in the lock.

Once inside the hallway, I let my back rest against the wall. Sweat was running between my shoulder blades, down to my underwear. Perhaps I should hide in here for a while, I thought. Let those two argue it out and head back to the car only once they'd come to some resolution and Lawrence had left.

Leon revved the engine again. Translation: hurry up.

I hated it when he got like this. Sure, he loved the cat but that had nothing to do with this. He'd reached the stage with Lawrence where he wouldn't back down about anything. And Lawrence was *old*. I kept telling Leon that's what old people were like. They got upset about things and complained. That's what gave them purpose. Well, that, and taking drives out to garden centres for cups of coffee.

I grabbed a couple of cans from the bottom of the fridge and poured myself a glass of water. I drank it slowly. Then I refilled the glass and I drank again. I was giving Leon the chance to calm down because if he didn't he'd be yelling at every other driver all the way to Formby.

I went into the hallway. I could still hear muffled voices from beyond the front door, so I delayed going out for a little longer and it was then that I noticed the telephone answer machine blinking.

I hit play.

'It's your mother . . .' Then there was a long pause as my mother figured out what she needed to say next. She cleared her throat. 'Can you pick me up some . . .' Another pause. Her speech was slurred. 'Christ,' she said emphatically, 'it's gone clean out of my head what I needed. I'll call you back in a bit.'

This wasn't unusual because my mother took pills.

Lots of them.

Sometimes her speech was slow and laboured in the morning because of what she'd taken the night before. Sometimes because of what she'd taken that morning. She lived in a mid-terrace house in Tuebrook, its front façade painted an ugly shade of muddied red like every other house on the street, and she took the pills so she didn't have to feel disappointed any more.

She was often quite out of it, but she could function pretty well. If you met her on the street you'd think her charming, an immaculately turned-out redhead – though more Rula Lenska than Rita Hayworth – and you might think her mildly eccentric. She liked to shock. She said outlandish things. This was how she hid her problem. If you expected a certain strangeness from her you weren't then suspicious when she said or did something that didn't quite add up. Such as if she held her gaze on you for a moment too long. Or laughed inappropriately. Or had lipstick on her teeth.

I didn't wait for her to call back. Instead, I headed out.

Lawrence was now gone and so I shut the garage door. Leon had done his usual trick of pulling the car right up in front of the garage, which meant I had to lower the door from the side so I didn't get squashed between the door and the bonnet – always tricky as there wasn't a lot of space.

I climbed into the passenger side and fastened my seat belt. Leon was staring straight ahead, still with that hint of madness in his eyes that he got whenever he had to deal with Lawrence, so I said, 'You're not going to carry this on all day, are you?'

He didn't reply.

'You're ignoring me now as well?' I continued crossly. 'What the hell did I do? It's not like it's my fault that Lawrence always—'

Without speaking, without checking his mirror, Leon stamped on the gas.

And the car flew backwards.

I cried out in terror. Cried out because my first thought was: *Are the kids strapped in? Are they safe?*

There was no time to check.

'Leon!' I shouted. 'Leon, stop!'

But by now we were already stationary again. The car having smashed into Lawrence's garden wall behind us.

Leon's forehead was on the steering wheel and he was unresponsive.

The children began to cry.

2

I didn't tell anyone about the argument.

I was frightened they would judge Leon. Think that this big, strong, clever man had been sent over the edge by a silly neighbourhood dispute and given himself a stroke. Or else a heart attack.

So when the paramedic asked me what had happened, I said, 'Nothing.' I told her nothing had happened, other than Leon looking marginally strange when I got into the car. She saw the beer in the footwell and asked if he'd been drinking. 'No!' I exclaimed, horrified. 'Of course not! The kids . . .'

'Sorry,' she responded. 'Had to ask.'

We were now on the pavement outside our house. Two ambulances were in attendance. Leon was in the back of one of the vehicles and they were preparing to leave. He was breathing but he was unconscious.

'Breathing but unconscious.' I said the words again, aloud, as if this might somehow settle me. Leon was unconscious and I didn't know why. They couldn't seem to tell me why. Jack, Martha and I had been examined inside the other vehicle but we were OK. The paramedics said I was probably more shocked than the kids. Martha sat in my lap now, thumb in her mouth, and Jack was at the kerb. Someone had given him a Coke and he was throwing his head back every few seconds trying to drain the last few drops from inside the can.

I stroked Martha's hair as I gazed at the ambulance. I thought of Leon inside it and the space below my ribs began to ache. Martha made a small whimpering sound and I kissed the top of her head. Then I looked at Jack and the breath caught in my throat. This family was everything to me. *Everything.* And it just didn't work without Leon in it.

A paramedic approached and squatted down beside me. 'There's some trauma to your husband's head,' she said gently.

'Trauma?'

'An injury,' she said.

I felt confused. There was no trauma that I'd seen. No signs of any injury. 'He's not had a stroke?'

'We don't think so.'

For some reason, I felt momentarily relieved by this development. Leon was too young to have suffered a stroke. But then his dad had died young, from a heart attack due to high blood pressure. And hadn't I read somewhere that black men developed high blood pressure younger than the rest of the population? I'd have to check, I thought, making a mental note. I didn't think Leon had ever had his blood pressure measured, something we'd have to rectify in the future because—

'Mrs Campbell. Did you hear what I said?'

My mind was drifting.

The paramedic's accent was soft Scouse. Just a hint of where she was from. I wondered if she'd tried to lose it purposely. Or perhaps she'd had aspirational parents. Parents who'd corrected her speech and told her she sounded like a scally if she lapsed into the local vernacular.

Had I heard what she just said?

'What did you say?' I asked, dazed.

'We're going to transport him to Fazakerley.'

'I don't understand.'

'We think your husband has a brain injury.'

I blinked slowly. 'Like . . . inside his brain?'

She nodded. How could Leon be injured inside his brain? How was that possible when I was sitting right next to him?

Wouldn't his skull be damaged? Wouldn't there be signs of . . . something? *Anything?*

'Do you have somebody who could take the children?' she asked, and I didn't respond. 'Because, if so,' she went on, 'you can travel with us. I'm afraid there's not room for all of you. We have your husband stabilized for now but—'

'Why aren't you taking him to the Royal?'

'Fazakerley specializes in brain trauma. They have a neurosurgical team there.' She placed one hand on my forearm. 'Don't worry. It's where he needs to be.'

I looked past her. The scene was busy with bodies. The police were here, dealing with the car. I was aware of Lawrence shaking his head at his crumbled wall, his wrecked standing roses, his felled bird-feeding station, his demolished flagpole that carried the Welsh flag . . . I couldn't see Rose. The woman from number 24 was here as well. Her husband had left her last year and she wouldn't let him see the kids. We'd hear banging in the early evening, him calling her a bitch from outside her front door, but no one ever complained because we all felt kind of sorry for him.

'Mrs Campbell?' the paramedic said. I couldn't focus my gaze on her. Her voice sounded far away.

There were other people in the street. Some, I recognized: people who passed by our house on their way into town; dog walkers on their way to Sefton Park. But there was no one here that I could ask to take my children for me. No one I knew well enough to trust.

'I can't,' I said weakly.

I looked again at the ambulance. The one with Leon inside. The rear doors were still open.

He had looked so unlike himself when they'd eventually lifted him from the car. His face had lost all of its tone and he looked both younger and older at the same time. Nothing like my husband. Nothing like the man I'd sat with only moments before. He'd also soiled himself, which made the whole thing shockingly, sickeningly real. I think up until that point I hadn't properly registered what was happening, and it was only then, as I focused on Leon's compromised body, that I heard myself yelling at the bystanders, 'Get back! Get the hell away from him!' I was scared suddenly that they would witness Leon in this state and commit it to memory. It would be the one thing they would take away with them from here today.

The paramedic made to stand. Her face glistened with sweat. The heavy green cotton of her uniform was too warm for this weather.

'Will he die?' I mouthed silently.

'He appears to be very unwell,' she replied carefully. 'But . . . I always urge people to hope. It's important to hope.'

'What if something happens and I'm not with him?'

She saw my panic and she glanced towards the children before replying.

'Listen,' she said. 'Do you have someone you can call who can take them?'

I thought for a moment and nodded numbly.

'Do that,' she said. 'Then come to Fazakerley. Don't rush to get there. Take as long as you need and take care when you drive 'cause you'll be shaky. They're going to be busy with your husband when he arrives, CTing his head and so on. They may even take him straight to surgery. There's not a lot you can do there, so my advice would be to get the children settled and pack some essentials for yourself before setting off. It's probably going to be a long day.' She reached down and touched my shoulder.

'Thank you,' I said to her. 'Please thank your colleagues too for what they're doing for Leon. Would you do that?'

She told me she would. 'Good luck,' she said.

I put the kids in front of the TV and, my voice shaking as I tried to sound authoritative, as though I really, really meant it, I told them not to move until I came back. They made like statues. Held their breath. And I went to sit on the bottom stair and put my head between my knees.

I wasn't sure I could do what I had to do next.

I took two more breaths and called Leon's mother. She answered, saying, 'Why aren't you here yet? Where are you?' in a stroppy, aggrieved manner that she would soon forget as I explained to her in the best way I could what had happened to her son. Her only son.

We arranged to meet at the hospital and she said she'd phone Leon's sister in Manchester. 'Juliana'll want to know,' she said, and it was only on speaking her daughter's name that she started to cry. Like, really cry. As if up until that moment she'd held the tears of a lifetime inside her. I'd not seen Gloria weep, not even when Leon's father died. I'd always thought it was something she must do in private.

'Gloria,' I said, but her sobs were choking and she was unable to answer. 'Gloria,' I said again, louder this time. 'I'm so sorry, I really don't want to leave you like this, but I really must get someone to take the children.'

And I replaced the receiver. I could apologize later.

Then I called my neighbour, Erica, on her mobile.

I knew she wasn't at home. She lived diagonally opposite and would have been straight out of her house at the first signs of commotion.

'There's been an accident,' I told her quickly. 'It's bad. It's Leon. It's his head. I don't know anything else, but they've taken him to hospital and I . . . I don't know what to do. Can you come and watch the kids for me? I—'

I heard Erica say to someone: 'Sorry, love, but I won't be buying these after all,' before saying to me, 'Fifteen minutes. I can maybe get there in ten.'

3

Leon's head.

That's what this was all about. They were trying to save Leon's head.

I was in the relatives' room. I'd been here for thirty minutes and there was no sign of Gloria yet. I watched the door, eager for her arrival.

There was another family in the waiting room – another family in crisis. They were big talkers. And criers. Ones for big shows of emotion, and I felt very alone. From what I could gather, Grandad had slipped outside his back door while dealing with his pigeons. 'Pigeons that should have been got shut of years ago.' And, as a consequence, Grandad's head was now full of blood.

Was Leon's head full of blood?

That's what they were trying to find out.

On arrival at Fazakerley, once he'd been stabilized, they'd taken Leon straight to CT. But now they needed an MRI scan as well and a doctor wouldn't be available to speak with me until they had the results of that.

Leon had a beautifully shaped head. When our children were born, his mother had insisted that I let them sleep not on their backs, in accordance with the advice on preventing cot death, but on their sides. 'You want to put your babies to sleep on their *sides*,' she'd stressed. 'Keep them in place with a rolled-up blanket. See?' This was to prevent the unsightly, flattened, back-of-the-skull problem which Gloria said made people look like they had lower than average-sized IQs.

Leon shaved his head, which Gloria didn't care for. 'Makes you look like a thug.' But I knew she was secretly proud of the shape of her son's head because I would catch her eyeing it sometimes, pleased.

The paramedic had mentioned surgery.

Which was an innocuous enough word until you realized surgery to the head meant brain surgery.

Leon couldn't stomach the night-time medico-trauma documentaries I liked to watch. He could be remarkably squeamish, even with his thirst for all things crime. But I'd sit through emergency amputations, spleen reparations, quadruple bypasses, because I found them life-affirming. The one thing I did know from my limited knowledge of head trauma was that, after injury, the brain would swell. And it was this swelling, often as much as the trauma itself, which could cause brain damage or indeed often death. Sometimes they would cut the top of the skull away to give the brain more room to swell. I tried to push away the thought of this happening to Leon.

Gloria arrived twenty minutes later with Leon's sister, Juliana. With them was Juliana's on-off girlfriend, Meredith. We hugged and cried. Cried some more. And then, never really knowing what to say to Meredith, I murmured, 'You made good time,' and she smiled sadly, saying, 'Juliana was driving. You know how she can be.'

What Juliana could be was erratic. Which was generally the reason they couldn't seem to live together for more than a few months before it was all over again. Gloria didn't like it. She thought that as a gay couple they should show the world that they could stick it out for the duration. 'Set an example,' she liked to say. Which Juliana told her was 'totally fucking insulting'.

Juliana was the only one who swore at Gloria. Gloria was quite churchy – a Methodist. Her father had come over from Trinidad and married a woman from Wolverhampton, whom he'd met at church, and Gloria was brought up 'knowing Jesus'. She met Leon's father on a church day trip to Liverpool and they married soon after. I'd never heard Gloria actually *say* she disapproved of profanity, but I took it as a given, and so it was not something I did when I was around her. I swore at my own mother all the time. But that was different.

The door to the waiting room opened and a plump young woman in a grey tunic gestured to the other family with a slight nod of the head. They filed out after her in respectful silence and Juliana's gaze followed them. 'I hate hospitals,' she said. 'Can't stand the smell.'

'So, what have they told you?' Meredith asked me.

'Not much,' I said. 'They'll let us know what's going on when they have his MRI results.'

'I just don't get how he did this,' Juliana said. 'How does he go and knock himself unconscious by reversing into a wall? Wasn't he wearing his seat belt? He can't have been going that fast, can he? You were in your driveway, Mum said. Is that right?' Then before I could answer, she said, 'Shit. I haven't asked about the kids. Sorry, Jane. How are the kids? Are they injured? Are the kids OK?'

'The kids are fine. They're with a neighbour.'

'And what about you? Are you OK?'

'I'm fine. Shook up, but fine.'

We sat down. Juliana put her arm around Gloria and pulled her mother in towards her tightly. Gloria was doing her utmost to appear stoic but had been weeping silent tears since arriving. 'Think positive, Mum,' Juliana instructed and Gloria said, 'I am, love. You know I am. I'm praying for Leon.' She closed her eyes and dipped her head before clasping her hands together in her lap. Her lips began moving, almost imperceptibly, and the effect was such that the rest of us saw fit to close our eyes as well.

A few minutes passed before I thought it was the right time to say what was on my mind.

'I think Leon may have had some sort of . . . thing before he crashed,' I began carefully.

Juliana's eyes snapped open. 'What kind of thing?'

'I don't know what to call it. A funny turn. When I got into the car he didn't look like himself.'

'Did he say anything?' Juliana asked.

I shook my head. 'It was as if he couldn't hear me . . . He was almost trance-like.'

'Do you think he could have been having a stroke?' Gloria asked.

'It crossed my mind . . . but I'm sorry, I'm no expert. I don't know what a stroke would even look like.'

'You're supposed to ask them to raise both arms,' said Meredith helpfully. 'Then ask them to smile and say a few words. If they can't do any of those three things, then it's probably a stroke.'

Meredith worked for the NHS, dealing with patient complaints. Sometimes, it could make her a bit moody. She did appear to have *some* degree of medical knowledge, but Gloria always said to take any advice from Meredith with a pinch of salt.

'I didn't think to do that,' I said quietly, and I neglected to tell them that by the time I realized there was something very wrong with Leon, we were in Lawrence's front garden, the kids screaming in the back seat and Leon slumped lifelessly at the wheel.

Gloria put her hand on top of mine. 'I wouldn't have known to do that either, love.'

The door opened and the four of us looked up expectantly.

'Are you Mr Campbell's family?' A woman in a smart taupe-coloured suit approached. We told her that we were. 'We'll talk in here then,' she said, 'if that's OK with you? Seeing as though it's empty.'

We didn't argue and she pulled a chair around so that she was sitting directly in front of us.

'I'm Dr Letts,' she began. 'I'm one of the neurologists here. I've had the chance to examine each of Leon's scans and so now we're fully aware of what we're dealing with.'

She cleared her throat.

'OK . . . it seems Leon has two fifty-millimetre nails lodged inside his brain.'

I repeated what she'd said silently back to myself: *Two fifty-millimetre nails inside his brain.*

Nobody spoke.

I could only assume the others were staring back at her with the same look of incredulity I was.

'One entered here,' Dr Letts said, gesturing to the area just above her right ear, 'and one here.' She moved her finger forwards, to her forehead.

I wondered if she'd got the wrong family.

Wrong family. Wrong patient. Wrong scans.

'How did they get in there?' Juliana asked, quietly stunned.

I looked at Gloria to see if she had the answer. For one mad moment, I had an image of her suddenly smacking her *own* forehead, exclaiming that Leon had fallen off a wall/bicycle/horse as a kid, and had run all the way home with a piece of wood stuck to the side of his head.

But instead, Gloria whispered, 'How long is fifty millimetres?'

The neurologist held her fingers two inches apart and Gloria swallowed, closing her eyes. She took a steadying breath and I saw it shudder inside her chest.

How had this happened? I didn't understand.

I once read about a woman who, having experienced some weird tunnel vision and tingling arm pain, had a head X-ray. She was told there was a bullet inside her brain; she'd been shot as a kid, and no one had thought to tell her.

Could the same have happened to Leon? Had these nails been inside his head for years?

'I'll be straight with you,' said the neurologist. 'It looks very much as though this is the result of a violent attack.'

And when each of us stayed silent, when each of us listened to her words and found they just didn't quite make sense, she said, 'It seems to me as if it was done intentionally.'

Juliana gasped.

'He was shot with a nail gun,' Dr Letts explained. 'We've contacted the police because, well, to be frank, this looks like attempted murder.'

Immediately, Gloria asked, 'How is he?'

‘He’s in an induced coma. And the—’

‘Attempted murder?’ I said, and the neurologist nodded her head gravely. ‘Murder?’ I repeated. ‘Who would want to murder Leon . . . ? No one would want to murder Leon. Are you sure you have this right?’

‘It’s important to stress that we can’t be completely sure of anything right now,’ said Dr Letts. ‘But we have notified the police. And unless Leon was working with a nail gun at the time, which, from what I understand . . . ?’ She looked at me.

‘He wasn’t.’

‘Then I’m afraid everything points to him being the victim of an intentional attack,’ she said. ‘I’m very sorry. It’s a shock to hear, I know.’

‘Will you remove the nails?’ asked Juliana.

‘We will. This afternoon if possible.’

‘Will it be you who does the operation?’ she asked.

‘I don’t perform surgery. It will be one of my colleagues, most likely Mr Jorgensen. He’s the one who leads the neurosurgical team here.’

‘Wait,’ I said. ‘Leon isn’t the kind of person who . . . Leon doesn’t *have* enemies. This isn’t something that happens to a person like Leon. And we don’t live in an area that . . . You’re telling me he was really shot? On purpose? In the head?’

I felt as if my blood was draining from me.

‘All I can tell you,’ she said, ‘is that we will do our very best to treat Leon and help him recover.’

Dr Letts was calm. Softly spoken. She had small pearl earrings that fitted neatly against her skin and she wore a layer of barely-there make-up. We knew we were in the presence of someone exceptionally clever, someone with great authority, and that seemed to make us go against our instincts. We should have been screaming. I felt as though I wanted to tear my skin off, and yet I sat there listening to what she had to say, my manner remaining composed.

'I think the police will have more information for you when they arrive,' she said. 'Maybe they'll be able to shed some light on things. In the meantime, I know you have a lot of questions. And I'll do my very best to answer them. But I'll be honest with you: I'm not going to be able to give you definitive answers at this early stage. It's going to be a difficult time and we'll keep you informed at every step. But right now we just don't know what the outcome will be.'

'Outcome?' Juliana said. 'You mean you don't know if Leon will actually survive this operation?'

Gloria glared at her daughter's insensitivity. And Juliana glared back, saying, 'What? We need to know, Mother. We need to know what his odds are.'

Dr Letts smiled sympathetically. 'Mr Jorgensen will talk to you in more detail. But as with any operation there are risks. And it goes without saying that any surgery to the brain comes with *significant* risks. But we wouldn't be attempting this procedure without the belief that it's absolutely necessary. The foreign bodies must be removed from inside the brain if Leon's to stand any chance of recovery.'

'The nails can't stay in there?' I asked.

'Afraid not.'

'But why didn't I see them? I don't understand. I was with Leon when this happened. Why didn't I see the nails in the side of his head? It doesn't make any sense to me.'

'Perhaps because they were the last thing you were expecting to see,' she suggested. 'And also, the heads of the nails used in nail guns are relatively small in diameter. You're maybe imagining the size of a drawing pin. Well, these are actually much smaller than that and . . .' She paused, checking each of our faces before continuing. '. . . they're currently sitting just beneath the surface of the skin.'

So they were really in there. Those nails had gone right into Leon's brain.

I tried to remember the accident.

Did Leon have blood coming from above his right ear? It was certainly possible. But I'd been sitting to the left of him, and by the time I was out of the car I was pretty much hysterical, trying to get the kids out, trying to keep people away from Leon. I wasn't the one who called for an ambulance. I wasn't sure who had.

Dr Letts made to stand. 'For now, if you'll excuse me, I need to be getting back. I'll bring you more news as I have it,' and when she left it was as if she took all the air out of the room with her.

Suddenly I needed to escape. Blood was thrashing around my body making my head woozy. I was hot and clammy and the muscles of my throat were constricting.

Someone had meant to do this to Leon. Someone had shot him in the head and had actually wanted him to die.

Perhaps they'd even hung around for a moment *waiting* for him to die.

And they'd shot him in front of his children. His own children.

4

I was heavy-limbed and numb. We were in my kitchen. The front of the house was ribboned with blue and white tape and my home was now a crime scene.

'I think I must be in shock,' I apologized to the woman detective, because I was finding it hard to speak.

She had asked me to talk about Leon. About *me* and Leon. 'Tell me anything,' she'd said, but my thoughts were jumbled. I couldn't seem to hold things in my mind for longer than a few seconds; thoughts were evaporating before I could turn them into words.

I put my hands to my face.

Someone had shot Leon in the head. Had *Lawrence* shot him in the head? He was with him before it happened.

I felt sick.

It was only a few hours ago that I'd been in this kitchen preparing for our day at Gloria's. And now I was back here again, but this time I was without my husband. Somehow, in his place, was Detective Inspector Hazel Ledecky, and she wanted to know about Leon, she wanted to know about our marriage, so that she might have a starting point. So she might have some clue as to what would make a person want to try to execute Leon as he waited in the car.

It didn't feel real.

'Take your time, Jane,' she said.

I couldn't concentrate. I was running through suspects. Could Lawrence Williams have done this? He was the last one to see Leon fit and well. But he was a *pensioner.* Lawrence was a nuisance, yes, but this? It seemed implausible.

I blinked hard a few times and then opened my eyes.

DI Ledecky was a tall, lean woman in her early sixties. She had the physique of a dedicated runner and I'd seen her on *North West Tonight* several times when commenting on behalf of Merseyside Police. She spoke well on air. She was contained. Discerning. And to have her in my kitchen felt almost hallucinatory.

She wore her hair in its natural grey – short, tidy, pushed neatly behind her ears – and aside from that, the only real telltale signs of ageing were the two heavy bags sitting beneath her eyes. They spoke of cumulative late nights, of ploughing through case files, of a dedicated police life.

'What happened this afternoon,' Inspector Ledecky said, when still I hadn't spoken, 'was incredibly traumatic. I'd wager that this is probably the most traumatic thing that's ever happened to you?'

I nodded. Each time I thought about it I felt as if I'd walked into a plate-glass window.

'With that in mind then,' she went on, 'I want you to know there are no rights and wrongs here.' Her voice was low and level. 'I know you're traumatized, but this is a safe space in which you're free to talk. You're certainly not being judged as to how good a witness you are. For the moment, I'm simply here for support. Anything you can tell me as to—'

'I'm scared Leon won't get through this,' I blurted.

I'd been holding this inside since arriving at the hospital, unable to voice my fear in front of Gloria, Juliana, Meredith.

'How is Leon doing?' Inspector Ledecky asked. 'Do we know if he's stable yet?'

'He's alive, but only just. That's all we've been told.'

'It's an induced coma, as I understand it?'

I nodded.

'Any indication of when they'll bring him out of it?'

'They didn't say. They don't want to say much really. I suppose they don't want to get our hopes up. His mother is with him. She sent me home to see to the children. I really didn't want to leave him but . . . the kids . . . I had to come back and I'm scared to be alone here,' I told her, panicked. 'What if . . . what if the person who did this comes back? What if he comes back and hurts the kids?'

I'd been asked if there was anywhere else I could go. Anywhere I'd prefer to spend the night. But I'd shaken my head numbly at the time because I hadn't been able to think through what spending a night here, alone with the children, would actually mean. I hadn't considered how utterly vulnerable I was.

'I can't talk you out of worrying about your husband,' Inspector Ledecky said. 'But I can offer you complete assurance that there is nobody outside your house tonight. We have a uniformed officer at the front. You and your children are very safe.'

'What about tomorrow?' I said. 'What about the night after that?' I started to shake. 'I can't just go on as if nothing's happened.'

'Let's worry about tomorrow *tomorrow*,' she replied gently. 'For now, tell me more about Leon.'

I tried to get control of my breathing.

'Tell me about the two of you,' she coaxed.

'I don't know what you want me to say.'

'Anything. Anything at all. What's your marriage like?'

'It's good . . . we're happy. We like being together.'

'No small feat,' she said. 'Is it always like that between the two of you?'

'Mostly. But we've been together a long time, and we have Jack and Martha to take care of, so it's never going to be all hearts and flowers . . . Leon's job can be stressful sometimes, so sure, there are days when we probably both want to kill each other, but we're united. We're strong together. We really love each other, you know?'

She nodded as though she did, and this made me tearful again. 'I'm sorry,' I said. 'I'm not really sure what else you want me to say.'

'Tell me about the small stuff,' she said. 'Whatever pops into your mind. It's good for me to get an idea of who Leon is . . . Often, as investigations progress, there isn't time to talk about the details, to gather the facts that make up a person . . . How about you start by telling me how you met?' She fixed me with a well-meaning smile.

I told her I met Leon eight years ago through Frankie Ridonikis. I was thirty-one at the time. 'If you're a reader,' I said to her, 'you might have heard of Frankie,' because he too had made a good career from writing novels.

'I'd gone to a book signing,' I told her, 'a joint book signing between Frankie and Leon, but because Frankie's queue snaked out the door and along the street, I ended up chatting with Leon.

'Anyway, that's where it started,' I said. 'I think part of the reason I fell for Leon originally was because I wanted to be a writer so badly myself.'

'That still the case?' she asked.

'Up until today, yeah. Hardly seems relevant now though.'

I glanced towards the back door. It was around nine and the last of the day's sun was fading. Moths and midges circled the outside lamp.

Fear rose up again as the image of Leon with a nail gun held to his head flashed into my brain.

Suddenly, I heard a noise from somewhere inside the house. 'Can you hear crying?' I asked the detective.

She craned her ear in the direction of the hallway. 'I don't think so.'

I stood. We both waited, listened. I took a mouthful of water from the glass on the table. It was over-chlorinated, and it burned the back of my throat.

Then there was a bang. And a wail.

DI Ledecky said, 'That, I heard.'

Martha's room got the evening sun and so I'd put her to bed earlier in just a vest and nappy. Now, when I reached the top of the stairs, I could hear her sobbing softly. She'd climbed out of her crib and was sitting, her back up against it, her small legs straight out in front of her. She held her nappy in her hands. She did this sometimes. Took the nappy off in her sleep, and then woke when her bed was wet. Her skin would be chilled and clammy like freshly dug clay.

'Hey, baby, let's get you sorted out.'

She was almost three so I was trying to wean her off the milk before bed. Then we could do away with nappies entirely and we wouldn't have this problem. Martha didn't want to wear the nappies, but she didn't want to give the milk up either. 'A bottle,' she said, hiccuping with tears.

On another night, I would have stood firm. I'd have said, 'We're done with all that, sweetheart. You're a big girl now,' but as I carried her into the bathroom, wiping her down with a clean wash cloth, I whispered, 'Won't be a minute and Mummy'll fetch your milk.'

Back in the bedroom, she was already limp with sleep. I pulled the curtain aside slightly, checking outside for any signs of movement, anything lurking in the shadows. Was he out there? Whoever he was, was he out there, watching, waiting? Was he waiting for Leon to come home so he could finish what he'd failed to do on the first attempt?

I changed Martha's sheets. She rested on her tummy on the rug, her knees tucked under her, her tiny bottom stuck up in the air. She looked like a snail. She was so small. So unprotected. I dressed her in a onesie (harder to get the nappy off again) and lifted her, thinking that the milk probably wouldn't be necessary now, when she murmured, '*Bottle . . . bottle,*' and began to whimper. It was the kind of whimper that could go either way, so I bundled up the bedding and told her I'd be back.

Downstairs, I threw the sheets into the machine and poured out a few ounces of full fat milk into a bottle. Then I set the microwave for fifteen seconds.

'Have you got kids?' I asked Inspector Ledecky as I watched the numbers count down.

'A daughter.'

'Close by?'

'Woolton,' she said. 'She married a footballer.'

'Do I know him?'

'He plays for Tranmere, so probably not.'

'No,' I agreed. 'Probably not.'

I returned to Martha's room and pushed the teat gently into her mouth while guiding her hand around the bottle. She gave three half-hearted sucks before her mouth went slack and she turned her head away. A fine line of milk ran from her lips down on to the pillow. I removed the bottle, kissed her on her tummy, and pulled the door closed. *Please sleep through,* I willed. *Please. Just tonight. Sleep through, sweetheart.*

Sometimes she did. Sometimes she didn't.

The children hadn't asked where Leon was when I returned home from the hospital. It was as if the events of earlier had been wiped clean from their memories and by the time I got in Jack was bursting to tell me what they'd been doing with my friend and neighbour Erica all day. 'We made bread!' he announced proudly.

Erica said, 'Play dough. But we pretended it was bread. It's wrapped in cling film if they want to play with it again tomorrow.'

That's when I told her Leon had been shot in the head and Erica's hand flew to her mouth and she made a sound as if she'd been bitten.

'What did they tell you?' she said. 'Who did it to him? Christ, that means whoever did it is . . .' and her words trailed off as she thought about her own family's safety.

This was Liverpool, yes. People occasionally got shot in some gang-related matter. But not in this area. Not on our street.

Erica grabbed her bag. She was a big-boned woman of fifty-four with a shelf-like bosom and square hips.

Usually, she was unflappable. Usually, her easy approach to life had a calming effect on those around her, but right now, she started to ramble.

'They had beans on toast for lunch. Hope that's OK. I knocked up some macaroni cheese for tea. Tried my best to get some broccoli into them . . .'

'You're an angel.'

'I was glad to do it,' she said quickly. 'Now, do you need anything else before I leave? Have you eaten? I made extra pasta just in case . . . *Jesus*, I can't believe he's been shot . . . I can't believe that could happen. Here. Of all places.'

She kissed me on the forehead and when she'd left I could smell the scent of her perfume lingering on my clothes.

Detective Inspector Ledecky gestured to the kitchen window. 'Your cat wants to come in.'

Bonita was there, attempting to meow, but she had a huge Magnum P.I. mouse moustache and couldn't generate sound.

'She a keen mouser?' Inspector Ledecky asked, and I wondered if this was a genuine enquiry or just a veiled attempt to keep me calm and focused on the ordinary.

'She kills everything,' I said. 'Not just mice. Chicks, frogs, moles. It's because she's a rescue.'

DI Ledecky raised her eyebrows as if to say why would that matter.

'At her last home she had three sets of kittens back-to-back, which stunted her growth,' I explained. 'Well, that, and the fact that they never fed her. She came to us half-starved.'

I reeled off this explanation whenever Bonita came home with something she'd caught and we had company. *So sad.*

So full of neglect. Whether her previous life accounted for all of the killing she did, I wasn't sure. I think it may have been simply *in* her. She was a small killing machine and if she didn't get her fix she'd stand on the kitchen windowsill making loud, strangled-sounding mewing noises, almost clutching her little throat with her paws.

'Your neighbour mentioned a cat,' Inspector Ledecky said neutrally.

'Lawrence?' I said, taken aback, and she nodded. 'I'm surprised he told you about that.'

'Because . . . ?'

'Because they were arguing about her. Just before it happened. He was the last person to see Leon. Well, you already know he was the last person to see Leon, I assume.'

Inspector Ledecky nodded again. Her expression remained impassive.

'They were having cross words about Bonita and sometimes their conversations can get a little heated. Well, more than a little heated. Leon and Lawrence don't really get on,' I said carefully.

'Why do you think that is?'

I exhaled. Why does anyone not get along with their neighbours? Small things turn into big things. Things that wouldn't ordinarily bother a person needle away until such a state of irrationality is reached, someone blows.

'It's all over nothing,' I explained. 'To start with, we had parking issues. Now Lawrence doesn't like our cat going in his garden, and Leon doesn't like Lawrence's creepy son coming around here bothering me when I'm dealing with the kids.'

'This is Glyn Williams we're talking about?' she said. 'Does he live with his parents?'

'No. But he's there a lot. And creepy's probably unfair. He's harmless really.'

'Why does he come over?'

'He dabbles in a bit of short fiction. Horror, mostly. He likes to talk about it sometimes. Leon hasn't got time for him, so I end up listening, but Glyn doesn't always pick up on the normal social cues, and he can be pretty awkward to talk to. I'm sure Leon wouldn't mind him as much if he wasn't related to Lawrence.' I was about to say more but I stopped. 'Are you considering Lawrence a suspect?'

'Right now, everyone's a suspect. So, yes, my colleagues are with Lawrence Williams . . . Did you witness the entire argument between Lawrence and Leon?'

I shook my head. 'I came inside to get something.'

'Something?'

'Beer. Leon wanted beer. He wanted to take it to his mum's house. It was his birthday. *Is* his birthday,' I corrected.

DI Ledecky delayed responding; she seemed to be processing her thoughts. She looked across to the stacked bookshelves which ran along the opposite wall in the dining area of the room. 'Tell me,' she said, 'did your husband ever have problems with fans coming to the house? Anyone ever bother him at home?'

'By fans, you mean readers?' I asked.

'Yes.'

'Readers don't tend to do that sort of thing . . . They're generally a very well-behaved bunch. They contact Leon via his author page, via Facebook and Twitter. Most of the correspondence is nice: "Love your work", "When's the next book out?" That sort of thing.'

'Most?' she said.

'Well, you're always going to get the odd nutter.'

'I see. But has anyone ever tried to track him down?'

'Not that I'm aware of, and I'm sure Leon would have said if . . .'

I paused.

My thinking stuttered for a moment and Inspector Ledecky frowned a little as she waited for me to go on.

Eventually I said, 'Look, I really don't want to send you on a wild goose chase with this.'

'But the occasional goose pays off,' she said.

She was watching my face intently. Waiting for me to say more.

The subject was something I rarely spoke about and she seemed to sense my unease. She stayed motionless. When I still didn't answer, she relaxed her face into an expression that seemed to say, *It's OK . . . we're all friends here.*

'There's a guy,' I said.

She waited.

'Sometimes he turns up at readings,' I said. 'Sometimes he comes to events, and, well, he can make a bit of a nuisance of himself.'

'He heckles Leon?'

'He has done. Though that's since stopped. He did it once when Gloria, that's Leon's mother, was in the audience. She'd taken some pals along to watch him speak at the Manchester Literature Festival and the guy, Alistair Armitage, began shouting stuff from the stalls.'

'What kind of stuff?'

'Accusations. Expletives . . . Apparently, Gloria marched over to him and insisted he stop at once. When he told her he had every right to say what he was saying, she ejected him from the theatre herself.'

'Has Leon mentioned Alistair Armitage recently?'

'Not that I recall. But I'm not sure if Leon *would* tell me even if he had turned up again. He found the whole thing rather unsavoury. It was embarrassing, distressing, and when I tried to talk to him about it, when I said perhaps we should get the police involved, he always told me no. He said if it got any worse he would do something about it himself.'

'Do you think Leon *did* do something about it himself?'

I thought for a moment. It was possible. Leon could be a secretive sod when he wanted to be, and, of late, he'd been more distracted, more short-tempered, than was usual at this stage of the book. He was on the opening. The part he usually loved to write. Once he got to thirty thousand words he would have a wobble, think every word he'd written was drivel, and would require huge amounts of persuasion to continue.

Had Alistair Armitage been bothering him again?

'My instinct says no,' I said finally.

'But you can't be sure.'

'I can't be sure.'

'What exactly was Mr Armitage so upset about anyway?' Inspector Ledecky asked, by way of an afterthought.

I swallowed more water.

'He said Leon was a liar and a cheat and he accused him of stealing his book.'

'A book?' she replied, confused. 'That doesn't sound like something to warrant such a reaction.'

I shook my head. 'Not *a* book. His own novel,' I explained, setting down my glass. 'Alistair Armitage accused Leon of taking his ideas. He accused Leon of stealing his work.'

5

The following morning, they found the weapon.

A DeWalt heavy-duty cordless nail gun. Later, I would look it up online and find it to be a monstrous, evil-looking piece of equipment. Something capable of inflicting a staggering amount of damage.

It had been discarded in a privet hedge further along the street and initial analysis showed there were two sets of fingerprints on it. As well as another, partial, smeared print. I agreed to have my fingerprints taken readily, although I did tell the police it was pointless as I had never seen that gun before in my life.

I thought about what it would take to pick up a weapon like that and aim it at someone's head and my insides went slack.

We were at the hospital when DI Hazel Ledecky called me with more news. My phone rang at just about the worst time as, minutes earlier, we'd been told that even though Leon was initially stable after his surgery, his brain was now beginning to swell.

'Fast,' Dr Letts had informed us, solemnly.

And when we'd asked what that actually meant for Leon, she'd refused to commit. She'd said these were the early stages of what could be a very long process, but again that they were doing everything they could to ensure a good outcome for Leon.

She'd kept using that word: outcome. And each of us had accepted it, as though it meant something to us. As though we actually had some clue of what might lie ahead.

We were at Leon's bedside, Gloria, Juliana and I (Meredith had gone home for now), and we were helplessly willing the pressure inside Leon's brain to recede when my mobile rang and Inspector Ledecky said, 'It's your nail gun, Mrs Campbell. The nail gun belongs to you. The two sets of prints on it are yours and Leon's.'

I noticed immediately that she'd reverted to using my surname.

'Hold on,' I replied, quickly moving from ICU to the corridor outside. Once there, I said, 'But I've never seen the nail gun before,' totally baffled by this piece of news, certain the police had somehow got their wires crossed.

DI Ledecky seemed unsurprised.

'Would you know if you owned an electric screwdriver, a power sander, an angle grinder?'

'*Do* we?'

'You do.'

Leon had a whole cornucopia of power tools in the garage that I was unaware of, it seemed. Which was peculiar to say the least, since I couldn't remember the last time Leon had attempted any DIY. Leon tended to break things. Tended to make matters worse. He had very little interest in home improvement and didn't derive any pleasure at all from, say, tinkering around in the garage the way some men did.

'But how would my fingerprints even get on that gun?' I asked.

'Well, aside from the obvious,' Inspector Ledecky said, and then she paused, waiting for me to play catch-up, waiting for me to comprehend her full meaning, 'aside from that,' she continued, 'you probably moved it without thinking. Perhaps when searching for something else.'

Her tone was different from the night before. I was no longer somebody to be consoled. To be supported after a traumatic event.

Her voice was cold, level. Unsettling.

'The obvious?' I repeated. 'What do you mean *the obvious*?'

Inspector Ledecky lowered her voice. 'Mrs Campbell, do I really need to spell it out?'

'No,' I said quickly. 'No, you don't.'

I put my back against the wall. A porter was wheeling an empty bed along the corridor. He looked hungover.

My prints were on the weapon used to try to kill Leon.

'Am I under arrest?' I asked quietly.

'Not yet,' she said.

I thought of the open garage door, the nail gun on show. Someone must have simply picked it up and walked the two or three steps to where Leon was sitting in the driver's seat, raised their hand, and fired. Leon would have been trapped. He couldn't have escaped even if he knew what was happening.

We were told that one nail had entered Leon's temporal lobe, from just behind his right ear, and they thought that this was the first nail to be fired. Then, on realizing he had been shot, perhaps, Leon turned his head to the right, and this was when the second nail was fired straight into his forehead. This nail had lodged itself in his frontal lobe.

I made myself avoid Google. I told Juliana if she wanted to look up the consequences of the positioning of the nails then that was up to her. But I didn't yet feel ready to speculate on whether Leon would lose his mobility, his sight, his speech.

I didn't want to know what his 'outcome' might be. I just wanted him to get through the next day. To stay alive.

I needed him to stay alive. I needed him back where he belonged.

Leon's protection was something I'd always taken for granted. If there was a noise in the night, I would move a little closer, feel almost smug in the fact that I'd bagged myself a real man this time. Because the men I'd dated up until Leon were just boys really – boys, who had played at the game of being grown up.

Leon was my security. My shield. It was *his* job to safeguard us. *His* job to keep us out of danger.

But now Leon wasn't at home. And as the days began to pass I felt his absence keenly at every moment.

I'd never been afraid before. Never sat in my house with the lights off watching for signs of movement outside. Never been startled by the sound of the phone, the doorbell. Never made it my business to watch Lawrence Williams in the house opposite as he went about his chores, as he moved from room to room, all the while wondering: Had he tried to kill Leon? *Why* had he tried to kill Leon? And, if so, why hadn't he been arrested by now?

Or was this person a stranger? An opportunist?

Leon had talked about installing CCTV once. This was after someone had stolen a crate of beer from our porch (which miraculously turned up in the boot of his car). I'd pooh-poohed it, said we didn't need CCTV. 'Only crooks need a deterrent like that,' I'd said. Now I wished we had it.

The police remained tight-lipped when I asked about the progress of the investigation. I'd given a formal statement and Inspector Ledecky had not been present. And she was right when she said that as the investigation went on there was less and less time for victimology.

As we moved into day three, day four, day five, appallingly, no one was asking questions about Leon any more. About the type of person he was. Leon was now referred to as 'the victim', and when he was discussed, it was as if he was completely without personality, without character.

I could feel Leon slipping away.

And this wasn't merely because of the way the police now referred to him; there were physical changes to Leon too: Leon didn't look like Leon any more.

His brain had continued to swell, and he would need to stay sedated, kept in an induced coma, until it showed signs of receding. He had a probe inside his skull that measured intracranial pressure and it was this, this probe, that I tended to fixate upon most when I was at his bedside, because, suddenly, gone was his beautiful face. Gone was the face I knew so well, and in its place was a bloated, piggy-eyed version of the man I loved.

Add to that that Leon's hair had started to grow back. I'd never seen Leon with hair, except in photographs of him as a child. He shaved his head every second day in the shower and, with the beginnings of a head of hair, he looked like another man entirely. Somebody else's husband.

But it was his face. The face that had always been so pleasing to me, the face that evoked a real, visceral reaction:

a blooming in the chest, a warmth spreading throughout my limbs; feelings that when I looked at him meant there was quite simply love present. That face was no longer there and it had been replaced by the countenance of a very different man. A man of hard living and excesses. A man who looked as if he'd abused his body. A man who didn't like his own mind.

'Come back to me, Leon,' I would whisper.

'When *is* Daddy coming back?' asked Jack now. We were coming in from the car after I'd collected them from my mother's – again. My mother, whom I called every night and again each morning to check she'd not over-medicated.

'I don't know, honey,' I told Jack. 'Soon, I hope.'

I'd not told them very much. Daddy was unwell and he was in the hospital: that was the extent of it. They didn't know he had a brain injury and Jack, particularly, was starting to suspect I was withholding information. Inspector Ledecky had arranged for another detective, a young woman with experience in dealing with traumatized small children, to question Jack and Martha that morning. And she went at it very softly-softly. She spent a long time 'establishing trust' before coming out and asking them directly about the day of the attack, and what they remembered.

They remembered nothing. I could've told her that. It wasn't like I hadn't asked them myself: 'What happened when I left you in the car?' 'What happened to Daddy?' 'Who did you see?' 'Did Lawrence hurt Daddy?' 'Did you see *anyone* hurt Daddy?' 'How could you have seen nothing at all?'

But they'd had their earbuds in and their eyes on their

iPads and the outside world had ceased to exist for them at the exact moment someone was trying to execute their father.

When the young detective was clearly getting nowhere fast, Inspector Ledecky stepped in and raised the idea that perhaps Jack and Martha were so very traumatized by the event they'd witnessed that they'd buried it immediately. So deep that they couldn't access the memory.

'Young children do that sometimes to protect themselves,' DI Ledecky added helpfully, and Jack shot me a withering look, like, *That's not what I'm doing here.*

I went along with the notion all the same though because Inspector Ledecky was still cool around me. She was still watchful of my movements, distrustful of my behaviour, and I didn't want to give her reason to think I was trying to stop my own children from outing me as the perpetrator. As ridiculous as that was.

'Grab your rucksack, honey,' I said to Jack now. I had Martha in one arm and a bag of groceries in the other, and I was trying to close the car door with my hip. Martha was sleepy and heavy. She'd nodded off on the way home from my mother's and if I didn't get her inside fast and lay her down on the sofa, with either her comfort blanket or something sweet to suck on, she would cry pretty much until bedtime. And then, once in bed, she'd cry some more, and I'd have to resort to letting her cry herself to sleep while I sat on the bottom stair, listening, hating the fact that she was so distressed.

My mother's generation had none of these problems. As kids, we were all tucked up asleep by seven o'clock apparently. Night-time misery was alien to them. They just *got on with it*, according to my mother.

I was struggling to get the key in the lock and hitched Martha higher on my hip so that I could reach when I became aware of a sound behind me. A scraping sound. A foot on gravel.

I turned.

There was no one there.

It must have been someone passing on the street. Or else my imagination.

Since the attack I'd become hyper-aware. I seemed to sense stuff I'd been blind to up until that point, and my brain now felt assaulted by the sheer number of stimuli.

Martha whimpered, and then, without warning, she flung her head back hard and I almost lost my grip on her. She writhed in my arms as she began building up to her biggest cry when I heard footsteps. Footsteps right behind me.

I pulled Martha in close. She fought me. I held her so tightly that I knew I was hurting her as I battled with the lock.

I'd envisioned this.

I knew I was vulnerable. I knew that whoever had attacked Leon would be back. Knew they wouldn't be content with leaving him as he was and—

The lock released and we crashed through the door. I pulled Jack along with me by his hood, hurting him in the process, for he shouted out. I practically threw Martha to the floor and shoved the two of them inside as I slammed the door shut behind me.

There *was* someone there.

I saw him. Just glimpsed. But there was definitely someone in my driveway. He was standing, unmoving. He was watching me.

I gripped both children and put them in the kitchen before grabbing my phone. Then I ran back towards the lounge at the front of the house so I might catch sight of who was out there.

It was when I was dialling the first 9 that I saw him.

Glyn Williams.

Glyn Williams, Lawrence and Rose's oddball son.

Glyn was in my driveway and he was rubbing his chin with his palm as if he was undecided what to do next. He took a step forward and then stopped.

I dialled a second 9.

He appeared to be talking to himself. Reciting something. He seemed almost trance-like.

I eased away from my spot and angled myself behind the edge of the curtain so I couldn't be seen. He seemed to catch my movement and for a minute he focused on the window. They weren't visible to me now, but I knew Glyn Williams had the palest, roundest blue eyes. They appeared as though all the colour had been washed from them and he would hold them steady, too steady, on anything except the person he was conversing with.

My heart raced. There was an unpleasant taste in my mouth.

What was he doing here?

Did he know I was watching?

He looked troubled.

He took a step forward and then stopped again.

He looked like he had something he really needed to say.

Or else do.

But for whatever reason, Glyn Williams didn't approach further; he seemed almost blocked. As if an invisible barrier thwarted him. I stood with the phone in my hand, ready to redial the emergency services should he move.

Did he know something?

By now, my brow was slick with sweat. My heart hammering. The kids were being quiet in the kitchen – too quiet; I needed to check on them. But the sight of Glyn Williams there, static, unmoving, was strangely arresting.

He was such a peculiar man. Until this moment, he'd never done anything to make me feel really fearful of him, but there was something always a little 'off'. I tended not to turn my back in his presence, tended to wonder where exactly in the house Leon was whenever Glyn called around. He had the creepy habit of turning up at the back door, unannounced; just appearing there, even though he knew the front door was our main point of access, and once inside the kitchen he would stroke his hand backwards and forwards across the kitchen work surface, repeatedly, as if checking for imperfections in the granite. And he always wore the same waterproof jacket. He was wearing it now in fact.

Bonita began snaking around my legs. She leaped up on to the windowsill and the sight of her through the glass seemed to startle Glyn. A look came over him. A look of confusion. As if, suddenly, he wasn't entirely sure how he'd got there, the last few minutes a mystery to him. He appeared quite stricken and, as he turned on his heel, he stumbled. He completely lost his footing and had to put his hand out fast to steady himself by holding on to the car.

He paused there for a while, smoothing his hair down, checking his laces, before slinking away, and I watched him, my teeth cutting into my bottom lip.

I exhaled. I tried to calm my breathing. I reached for Bonita and she headbutted my hand to ensure a firm stroke, when – there was a scream from the kitchen.

Martha.

She was ratcheting it up for a full-blown meltdown, so I hurried in, straight to the cupboard, ready to pacify her with something inappropriate. Something that would destroy her appetite for the rest of the evening and mean dinner would be a total write-off.

Then I called Inspector Ledecky.

'Hazel Ledecky,' she said upon answering, and I sensed she was in the car. I could hear the extra static from the speakerphone and she was projecting her voice as though talking to someone in the next room.

'Glyn Williams was in my driveway,' I said. My voice had a distinct tremble to it. 'It's Jane Campbell.'

I paused.

'Glyn Williams was in my driveway and he was acting strangely. I don't know what to do.'

'Was he acting in a threatening manner?'

I hesitated. 'I'm not sure if you'd call it—'

'What did he do exactly?'

'He just stood there . . . But I'm on my own with the kids, and you appreciate I'm not exactly relaxed here, obviously.'

'He didn't threaten you physically?'

'No.'

'And he's not out there now?'

'I don't think so. I'm in the kitchen—'

'Mrs Campbell,' she interrupted, 'would you mind going to the front of the house and checking? I'll stay on the line.'

I heard the click-clack of Hazel Ledecky's indicator as I went through to the lounge. Bonita had remained on the windowsill and arched her back in readiness, thinking I'd returned with the sole purpose of petting her again.

'He's not out there,' I said, scanning the driveway, scanning the street beyond that.

I almost felt disappointed. Ledecky, in her usual businesslike manner, was making me feel as if I was wasting her time. Making me feel my unease was unwarranted.

But then she surprised me.

'I'm not far from your house, Mrs Campbell,' she said evenly. 'Leave it with me. I'll talk to him.'

6

Half an hour later, Hazel Ledecky was in my kitchen.

'Why was Glyn Williams out there?' I asked.

'I've requested he not come around here for a while and he agreed. As have Mr Williams – Lawrence – and his wife, Rose. Glyn apologizes if he startled you, and says he won't come here again. It's probably best if you do the same.'

'Not talk to them, you mean?'

'Don't go over there,' she said.

'I wasn't planning to, but why?'

'Because it makes life simpler.'

I looked at Inspector Ledecky as if to say, *That's your answer?* but she didn't take the bait, she merely held my gaze, almost challenging me to say something more.

Something incriminating perhaps?

In that moment, I was very aware that, as far as she was concerned, my fingerprints were on the weapon and I had no alibi for the time of the attack. I was still on her list of suspects. Which was absurd because while she was considering my part in this, the person who actually did it was roaming free. She was wasting time.

'Why don't we know who did this yet?' I said. 'This is attempted murder, for Christ's sake, and you don't seem to be doing anything. What is it? Is Leon not important enough? Why haven't you arrested Lawrence? He was here, wasn't he? They were arguing. He could have wiped his prints from that gun before he threw it in the hedge. Surely you know that.'

Inspector Ledecky maintained her self-possession. 'I know it's frustrating. And I know you feel like you're being left out of the loop, but that's because our investigation hasn't generated enough evidence against one particular suspect. We can't arrest someone until—'

'But Lawrence!' I snapped. 'He was here and—'

'Mrs Campbell,' she said, firmly, to shut me up, and then she paused. 'Jane,' she said, more quietly, 'I'm sorry that there's not been more progress. It's frustrating for us too, and we're doing everything we can, I assure you. But there's something else I need to make you aware of that's' – she took a breath – 'well, it's not exactly what we were hoping for.'

'Tell me,' I said flatly.

'The nail gun was from here,' she said. 'It belonged on the site of the property. So that means we will have to charge anyone we arrest now with grievous bodily harm, and not with the increased charge of attempted murder.'

'What?'

'Whoever did this to Leon,' she explained, 'did not come here specifically with the intent of murdering Leon.'

'How can you know that? They aimed that gun at Leon's head!'

'They picked it up and inflicted damage in much the same way as if they'd picked up a brick and aimed that at Leon's head. That would warrant a charge of GBH too.' She took no pleasure in telling me this, I could tell. 'I think it's important you know that it's unlikely the CPS would now authorize a charge of attempted murder,' she said. 'Even though I must stress we'll continue to push for that.'

'But GBH? That means the sentence will be a lot less. It could be as little as a couple of years.'

'Yes,' she said.

She didn't take her eyes off my face, and it dawned on me that she was watching to see if *I* appeared relieved.

Would the news that *I* would be going to prison, if I was convicted for attacking Leon, for a much shorter duration have any effect?

'You're not seriously still considering me for this, are you?' I said.

'As I've made clear before, we're considering everyone.'

I passed Ledecky her coat.

Intimated it was now time for her to leave.

'You know,' I said, holding the front door wide for her, 'at the rate you're going with this investigation, it'll be quicker to wait for Leon to wake up to find out who actually did it than rely on you and your officers to provide answers.'

And she left.

But another week passed, and still we didn't have answers. Still we didn't know who did it.

When the kids were asleep, when I *couldn't* sleep but was sitting, the cat curled up in my lap, my mind Rolodexing through thoughts, thoughts that I'd had to put aside whilst ministering to Leon at Fazakerley Hospital throughout the day, I'd think: Who *had* done this? Why Leon? And what did Glyn Williams *want* when he was loitering there in the driveway? There was nothing in Leon's life that pointed to him attracting trouble. He'd never really crossed Glyn, or anyone else that I could think of, never been violent. It made no sense that someone would want him dead.

Lawrence, Rose and Glyn did stay away from the house after that incident, as Ledecky had predicted, and I, in turn, stayed away from theirs. I ducked inside if Lawrence was filling his recycling bin or backing out his car. I felt hopelessly in the dark about it all, but there wasn't a lot I could do.

Instead, I tried to focus on Leon.

He'd been in a coma for twelve days now and there was no change. Each passing day was another in which he'd managed to stay alive, but also one when he didn't improve either. It was the worst kind of limbo.

Time seemed to have taken on a different quality, and days that had slowed by an absurd degree in the stretch immediately following the attack now felt as though they'd come to a complete stop altogether. I'd arrive at the hospital and Leon's mother would be there. She played music to Leon, but it was the wrong music. She read books to him, but they were the wrong books. She massaged the skin of his hands with cheap, lavender-infused oil that made Leon smell like the contents of my own mother's underwear drawer. All of these things began to irritate me. I hated the way she seemed to have no interest whatsoever in the police investigation. Hated how she spoke of caring for Leon as if it were more her job than mine. As if she'd been elected chief care-giver, because my attentions were elsewhere – as in, with her own grandchildren.

It had been explained to Gloria that Leon would not

wake from his coma of his own accord. That his state was under the neurologist's control. But still, she acted as she had seen people do in the movies. She spoke to him incessantly.

Open your eyes, son. Open your eyes. I'm here for you. Open your eyes.

And she had these one-sided conversations, conversations where she somehow managed to natter away to him for hours without posing any actual questions.

When, after over a week of this behaviour, I asked her, as gently as I knew how, if she thought talking to him like this might somehow bring him round, she said, 'No, dear,' and she carried on.

When I pressed her on the matter, she became somewhat brittle. 'I just want him to know that he's not alone in here,' and she looked at me in such a way as to suggest that my absence of chatter, my absence of providing props to keep Leon occupied, might want addressing.

As though Leon might suddenly wake and glare at me, saying, 'Where the hell have *you* been?'

So I asked Gloria if we might switch. Asked if perhaps she could take the children for a few hours and let me spend some more time with Leon. I neglected to add *alone*, but I thought she'd take the hint and come over all apologetic. *Oh my word, it never even entered my head. How remiss of me to—*

No.

Gloria ignored my suggestion and simply said, 'I'm needed here.'

But the children were getting fed up of being with my mother all the time. Her skills as a grandma didn't really extend past teaching them how to put on make-up and allowing them to dress up in her old furs. And *she* was getting fed up of them. 'You're here! Again!' she'd exclaim as they ran past her legs each morning. Then she'd bid me a weary wave and pull her dressing gown around her body before closing the front door.

Later, when I would return at five o'clock, she'd pull the martyr routine: 'This is bloody hard work for one person. I've not stopped all day. I've only had a cracker for my lunch and I'm not as young as I was, you know. And why does Gloria get to sit at his bedside all the time, reading that sodding bible, or whatever it is that she does? You should tell her you need *proper* help. You should tell her what you really need is help with these children. They're her grandkids as well, aren't they? It's not on that it all falls to us to . . .'

But it was now the end of August, and school started in a week, so our routines would be altered anyway. Jack would be starting school for the first time and I'd not bought the uniform, shopped for school shoes, pumps, PE bag, pencil case. Erica had offered to step in and cover it. She said she would be absolutely thrilled to whisk Jack off and sort out the essentials. (Erica's sons were in their early thirties and were showing no signs of procreating, so she said she had to get her fix of small children wherever she could.)

But I didn't want Erica to do it. It was something I should do. Something I *wanted* to do. How many of these milestones were there in a child's life?

Trouble was, I couldn't seem to summon up the nerve to actually get it done.

Jack starting school had me conflicted. Yes, the fact that I wouldn't have to think about childcare for *two* children any longer would be useful, when ministering to

Leon took up so much of my time, but I didn't feel ready to let Jack go yet. Not without Leon by my side telling me it would be OK. Telling me Jack was ready, that he *needed* this next stage. Without Leon here to buoy me up, sending Jack off into the unknown made me horribly anxious. And so I avoided, delayed, did what I always did when I couldn't face what had to be done.

Today, I arrived at the hospital later than planned. Leon had been moved to the end of the unit and Gloria was there, playing music to him again on her red mini cassette recorder – circa 1986.

I sighed. Because the thing was, Leon had very particular tastes in music. He really only liked dub reggae: Jamaican producers such as King Tubby and Prince Jammy. Artists like Sugar Minott, Eek-A-Mouse. Along with some awful nineties house.

I used to hear him coming down from the attic room – where his office was located – at the end of the day, chanting, '*ONLY* house music,' and I'd know he'd been up there reliving his youth again.

Today, Gloria's cassette recorder was playing Michael Bolton (*The Essential*); yesterday, she'd been playing that nauseating Dutch violinist, André Rieu; it was Chris de Burgh, the day before that. She played the music not so loud as to disrupt the other patients, but she'd put the cassette recorder right next to Leon's ear, so close that today I wanted to hit her over the head with it.

'I'm getting a coffee,' I told her shortly after arriving.

'But you just got here.'

'Do you want one or not?'

I was turning on my heel when she said, 'They want to talk to us.' Her voice was hushed and there was panic in her eyes. 'They want a meeting,' she went on, afraid. 'They said they'd wait for you to arrive.'

'Did they say what it was about?' I asked carefully.

'No,' she said. 'But I expect . . .'

'What did they actually say, Gloria?'

I was being short. I was being short with her and this was not who I wanted to be, but I couldn't help it. We'd been in each other's company pretty much all the time and though I'd tried, tried so hard to keep my emotions under wraps, sometimes it was as if the words shot out on their own.

Gloria looked wounded. She stood up. She tried to brush out the creases in her skirt that had formed across her tummy from sitting.

She said, 'I'll tell them to let Dr Letts know you've arrived.'

Dr Letts's office was impersonal. Like a corporate space rented in a hurry. There were no photographs, no personal items, just a vase without flowers and a bowl containing over-sized pine cones.

'How are you both?' she began by asking.

'He's doing OK, isn't he?' Gloria ignored Dr Letts's question, eager to discern the reason for this meeting. 'Nothing's happened overnight? The nurses didn't seem to want to say when I asked them and—'

'Nothing has happened.'

Gloria exhaled.

Today Gloria was wearing a wig. She often used wigs when her own hair needed relaxing or colouring and today's offering was one of the better ones. Some were a bit on the shabby side.

'I have good news,' said Dr Letts, and she placed her palms flat on the table. 'Leon's intracranial pressure has dropped. It's dropped to a level that we now consider safe.'

She bestowed a beatific smile on both of us that I'd not seen before. This was her Good News smile, clearly. Her whole face was changed. How pretty she is, I thought absently. How—

'What does that actually mean, doctor?' Gloria asked.

'It means, Mrs Campbell, that we're ready to wake up your son.'

I had not been prepared to hear this news today.

I turned to Gloria. A tear was welling in the corner of her eye and, suddenly, she reached out and clutched my hand. She placed her fingers over mine and squeezed twice in a kind of victory celebration: *We did it.*

Then she hugged me and I felt ashamed of my behaviour earlier.

We did it.

Leon was waking up.

I hadn't really allowed myself to think about this in case it never happened. Up until now, the focus had been on keeping Leon alive: keeping his skin intact so he didn't develop pressure sores, keeping his joints moving, his muscles stretched, so he didn't develop contractures. Keeping his airways clear of phlegm so he didn't develop pneumonia. We were bombarded with information about Leon's medical state and Gloria and I had lapped it up willingly. It was something to focus on. It gave us *attainable goals.*

But now Leon was going to wake up. Finally, he was coming back to us.

I took out my phone. 'I should call DI Ledecky.'

7

It was planned for the following day. Dr Letts and her team would bring Leon out of his coma, early in the morning, the hope being that Leon would regain consciousness and begin breathing again on his own.

After that there were a lot of unknowns.

Leon, we had been warned, might not wake up straight away. There was even a possibility that he might *never* wake up. A proportion of brain-injured patients live on for years in that state: unconscious, in long-term residential care, their families neither able to mourn the passing of their loved ones, nor hope for any kind of future with them. But Leon's brain activity readings had caused Dr Letts to be optimistic. 'Still,' she warned when she'd explained the worst-case scenario, 'always best to have the full picture before we begin the process, I think.'

By mutual agreement Gloria and I had decided to keep Jack and Martha away from the hospital until now. 'Not a place for children,' she'd stated, but that's not what she really meant. She meant that the sight of Leon would scare them. And she was right. Sometimes, the sight of him scared me. But I didn't say it. Secretly, I worried that Leon would remain the swollen, bloated-fish version of himself, even when he began to recover. Even when I envisioned him sitting up, joking, eating ice cream, castigating his mother for playing all that shitty music.

'You'll bring the children along tomorrow, then?' Gloria said, and I told her I would. But I was hesitant. Was it the right thing to do?

Gloria fixed me with a glare. 'It's the right thing to do,' she said, sensing my unease.

She'd also called Juliana and told her to be at the hospital. Juliana would be bringing along her sixteen-year-old son, Eden, but she wasn't certain if Meredith would be able to make it. 'Which means they've been rowing again,' Gloria said. Then, without warning, she declared, happily, 'I'm going to make a cake! Sweet potato and rum! Leon's favourite. The cake he never got to eat on his birthday.'

It struck me that Gloria was treating this as a celebration – Leon's unveiling. Which I supposed it was, but I did wonder if she wasn't jumping the gun by gathering the whole family, passing out cake and wine for the staff. What if Leon didn't wake up? What then?

'Shouldn't I bring the children in when Leon has had a couple of days to come around instead?' I suggested to Gloria.

But I think she had this image of Leon in her head: Leon regaining consciousness, casting groggily around the room, his eyes alighting on Jack and Martha, smiling as the children jumped into his lap, all being well in the world once again.

'Leon will want to see his children,' she said. 'Do *you* want to be the one to say that we didn't bring them to see their daddy?'

I didn't.

'No,' I conceded quietly, but I couldn't shake my misgivings.

The following morning, I rose early. An hour earlier than usual.

I opened the curtains and was about to head to the bathroom when I caught sight of Rose, opposite. She was standing in her front garden in her dressing gown staring at our house.

Rose had not made eye contact with this side of the street since the visit from Hazel Ledecky, so what was she doing now?

Perhaps she's talking to her plants, I thought idly. Like Prince Charles.

I edged away from the window and watched. Rose was not someone you ever caught stationary. She was a doer, a woman on a mission. She and Lawrence were always busy, busy, busy! Retirement didn't give them a minute, they liked to say.

Lawrence and Rose's wall had been repaired after Leon had ploughed into it, but they'd lost a good proportion of their shrubs; they'd had to plant anew. But Rose wasn't looking at her plants. And her lips weren't moving. In fact, her expression, no longer vacant, was now rather stern.

Was she lucid?

She didn't look it.

Suddenly, all at once, out of nowhere, Rose bent at the waist, as if she was ducking a shot, and her action had the effect of making me flinch. I watched as she fidgeted around by her slippers, her gnarled fingers trying to gain purchase on . . . what? What was she trying to pick up?

She straightened.

And her eyes narrowed further.

Then she pulled her right arm back and took aim. Launching a rock? A dropped quince? Straight at my wall.

Straight at my cat.

Bonita fled the scene and I stared, agog, too shocked to react at first, as Rose quietly smiled to herself.

The bitch.

I hammered on the window. 'Rose!'

Is this what she did each day? Before I woke up? Had she been terrorizing Bonita? No wonder Bonita could be skittish.

Inside the house, Bonita was all smiles, rubbing up against your ankles, purring loudly whenever she settled herself upon you. Outside she was a different cat entirely. Try picking her up and her claws would turn to talons. Her entire body would stiffen, her legs held out rigid at right angles, and she'd scratch at you until she was deposited. Whereupon she would tear off as if she'd been shot at.

Leon used to say it was as if Bonita didn't recognize us outside the house. 'We're strangers to her out here,' he'd say. 'She can't trust us.'

Now I knew why.

'Rose!' I yelled again, hammering on the glass.

But it was as if she couldn't hear me. She turned and pootled off, the picture of innocence.

I stared after her, stunned that she could perform such an act of malevolence so openly. I began pulling on my jeans, grabbing yesterday's T-shirt from the top of the washing basket. She couldn't just—

I checked the clock. There wasn't time for this today.

As soon as I got back from the hospital, I'd go over

there. Have it out with her. Demand Rose tell me what was going through her nasty little mind. But now there wasn't time. Now, I needed to get the kids their breakfast and get them ready to go.

I lifted Martha out of her *Frozen* dressing-up outfit that was covered in jam (which she'd demanded she be allowed to sleep in rather than pyjamas for the past three nights), and I put her and her brother straight in the bath. Then I rinsed and conditioned their hair, dressed them in clothes I would normally reserve for a party, or dining out at a restaurant, and I explained to them what I hoped would happen later that morning. They knew Leon had been injured. They knew he'd been unconscious. This, I'd explained to them, was the reason for their not coming to the hospital with me each day. And when they'd whined, when they'd complained that they wanted to visit Daddy nonetheless, I'd resorted to the kind of lie my mother would have told me when I was little.

'Doctors don't allow children inside the intensive care unit.'

Inspector Ledecky planned to visit Leon later in the day if he was deemed well enough for questioning, and I felt queasy with excitement when I thought of this.

Soon we would know.

We'd know for sure.

We'd get our answer on who attacked Leon and I'd be able to say goodbye to that mounting terror I'd experienced every time I got into my car in the driveway, every time I went to bed each evening, that feeling that someone was going to put a gun to *my* head and pull the trigger.

We were walking across the hospital car park when my phone began ringing inside my bag.

Juliana.

She didn't wait for me to say hello. She said, 'He's awake!' before I had the chance to speak.

She was sniffling and crying and I was aware of voices in the background. It sounded as though she was in a busy office rather than the ICU ward. 'He's sitting up and he's awake!' she said breathlessly. 'Are you far away? Because he's desperate to see you. Come fast. Come now. He wants you.'

'How is he?' I dropped my voice. 'Is he . . . OK?'

'He's confused and he's a bit all over the place, but he's fine. He keeps asking for you. He just wants you, Jane.'

I lifted Martha into my arms so that I could get across the car park faster. 'Come on,' I said to Jack, pulling on his hand a little. I was trembling. 'Let's hurry. Daddy's awake.' He looked up at me, his expression serious. In his white shirt, navy tank top and cream chinos he looked as though he was on his way to a job interview.

'You all right?' I asked, and he nodded without speaking. He was nervous. Me too, but I tried not to let him see it. This was what we'd waited for. This was what we'd prayed for and now it was finally happening.

As we passed through the main reception area, we got an excited wave from one of the records clerks. 'I've heard!' she called out to us. 'Such great news!' she said, before her gaze landed on the kids. She put her open palm to her breast, tilting her head over to one side. Her expression was one of *Oh, those children are just adorable,* and I could see she wanted to approach. Pet them. Fuss over them. The kids tended to do that to people.

Another time though. She curled her fingers into a childish wave and mouthed, 'Good luck.'

We turned on to the main corridor and I put Martha down. 'You can walk now, honey,' and she and Jack held hands while I adjusted my handbag and the bag of nonsense items Gloria had insisted I bring: bunting, balloons, a banner with 'Welcome Back', paper plates for the cake, plastic cups, candles, a disposable lighter.

Coming towards us was Becky, one of the staff nurses from ICU. Her blond ponytail swung rhythmically from side to side and her trainers squeaked softly on the polished floor. Such a huge sense of indebtedness overcame me whenever I saw these people, such a surge of emotion, I could be literally knocked sideways. Particularly if I saw them outside of the unit, say, in the canteen, or, as happened a few days ago, by the tills at Primark. I'd been picking up some extra underwear and socks for the kids as I wasn't getting through the laundry as often as usual and when I saw him, Lorenzo, the small, stockily built nurse from Madrid, buying a school uniform along with his wife, I felt as if I'd spotted some long-lost relative, who'd been thought of as dead up until that point. I started to sob spontaneously on the spot and Lorenzo rushed to my side. I apologized. Said I didn't know what had come over me, and he assured me that it happened to him all the time. That he had that effect on lots of the patients' relatives. He didn't mind, he said, and then he and his wife insisted on taking me to a nearby café and buying me an omelette. 'For jour *es*trength,' he explained earnestly.

I think the problem was that we owed the nursing staff so much. When you saw how they dealt with Leon: with such tenderness, with the kind of simple – I hesitate to use the word 'pleasure', but I can't think of a word more fitting – simple pleasure at being able to keep a person comfortable, clean, alive. Well, it could take your breath away.

'Today's the day, folks,' Becky said as she approached.

Then she squatted on her haunches in front of Jack and Martha so that she was at Martha's eye level. *Hospitals are scary places,* I could feel her thinking. *Make yourself small.*

'Your mummy's told me all about you two,' she said brightly. 'How you've been so brave whilst your daddy's been in hospital.'

This was not true. Not one word. I'd never told Becky this, but bless her for saying it all the same.

Jack beamed back at her, proud that his behaviour had been noted, commented upon, but Martha turned and clung to my leg, hiding her face from this woman in the strange uniform. Martha couldn't give a hoot if she was told she was a good girl or not. Which was something I admired in her and hoped would continue through to adulthood.

Becky straightened. 'He's asking for you.'

I nodded.

I was pleased she knew. Like Jack, I was proud that my behaviour had been noted. That it had been noted I was a good wife and my husband needed me. More than anyone else, it was me he needed.

Then a thought struck: *Does he remember the children?* I intimated as much to Becky and she smiled sympathetically, before whispering, 'Not yet. But don't let that worry you. It's entirely normal.'

I felt as if I'd been dealt a blow to the centre of my chest.

He didn't remember the children. What if he *never* remembered the children?

How did I go about shielding them from this? This would scar them. They wouldn't be able to make sense of it. How could their daddy not know who they were?

Becky sensed my alarm. 'Go to him,' she said. 'It'll all work out.'

The corridor had never seemed so long. Once at the ICU, I pressed the buzzer, smoothed down my hair, repositioned the straps of Martha's rucksack. 'Don't worry if Daddy doesn't seem exactly himself,' I whispered, and Jack looked up at me, panic in his eyes.

'Mummy?' he said, but the door opened too fast and there wasn't time to offer more in the way of explanation.

I grabbed both kids by the hand and made my way to the far end of the unit. Martha pulled back, as she sometimes did, wanting to turn this into some kind of game: half hopping, half skipping. I yanked on her wrist and she stumbled.

At Leon's bedside were Gloria and Juliana. They both had tears in their eyes and they glowed with happiness. On the chair against the wall sat Eden, Juliana's sixteen-year-old son. He smiled quickly my way. I'd not seen him in a few months, and his chest had broadened, his short dreads had grown longer. Though usually an affable, relaxed kind of kid, Eden was clearly uncomfortable in this setting. I said hi and he dropped his gaze and began scrolling through his phone.

I made my way to Leon.

He was sitting up.

ICU patients are generally kept naked but now Leon wore a T-shirt and I wondered where it had come from.

'Leon,' I said, my voice catching.

And he smiled.

'Hi,' he said and something inside me released.

'How are you feeling?'

'I'm OK,' and he continued to smile.

But then I realized that it wasn't really *his* smile. And a layer of alarm crept over me.

Leon's whole face usually shone. It was a gift he bestowed upon the recipient. This new smile was cautious, guarded; it was the kind of tight smile you'd use when entering a shop selling luxury items: *I'm just browsing, thank you.*

I took his hand and he looked down at my fingers.

Then he looked up at me with confusion.

'Please will you get my wife?' he said.

What?

When I didn't answer, when I was too gobsmacked to respond, he said, 'My *wife*,' firmly, as though saying it twice might change my reaction.

'I don't mean to be rude,' he said, 'but I really want to see my wife.'

8

'Where's Gina?' Leon demanded now. 'What have you done with her? I'm sick of this. Where. Is. Gina?'

He was shouting and thrashing about like a mad thing. And he'd lost none of his strength. For two weeks he'd lain completely still, no tone at all in his muscles. Now his body rippled with energy and for the first time in my life I was afraid of my husband.

Eden had got the children out of there quick sticks and had headed to the canteen to buy sweets. I'd thrust a tenner into his hand, saying, 'Buy them anything! Anything they want . . . ! Try to be gone for at least half an hour.'

And Eden had set off fast before suddenly freezing in his tracks. 'What if . . .' and he'd looked at me, stricken, '. . . what if Martha needs to take a shit or something?'

'Ask a nurse!' I'd yelled, desperate for him to get out of there so the kids didn't witness their daddy like this. 'Ask a woman with a child! People like to help, Eden. Let them.'

Gloria was trying to soothe her son. 'Leon, dear,' she was saying, 'just calm down. There is no need to get yourself worked up like this. Today is a happy day, my child. Today, you came back to us. We are so blessed to have you return. This is your wife. This is Jane right here. She's been by your side since the accident. She loves you, Leon.'

With his eyes never leaving mine, Leon beckoned his mother to come closer. 'I would *never* marry that woman,' he said between his teeth.

Gloria put her hand on his shoulder but he shrugged her off.

'You're not listening to me!' he shouted. 'That is not my wife. I would never marry a woman like that. Look at her hair. Red? Are you kidding me? She has skin the colour of skimmed milk. Fuck. I don't love her. I don't even *like* her. Where's Gina? Get Gina.'

No one knew what to do. No one knew how to calm him. It was an impossible situation. I gripped the side of the bed.

'Gina doesn't love you,' I blurted out.

And he looked at me with real hatred in his eyes.

'She's gone,' I stammered on. 'She left you. Gina's gone, Leon.'

Leon folded his arms and turned his head away.

After another minute, he said, 'Somebody get this woman out of here.'

'It's called post-traumatic amnesia,' Dr Letts explained.

We were back in her office. An emergency meeting had been called. She wore a look of concerned empathy and that was almost more worrying than Leon's behaviour. Something bad was ahead. I could feel it. Dr Letts's mouth was pulling downwards at the edges and when she spoke she appeared to be choosing her words extraordinarily carefully.

'Does that even exist?' asked Juliana. 'I thought that was something Hollywood cooked up for the purposes of dramatic storytelling.'

'It *does* exist, but perhaps not in the form you've seen in the movies. Post-traumatic amnesia happens to almost all patients after a period of coma. They don't wake up entirely themselves and, the longer the period of coma, the worse the symptoms of PTA can be . . . The patient can be conscious, generally quite alert; they can be conversing with staff, relatives, in a manner that's considered normal. But there's something not quite right. It's as if the wiring is faulty and the patient may not be able to remember certain things. He may not know what year it is or where he is, for example. And he may become distressed easily. Which is what you've experienced with Leon today.'

'We thought he'd wake remembering who attacked him,' I said. 'Will this amnesia be permanent?'

Dr Letts shook her head. 'Rarely. We're usually looking at a period of days . . . weeks, rather than months.'

'And then Leon will return to normal?' Gloria asked.

At this, Dr Letts didn't exactly flinch, but there was a twitch in the muscle of her right temple. A tell, so to speak.

She took a breath and I got the impression that this was a well-rehearsed speech she took no pleasure in delivering.

'At this point, we've no way of knowing what Leon's long-term outcome will be. What his *normal* will be, if you like. What I can say is that the period of post-traumatic amnesia is often the most challenging for all involved, but it doesn't last forever. The Leon we have right now will not be the same as the Leon we have in a few weeks' time. That's certain. And by then we'll have a clearer picture of what his needs will be.'

'Needs?' said Gloria. 'What do you mean, his needs?'

'Mrs Campbell, the brain is a highly sophisticated computer. It controls every single process in the body. After a traumatic injury we don't always know how it's going to respond. Right now Leon is confused, disorientated and agitated. But he's been lucky. The position of the nails in his brain means that Leon suffered no physical disability and no disruption to the speech centre. He will continue to walk and talk without difficulty. But there may be other issues.'

'Like?' asked Juliana.

'He may have memory problems, tiredness. He may have trouble concentrating for any length of time. That's very common with the brain-injured patient.'

'Doctor,' Gloria said, 'are you saying he may never write again?'

'I'm not saying that, no. But your son won't recover overnight. Recovery from brain injury is a long, arduous journey and you may find yourselves confronting very painful difficulties. Your courage and patience can be pushed to the absolute limit . . . What I'm saying,' she said, 'is that's not going to be easy.'

'Why didn't you make us aware of this before?' demanded Juliana, annoyed that she was only learning about post-traumatic amnesia now. And Gloria, though probably thinking the same thing, felt the need to apologize for her daughter's rudeness.

'It's all right,' said Dr Letts. 'I understand your frustration. Hearing all of this has come as something of a shock. But we believe families tend to do better taking this process one step at a time. Bombarding you with information about the difficult road ahead would do nothing to help whilst your loved one is still in a coma. You have enough on your plates worrying if they're going to come out of it alive. And that's what you must remember. Leon *is* alive. Yes, right now he's not exactly the Leon you know and love, but you do still have him. A lot of families aren't so fortunate.'

'What about Gina?' I asked. 'Do you think that when the post-traumatic amnesia has worn off he'll stop mentioning Gina?'

Dr Letts said she was optimistic. 'Let's hope so,' she said.

By the time Detective Inspector Hazel Ledecky arrived Leon had become calmer. This was, in part, down to the administration of sedative medication, and the fact that I'd left the room. Leon didn't want me there. He wanted Gina. And there was no pacifying him on this subject as he was convinced we were keeping his *real* wife from him. Convinced we were holding her somewhere and trying to fox him into thinking that he was married to me instead.

I crawled off to the canteen and sat with the kids and Eden and tried to act as if the bottom of my world had not fallen out.

'He's just come out of a coma, Auntie Jane,' Eden said reasonably. He could see I'd been blown sideways. 'His head's all messed up.'

'I know.'

But it was one thing for Leon not to recognize me. For him not to recognize the kids. I reasoned that I might have been able to rationalize that. Tell myself, as Eden had pointed out, that it was very early days, and not to expect too much. But to have the sight of me provoke such a reaction in Leon, a reaction of real disgust, well, that was crushing.

I wondered how long I could keep it together. I felt as if our lovely life had been erased. Leon woke up wanting Gina. He thought he was still *married* to Gina. And, for now, I was powerless to do anything about it.

Eventually, we received word that Leon was doing a little better, and it was deemed safe enough for me to return to his bedside. This was when I met Inspector Ledecky. She was also making her way along the corridor and was accompanied by someone she introduced to me as Detective Constable Payne – a guy in his early thirties with colourless hair and a forgettable face.

'We've been told Leon doesn't remember much,' she said.

DI Ledecky wore a navy suit with a navy silk blouse beneath. The trousers were a little short in the leg. She had to be close to six feet tall.

'Well, he doesn't remember me,' I said to her.

And Hazel Ledecky stopped in her tracks. She turned towards me. She put one hand on my shoulder, and said, 'I'm so, so sorry to hear that, Jane.'

Whether she truly meant it, or whether this was Ledecky doing her best supportive act again, I didn't know, but I found myself dissolving in response to this stern woman's touch.

She didn't speak. She let me weep in the hallway, people passing by us on both sides, her junior officer averting his eyes in polite embarrassment – the way you might when a person undresses in front of you.

When I was done, Inspector Ledecky fixed me with a look. One that said: *Ready?* But one which also seemed to convey strength.

I nodded.

'Then let's go,' she said.

They were in the process of moving Leon from the ICU to a ward. We waited outside as his personal effects, his notes and Leon himself were arranged into his new home for the time being. The hope was he wouldn't be here too long before being moved to the rehabilitation unit nearby. The hope was he would recover pretty swiftly. He was young. He was strong. He hadn't been a substance abuser. His medical history was, apart from the two nails inserted into his skull, mostly uneventful.

Gloria and Juliana took the opportunity to slip away for something to eat and to relieve Eden of his babysitting duties for half an hour. As they left the ward they looked strained. Weary. The jubilation of Leon waking up already long gone. Gloria's wig was askew and her face was perspiring. 'He's resting now, my love,' she told me. 'He's a lot more settled,' and I could see she was apprehensive about what lay ahead.

Leon appeared to be sleeping when we went in. I hung back in case of another attack and DI Ledecky took the lead. The other officer – DC Payne – took out a pocket notebook ready to transcribe whatever was said.

'Mr Campbell,' Ledecky said, her voice soft, cajoling. 'I apologize for waking you.'

At first Leon didn't stir.

Then, as Hazel Ledecky repeated her introduction, his left eyelid lifted halfway and he gave her a grin. It was almost lascivious in nature, as if Leon was waking from a sex dream.

I held my breath.

'Who are you?' he said, still grinning.

Ledecky's usual unyielding exterior cracked and she seemed surprised to find herself smiling back at Leon. 'I'm a detective, Mr Campbell. I'm here to ask you some questions. Do you feel up to talking?'

Leon blinked a few times before attempting to sit up. His T-shirt was bunched up around his chest and I feared he might expose his genitalia, but, as the covers loosened around him, I could see the staff had decatheterized him and got him into some underwear. He looked down at the T-shirt, caught under his right arm, and he seemed perplexed as to what to do with it. My instinct was to rush forward, untangle him, but I didn't. I stayed where I was.

'I hear you're having some memory problems?' Inspector Ledecky said.

'Am I?' Leon said. 'I really can't remember.' Then he shot her another smile. 'Nah, I'm just messing with you.'

'Nice to see you've kept your sense of humour,' Ledecky said.

That's when Leon noticed me standing off to the side, trying to look invisible. I dipped my head, braced myself for a repeat of the onslaught of earlier, ready to be ejected from the room, but Leon said, 'And who are you?'

I struggled to come up with an answer lest it send him into a fury again but DC Payne looked up from his notebook, glanced at Leon, then at me, then back at Leon again.

'That's your wife,' he said, frowning. 'Don't you recognize her?'

Hazel Ledecky rolled her eyes. 'Payne,' she said, her tone one of exasperation, 'far better to keep your mouth shut and to *appear* stupid, than to open it and remove all possible doubt.'

'Absolutely,' he said, castigated. 'Sorry. Sorry about that.' He addressed Leon. 'Didn't mean to cause offence.'

Leon spread his hands wide. 'None taken.'

Then Leon said, 'That's not my wife, by the way,' and when Payne went to correct him, Hazel Ledecky cut in, saying:

'Mr Campbell. OK if I call you Leon?'

'Sure.'

'Leon, I'm certain the doctors have already explained to you the reason you're in here. Someone attacked you. It's my job to find out what happened and I was hoping you'd be able to help me. How does that sound?'

She was talking to him as though he was a child. The Leon of old would have been incensed by her manner, told her to go fuck herself. But he listened attentively to her question before replying that he would very much like to help. 'Anything I can do, just let me know,' he said, as if it was not *he* who'd been attacked, but a stranger, someone he didn't know, and Leon was just a concerned bystander.

'Great,' she said. 'Let's start then with what you do remember.'

'That's easy,' said Leon. 'I remember having breakfast with Gina, going upstairs to work on my latest novel . . . I'm a writer,' he said proudly.

'I know,' said Ledecky. 'Some of my colleagues are fans.'

'They are?'

Ledecky nodded. 'Real page-turners, I believe,' she said.

Leon was pleased. He went on: 'Well, as I said, I remember having breakfast with my wife and then . . .' He paused. His gaze rested on me. He reached up with his right hand and tentatively felt at his scars, wincing as he touched the one above his ear. 'Who did you say you were again?'

I swallowed.

Hesitated.

'I'm Jane,' I said finally.

'I know you, don't I?' There was recognition in his eyes.

'I hope so,' I said.

He looked at Inspector Ledecky. 'I know her,' he said. 'I remember her. I know I've seen her face before. I'm absolutely sure of it.'

'That's good,' she replied, encouraging. 'What else do you remember about her? Can you tell me how you know her? Where she lives?'

Leon studied my face, willing the information to come. It was unbearably tense. His eyes were locked on mine and I knew he knew me. I could feel it. Feel the connection we had. It was right there.

Say it, Leon.

Tell them I'm your wife. Say it out loud for everyone to hear.

Leon's expression darkened.

'That woman is the person who attacked me,' he said.

9

'I've no idea why he's saying that,' I snapped at Hazel Ledecky outside Leon's ward. 'Just as I've no idea why he doesn't remember who I am, but knows who his mother is, and knows who his sister is. He even knows he's a stupid Everton supporter, but he doesn't know I'm his wife.'

'He's saying you were there. He's saying he remembers you.'

'I know what he's saying,' I said. 'And yes, I *was* there. He *does* remember me. But for some reason he thinks I was playing the role of assassin rather than his wife. You're not taking this seriously, are you?'

Ledecky's face was unreadable.

'Oh, come *on*.'

She looked towards DC Payne, nodded once in his direction, and said, 'We'll be back later.'

I felt helpless.

What if Leon continued with this? What if the part of his brain that was short-circuiting never recovered?

What if people *believed* him?

Would they really think I'd wanted to kill him? Would they try and *prove* I'd wanted to kill him?

I thought about my prints on the nail gun.

I thought about Ledecky's face when Leon told her it

was me. She was taking his claim seriously. She thought it was possible.

I needed him to remember.

I needed Leon to realize he was married to me. That he loved *me*. That I would never want to hurt him.

I needed him to look at me and say my name out loud.

So I did the only thing I *could* do. I called Gina.

'What the fuck do you want?' Gina said.

I should probably explain a few things.

Gina didn't exactly *leave* Leon, as I might have suggested earlier. I said that to hurt Leon. To make him remember. I said it in retaliation, whereas the truth was quite different.

Gina did not leave of her own accord. Leon and I had an affair.

I won't try to justify it by saying I'd never dated a married man before; that we didn't mean it to happen; that as soon as we knew we had feelings for one another we did everything we could to put a stop to it. All of which was true, but really, so what? It didn't make what we did any less painful for Gina, and it probably won't make you judge me any less.

All I will say is this: I thought I'd die if I could not be with Leon Campbell.

You know when you're a teenager and you ask your mother: How will I know? How will I know when the right person comes along? And your mother gives a wistful look, then gazes off into the middle distance for a time, remembering, before gathering herself and saying: Darling, you just *know*.

Well, I knew.

I knew Leon was the one. The one person in the world I was meant to be with, the person I couldn't bear to be apart from if only for an hour.

Never before had I felt pretty, stylish, sexy. My hips sashayed as I walked. I could write for hours and hours in a steady stream without getting tired. People who'd irritated me for my whole life: suddenly, I felt magnanimous towards them. Even a stubborn patch of eczema on the back of my knee cleared up.

It was as if up until meeting Leon I'd been living half a life. Something always missing, something not quite right.

Finally, I understood what all the fuss was about.

We were completely consumed by one another and so we navigated his really ugly divorce, Leon giving Gina everything he owned, including his beloved Weimaraner. And we started from scratch. There were no kids involved, thankfully. Gina had wanted to delay having children until she'd got her new store in Chester off the ground, and they'd just about started trying for a family when . . .

I came along.

Gina still hated me with a passion. And 'What the fuck do you want?' was probably the least I deserved.

'It's Leon,' I told her.

I was aware that Gina would of course know about Leon's brain injury. It had made the regional news, and the *Liverpool Echo* had also run a story on the assault being a possible hate crime, since a young biracial kid had been beaten up quite badly outside a kebab shop on Penny Lane. They'd alluded to the two crimes being linked.

'He's awake, I hear,' Gina said.

'Yes.'

'That must be a relief for you.'

'It is . . . but, Gina?'

'What is it, Jane?'

'There's been a bit of a complication . . .'

She looked amazing, as expected.

And I'm not sure if she'd agreed to come to the hospital because she genuinely cared about Leon's recovery, and wanted to help out in any way she could, or if she took some dark pleasure from the fact that Leon had woken up wanting her instead of me.

Would I have turned up at the brain-injury unit looking my absolute head-turning, off-to-a-film-premiere best? Full make-up, little black dress, hair glossy and loose?

Probably not.

But I wasn't Gina.

And I couldn't really blame her for the whole look-at-me-now routine. These moments of retribution were scarce in life and you had to take them whenever you could.

I stood at the end of Leon's bed. He knew Gina was coming and had asked his mother to bring his favourite Armani jeans and white, capped-sleeved T-shirt which clung to his chest muscles and biceps in a way that made him look borderline camp. A bit Dr Christian. Usually, I managed to talk him out of wearing it.

Here's what I was hoping would happen: Leon would clap his eyes on Gina and remember. He would see her, and Gina being a good eight years older than she was when they were together, Leon would think, Hang on, *that's* not the Gina I know . . . Perhaps I've got my wires crossed, perhaps—

She walked on to the ward and Leon's eyes welled up.

He got up from the bed. He was like a kid on Christmas morning. And in that moment my heart broke.

'Hey, baby,' he said to Gina as she approached, and he put his arms around her waist before kissing her deeply.

Gina didn't pull away and I looked at Leon's mother, stricken.

'Give him time,' she whispered urgently. 'He'll remember.'

I watched as Leon tenderly stroked the side of Gina's face, and though Gina was clearly uncomfortable with the situation, she didn't pull away.

Gloria and I didn't speak. We didn't know what to say for the best. Leon was smiling at his ex-wife as if he couldn't believe she was real.

With hindsight, this meeting should probably have taken place in the presence of a clinical psychologist, someone who could mediate, because I wasn't sure I had the strength to continue. I'd felt so sure Gina's arrival would trigger Leon's memory of me. That on seeing her his accusation of my attacking him would melt away. Now my limbs felt insubstantial. My stomach like lead.

Leon turned to his mother. 'I appreciate everything you've done for me. Caring for me while I was out, coming here every day and doing what you thought was best. But d'you think you could give me and Gina some privacy, now she's finally here?'

He did not address me. It was as if I was not even in the room.

'Gina'll take over . . . won't you, baby?' he said.

But Gina now had a strange look on her face.

I think up until this point she'd been kind of happy to go along with it. I'd explained the situation, in full, over the phone, and I think the romance of the thing had bewitched her. Her ex-husband loved her again! *Leon loves me! Take that, bitches!* She had waltzed in full of confidence, ready to calmly take control.

But now that she was here, now that she saw Leon was really quite maniacal, she was alarmed. It shocked her deeply and she started to panic.

She extricated herself from his grasp and when he tried to touch her again she shook him off. 'Leon,' she said, not meeting his eye, 'stop.'

'What is it, baby?'

'Stop it, Leon,' she said, firmer now. She seemed almost repulsed.

Leon gave a short laugh before reaching for her again, his brow furrowed excessively to show he didn't understand why she would pull away from him. 'You're my girl,' he said softly.

'No,' she said. 'No. I'm not.'

She was finding it hard to look at him. This was not the Leon she knew and her shoulders began to quake. She took a deep breath in, in order to gain charge over her body.

'Look,' she said, thrusting out her left hand for Leon to inspect, 'no ring. Not even the hint of a ring.'

'That doesn't mean anything.'

'Of course it does!' Gina looked at us, her eyes wide with dismay. She didn't know what to do.

'I'm not wearing a ring either,' said Leon reasonably. 'See?'

'We're not married, Leon!' she said. 'You have to listen to me. We're not together any more.'

'Don't say that. You're upset. I know. I understand. But don't say we're not married.'

Gina exhaled dramatically. 'Leon,' she said, gentler now, realizing perhaps that she was going about this all wrong, 'your brain is telling you something that just isn't true . . . And I'm sorry that this has happened to you. Really, I am. But you're all mixed up.'

'Baby, I—'

'No.' And she grabbed her bag from the end of the bed. She turned to Gloria and me. 'I'm sorry, but I just can't deal with this. It's too much. He's way worse than I expected.'

Gloria nodded.

There was hurt in Leon's eyes, but he reached for Gina once more, nonetheless, and she snatched her hand away.

'I have to go . . . It would be cruel of me to stay here and give you false hope,' she said, addressing Leon. 'I've moved on. I stopped loving you a long time ago.'

'Gina, I—'

'I don't love you and you don't love me.' She cast a brief look my way before saying, 'Jane is your wife.'

Leon was shaking his head. 'You're wrong. Don't say this. Please, I—'

'Jane is your wife now,' she repeated.

'Jane tried to kill me!' he yelled back.

'No, she didn't, you idiot! You love her! You left *me* to be with her! She's the one you wanted, Leon, even if you can't remember . . . But someday you *will* remember, because you fought so very hard for her . . . And you broke my heart in the process, you cruel bastard.'

Leon was looking at her as though this was all lies.

We were liars. All of us.

'I won't be coming here again,' Gina said quietly.

10

It was now 7 a.m. on 7 September, Jack's first day of school, and Hazel Ledecky was plaguing me.

She'd been plaguing me for the past week, in fact, and as much as I tried to chatter amiably to Jack and Martha as I set down their breakfasts, smeared peanut butter on to bread for Jack's packed lunch, my mind was on the interview scheduled for later that morning.

Another seven days had passed and though Leon had improved enough to warrant being transferred to the neuro-rehabilitation unit, he still hadn't recovered the memory of me, the kids, or his former life, and he was maintaining that I was the one responsible for his brain injury.

Ledecky treated his claims seriously, not once suggesting they weren't true, not once intimating that she might think Leon's allegations fantastical – even though Gloria and I had tried to persuade her otherwise. She had a duty to investigate, she said, and so had called me in for a second interview within the space of three days. I was feeling brittle and skittish, finding it hard to concentrate. I'd begun dropping things, losing my words mid-sentence. The prospect of a second interview, combined with Jack's first day at school without Leon by my side, had me feeling, in short, as if I was coming apart. So I'd asked my mother to come along to school with us. Not that she was particularly great at injecting calm into a situation, but I needed her, needed *someone*. She said she'd be here for eight thirty.

At eight twenty, I was washing up the breakfast bowls when I sensed a presence pass by the kitchen window. Like us, my mother always used the front door. And she was never early. I craned my neck to see if there was anyone out there but could see nothing, so I let it go.

I was seeing things. It happened a lot now.

I wrung out the dishcloth and was just about to start on the surfaces when I heard a noise. It was the softest tap-tapping on the back door.

My breath stuttered inside my chest.

I kept my eyes on the door.

The tapping continued but it was barely audible. It was almost apologetic in nature. No one used the back door as a point of entry. No one except—

I strode across and unlocked it. Pulled down on the handle fast.

'Glyn,' I said pointedly when I saw him standing there, his rounded, pale blue eyes looking back at me, before he immediately looked away again, holding his gaze steady at the level of my waist.

I'd not seen Glyn Williams in person since that strange episode in our driveway: when he'd loitered, unmoving, and had scared the shit out of me after Leon's attack. I'd seen his car over at Lawrence and Rose's often enough, seen the three of them together in Lawrence's driveway, each shooting furtive glances across to my side of the street, but our paths had not crossed.

'Glyn,' I said, 'you're not supposed to come here.'

And he nodded his head vigorously, as though yes, yes, he knew those were the rules, but said, 'I brought you this.'

He handed me an envelope with my name and address on the front. 'URGENT ATTENTION REQUIRED' was printed across the top and so I turned to fetch my reading glasses from over by the sink, and in the split second it took for me to reach them, Glyn Williams had stepped inside the kitchen and was closing the door behind him.

My pulse rate doubled. I'd never been inside the house with Glyn on my own before.

I checked the clock. My mother wouldn't be here for another ten minutes at the earliest.

'Glyn,' I said, 'you can't be . . .' but then I glanced at the envelope. 'This letter's been opened.'

He bit down on his lower lip. 'It was delivered to ours . . . I mean my parents' by mistake.'

The letter was from Liverpool City Council. Inside was a notice to say our council tax payments were in arrears. I would risk a fine if I did not settle the outstanding amount immediately. Must be a mistake.

'Who opened this, Glyn?' I asked.

'It's not been read,' he replied defensively.

'That's not what I asked. Who opened it?'

'Mum,' he admitted, and he began stroking the work surface, backwards, forwards, with his right hand.

I fingered the page. There was a circular coffee stain next to my address. It had definitely been read.

I thought about Rose aiming stones at Bonita.

'Glyn,' I said, 'does your mother have an issue with me?'

He didn't respond.

'Does she have an issue with my cat?'

Nothing. No answer.

This was what Glyn was like. Leon called him 'Oddball Glyn'. Or, when he was feeling less charitable: 'That Weird Fucker Glyn'. 'How old is he?' Leon would say. 'Forty-five, and he still practically lives with his parents?'

I could ask Glyn a question straight out and if it made him uncomfortable, or if he didn't quite know how to respond, he would stare at his feet until I could bear it no longer and I would have to break the silence myself. Then he would resume conversing as if this weird little episode had never occurred, filling the air with random facts he'd gathered, sometimes hanging around in the kitchen until I almost forcibly evicted him: *We're just about to eat now . . . I really must give the children their bath . . .*

'You know your dad was the last person to speak to Leon before he was shot in the head, Glyn,' I said. 'That means he's part of the investigation. Inspector Ledecky thinks it's best if we don't talk to one another until after things have been sorted out. Do you understand that?'

He looked crestfallen.

I really wanted to press him about his mother, but I wanted him to leave more. He was setting my teeth on edge.

'The letter said urgent,' he said.

'So why not just put it through the letterbox?'

Glyn shifted his weight on to his other foot.

'Does Lawrence know you're here?' I asked.

He shook his head. Then he lifted his gaze, just for a second, and said, 'I've written a new story . . . Would you like to read it?'

I sighed. Closed my eyes briefly. 'It's Jack's first day of school . . . I really have to get going shortly and—'

He was already withdrawing a folded sheet of lined paper from his pocket. He liked to read his work aloud and, in the past, I would sit, politely listening, nodding reassurance, when really I felt like driving a fork into my own hand.

He cleared his throat, ready to begin, but I stopped him. 'Glyn,' I said, 'what exactly were you doing in my driveway that evening? You looked as if you had something you wanted to tell me . . . Do you have something you want to tell me? Do you know something about Leon? About what happened?'

And Glyn stared at the sheet of paper in his hands as it started to shake wildly as if of its own accord.

'Are you sure you don't want to tell me because if you do know something then wouldn't it just be easier if—'

Jack came in with his rucksack over his shoulders and asked when we would be leaving. I turned to tell him he should go and get his shoes on and turn the TV off and tell Martha it was time to put her coat on.

When I turned back around, I found the kitchen empty.

11

Jack went ahead of us through the school doors into the changing area and seemed completely horrified when he came upon a knot of mothers, crying openly, hugging, consoling one another at having to leave their child for their first full day. Jack shot me a warning look before whispering, 'You're not going to do that, are you?' and I told him I'd try my best to hold it together.

We'd been to the school on a number of visits to prepare for today and, without being asked, Jack now found the peg with his name next to it, removed his raincoat and hung it up, before slipping off his new Start-Rites and replacing them with slippers that each child was required to wear indoors. My mother hung back. Let him get on with it. She was wearing her favourite seventies ladies' trench, red stilettos, and had her hair piled up high on top of her head. I noticed a few sidelong glances from mothers in trainers.

Jack took his lunch box out of my hand and, catching sight of a woman blowing her nose noisily into a tissue next to me, said, 'Will you be all right today, Mummy?'

I squatted down to his level. 'Look at me,' I said. 'Don't worry about me. I am very proud of you. And today, all that you need to concentrate on is having a lovely time.' I resisted telling him that Leon was proud of him too. Even though he would have been, even though it was true. I resisted, as I suspected it might unsettle Jack. Unravel him when he was doing so well.

My mother stepped forward. She planted a kiss on the top of Jack's head. 'Now, don't forget what we talked about, sunshine, will you?' and Jack nodded soberly.

'What did you talk about?' I asked her when we were getting in the car.

'I told him if anyone messes with him, he's to tell them his daddy will rip their head off.'

I just looked at her. 'Jesus, Mother.'

'What?'

'Like *The Hand That Rocks the Cradle*? Jesus, what were you thinking?'

My mother rolled her eyes. 'I always liked that film.'

Ninety minutes later and I was at the Merseyside Police Headquarters at Canning Place.

I'd driven past this ugly, red-brown brick building, next to the Salthouse Dock, a forgettable number of times. But I'd never actually imagined myself inside.

I'd asked DI Ledecky on my previous visit if we were at this location because of the severity of the crime, but she didn't commit to a yes or no. 'I'm based here,' she said simply.

Now, turning on the recording equipment, she looked at me, before glancing at DC Payne, finger poised, saying, 'Everyone ready?'

We nodded.

She cleared her throat and pressed record.

'I'm Detective Inspector Hazel Ledecky,' she said from

her script, as if we'd never met, 'and my role here today is to interview you in relation to the offence against Mr Leon Campbell. Also present is Detective Constable Kevin Payne. The time is . . .' She paused, checking the clock. '. . . eleven oh two on the seventh of September 2017. Can you state your full name, please?'

'Lucy Jane Campbell. But I go by my middle name – Jane.'

'And for the purposes of the tape can you confirm that there are no other persons present in the room.'

'There's no one else.'

'Good. You understand, Mrs Campbell, as with the last interview, that you are here voluntarily. That means you can leave at any time and you're not under caution.'

'That's been explained to me.'

'OK,' Hazel Ledecky said, 'then we can begin.'

That all sounded quite benign, didn't it?

Here voluntarily. Not under caution. Leave at any time. She made it sound almost cosy, as if this was nothing more than a friendly chat.

It wasn't. I'd learned that much by now. After a small amount of digging, I'd found that the police did this, not because they were wanting to come over as friendly, but because of budget cuts. Arresting people is an expensive business, so you'd better have all your ducks in a row before you went ahead and did it.

'Last time,' Hazel Ledecky said, 'we talked about the day of the attack, and you described to us what you were doing when Mr Campbell sustained the brain injury. I'd like to go back to that time and go over a couple of the details if that's OK with you?'

I signalled that it was and waited for her to go on.

She had an A4 folder in front of her. Inside were loose typed pages. She flipped through the first two or three before landing on what she was after.

'You said you were in the house for around seven minutes. Can you tell us what you were doing in that time?'

'Collecting beer for Leon. And listening to an answer-machine message from my mother. I've told you this.'

'Yes, but seven minutes seems rather long . . . Have you ever actually counted how long a minute takes to pass, Mrs Campbell? It takes more time than you might think.'

'I can count to sixty,' I replied flatly. 'And I can estimate how long seven sets of sixty would take. Or to put it another way, I know I was in there for more than five minutes but less than ten. I've also explained that the reason I was in there for that length of time was because Leon and Lawrence Williams were arguing.'

'Why would you want to avoid their arguing?'

'Because it's easier. Because I've heard it all before. And because I prefer to stay away from confrontation. I don't enjoy it.'

'Your children were in the car, Mrs Campbell. Surely if you were avoiding the two men because you found their behaviour threatening, you would have taken your children inside with you.'

I hesitated.

'It wasn't like that,' I said.

'What was it like?'

'Leon and Lawrence were bickering. I wasn't in fear of my life. And I certainly wasn't afraid for the children. They weren't at risk or I wouldn't have left them.'

Inspector Ledecky looked at me levelly. 'And yet, while

you left them unattended, your husband was shot in the head.'

'They weren't unattended. They were with Leon.'

'Who, as I said, was shot in the head.'

'He was,' I admitted.

She lowered her head and flicked to another section in her notes.

'So, you stayed inside the house,' she said after a moment, 'and you did *what* exactly? As I said, I'm struggling somewhat with the seven-minute timeline. It was incredibly hot that day, and to leave toddlers inside a hot car when the temperature was, quite frankly, stifling, seems an unusual thing for a responsible mother to do.'

I was starting to get rattled. Where was she going with this? Was she doing this on purpose? Trying to enrage me so I made a mistake? Or did she genuinely believe I'd left my children at risk?

'I was delaying,' I said. 'I was waiting for Lawrence to leave.'

I thought she might take this opportunity to say something about Lawrence. Explain exactly why he had not been charged.

But instead she said, 'Tell me about your marriage.'

'My what?' She had caught me off-guard.

'Your relationship,' she said. 'What were things like between you and Leon before this happened?'

'We were like any normal couple.'

'So it was a good marriage? Solid? Happy?'

'Of course.'

'Did you trust him? Did he trust you? Was it a loving relationship? Did you tell each other everything?'

'Yes!' I snapped. 'Yes, to all of those things! We were

close. We were happy. We told each other everything. I've told you before that there were no problems between me and Leon.'

'But . . .' she said carefully, referring to her notes, skipping forward a few pages, 'you confided to me shortly after the attack that Leon *did* indeed keep secrets from you.'

I frowned. Didn't answer.

Inspector Ledecky flicked over to the next page. I could see a section of text had been highlighted.

'You say here that you wouldn't have known if the author who accused Leon of stealing his work, Alistair Armitage, had been back in touch with Leon . . . because he kept that subject to himself.'

'What's that got to do with anything?'

'Did you say that, yes or no?'

'Well, if you're going to split hairs, then OK, we didn't tell each other absolutely everything. Who does? And why is that important?'

'You also said that you were jealous of your husband's career.'

'I don't think I did.'

'You effectively admitted that the reason you were attracted to him in the first place was because you were so desperate to be a published author yourself.'

I stared at her. 'I did not say that.'

Inspector Ledecky held my gaze. 'It's how you felt though, isn't it?' she said, goading me. 'You fell in love with him in the first place because you thought he held the key to fulfilling your dreams of becoming a writer.'

'That doesn't mean I'd shoot him in the head.'

Inspector Ledecky changed her expression. Gone suddenly was the hard stare and in its place was a look of impartial neutrality, as if she was open to anything I had to say. As if she could *understand* that I might have been driven to shoot Leon in the head. Under the right circumstances.

'That's not much of a motive,' I said.

'You'd be surprised what motivates people, Mrs Campbell. Particularly when they're unhappy at home.'

'I'm not unhappy at home!'

She glanced down. 'I quote . . . "We've been together a long time . . . it's not all hearts and flowers . . . there are days when we probably both want to kill each other." '

'Jesus Christ. I meant like any couple . . . ! Yes, we've had our share of ups and downs like *any normal married couple*! You're twisting my words. You're twisting what I said when I was upset.'

I pushed the chair away from the table, scraping it along the floor. 'You said I could leave at any time. Well, I'm leaving.' I stood.

'For the purpose of the tape,' Hazel Ledecky said, 'Mrs Jane Campbell is leaving the room and this interview is terminated at eleven oh nine a.m.' She stopped the recording.

'I thought you wanted to help us,' I said, grabbing my bag.

She stood and met my eye. 'My job is to help your husband, Mrs Campbell. And my intention is to keep going until I find someone to charge for the deplorable thing that happened to him.'

'Do you think this is easy? Do you think it's easy living with the reality that whoever did this to Leon can return at any time?'

She didn't respond.

'You waste your time asking me these bloody stupid questions when you can see that Leon doesn't know which way is up. Meanwhile, I'm scared shitless in my own home every day because you're doing nothing to find out who really did this. I don't get it. You're a woman. You must realize how frightening it is for me to be alone with two small children and not know who did this to him. You're wasting time questioning me for this, you're—'

'Mrs Campbell, I assure you I wouldn't be bringing you in here unless—'

'Unless what? Save it,' I said. 'And don't think of bringing me back here unless you've got something to charge me with.'

12

Ledecky didn't charge me. She couldn't. Leon was just about the most unreliable witness you could wish for, and so a couple of weeks passed, me hearing nothing from her, whilst Leon settled into the neuro-rehab unit. It was a welcome change from the starker hospital setting. Here, a team of professionals worked on Leon's cognition, memory, on his emotional state, and the place itself was much less clinical. It had been designed that way to mirror the home situation, so that patients might relearn the skills required to live in the outside world. The unit would have been a far less frightening setting for Jack and Martha to visit Leon in, but we couldn't take the risk. He had no memory of them. And this wasn't some experiment that we could keep repeating for Leon's benefit: *How about now, Leon? Do you recognize your own children NOW?*

So we kept them away.

But Gloria and I showed Leon endless pictures, videos of the kids, in the hope that it would jog something. But even though he could recognize himself in those pictures, even though he could see himself holding hands with me, loving me, it was as if his brain couldn't put all the pieces of the puzzle together. Sometimes I thought we were getting somewhere; he would allow me near him without flinching, without looking at me suspiciously, and I felt there was real recognition in his eyes.

And then we would be straight back to square one.

Gina remained at the forefront of his mind and every day was a sad, difficult, draining battle. A battle that was beginning to beat me because there seemed to be no end to it.

'Officially,' Dr Letts said, 'Leon's out of the post-traumatic amnesia stage. So we should begin to see signs of recovery.'

And we were. He *was* improving. Things that he couldn't remember a week ago – the titles of all his novels, for instance – now he could. He also knew that he lived near Sefton Park. Knew that he ran there on dry mornings, and that it was 2.5 miles around the perimeter. He knew that he could run it twice without becoming out of breath, and that its design had been based on Birkenhead Park, the first publicly funded civic park in the world. He also wanted to impart to anyone who would listen that in 1850, a visiting American landscape architect was so *impressed* with the design of Birkenhead Park that he used it as his template when later designing a park for New York. Central Park.

Leon was thrilled to have retrieved this piece of knowledge.

He also knew that the dreams he'd had while in the medically induced coma – about visiting Alaska, being awestruck by the mountains, the snowscapes, the migrating whales – were just that. Dreams. But they'd made such an impression on him that he was now planning to emigrate to Alaska the minute he got out of the rehab unit. Gloria thought the whole Alaska thing stemmed from

Leon's head being packed in ice to lower the intracranial pressure, but Dr Letts wouldn't commit.

'If he can only remember *parts* of his life from before the attack,' I said to Dr Letts, when she discussed Leon's progress, 'and you're saying that the post-traumatic phase is over, then when does the rest of his memory return?'

'Possibly never,' she said bluntly.

She went on to explain that he would probably always suffer from short-term memory problems and we would need to find ways of dealing with this. The position of the nails in Leon's brain might even have caused long-term memory issues.

'So, he might never remember being married to me?' I said.

Dr Letts had no answer.

And if that wasn't enough, now we had another problem: Leon had begun to have episodes of violent behaviour.

If we could have predicted the triggers for these, then perhaps they would have been easier to deal with. As it was, he could lash out when he was tired, when he was frustrated, when he was quietly sitting, seemingly lost in his own thoughts, and someone made the mistake of disturbing him.

I'd witnessed it only once since his brain injury, when he struck a porter, and so when it happened to me I was completely unprepared. Leon had never shown violence of any kind during our relationship, so when he raised his hand to me, I was mortified. I'd misjudged what I thought was a happy mood, absently gone to dust toast crumbs from his chest, and he'd grabbed my wrist. He'd held me fast, refusing to let go, because he knew I'd tried to kill him, he said. And when he still wouldn't let go, and my skin was beginning to burn, and he warned me – the whites of his eyes bulging, his voice low and menacing – that he could kill me so easily now if he wanted to, I'd had the first flash of awakening that I might not be able to see this through.

I might not be able to keep doing this, I'd realized, and that thought shocked me.

'Why don't you have a couple of days off?' Leon's sister suggested now.

Juliana was over from Manchester with her son Eden. Eden's dad had never been in the picture, so pretty much wherever Juliana went, Eden went too. Juliana had taken a week's holiday from work to spend some time with her brother; she missed him, she said, and she wanted to be with him. But I knew she was secretly hoping that she might be the one to unlock Leon's mind. I think we were all secretly hoping that.

'You look bloody awful,' she said to me. We were in the Ladies' washing our hands. 'And my mother says you're barely eating. She says she never sees you eat. Says you're living on fresh air.'

'I've not had much of an appetite,' I admitted.

'So, go. Stay away from here for a while. Go and see friends. Go shopping. Get drunk. Do normality for a bit, Jane. My brother will still be here when you return. You don't get a badge for running yourself into the ground and being no use to the kids in the process.'

'But what if he needs me?'

'He doesn't *know* you.' She saw how that wounded me. 'Sorry to be blunt,' she said, 'but what difference does it make whether you're here or not?'

'It makes a difference to me,' I said quietly.

Juliana regarded me levelly. 'Sure,' she said. 'I get it. You can't let yourself off the hook. You can't *not* come here because that would be abandonment, and what sort of wife would do that? But only you see it that way, Jane; we all know how challenging Leon is. The nursing staff are worried about you. They—'

'What have they been saying?'

'Don't get all defensive. They've just pointed out the obvious. That you're knackered. That you're rail-thin. That—'

'They said that?'

'They said it in a *nice* way,' explained Juliana. 'But so as to make sure we got the message.'

Usually, it annoyed me when women said other women were too thin. 'She's *soooo* thin,' they'd say, as if they were being complimentary. But the subtext was clear: she's not coping; she's stressed out with her life; she's unhappy in her marriage . . . *Something is going on here!*

But I *was* stressed out. Something *was* going on. And so today, I didn't mind so much that people had noticed. I felt kind of relieved. Perhaps someone else did need to take the reins even if it was for just a few days.

'Look,' Juliana said, 'Gina coming here was a good idea. It took real guts to call her up and make that happen. You did that for Leon, Jane, to help him remember. Bravo. I couldn't have done that. But this shit with the police accusing you means you're emotionally overwrought and we're concerned. Your feelings take a battering every time Leon looks at you and doesn't know who you are. A person can only take that day in day out for so long before getting sick themselves.'

'OK, but—'

'Use me,' she said. 'I'm here for a week. I'm planning on banning my mother for a couple of days too if that makes you feel any better. But that's because she's doing Leon's head in and he needs a break from her as much as anything. And besides, Eden's here,' she added, trying to sway me. 'He seems to get a buzz out of Leon's craziness, Christ knows why. And Leon's been responding to him well.'

This was true. Leon *had* been responding well to Eden.

Whereas Leon scowled and protested with the rest of us, with Eden he held it in. I hesitate to say he was normal around his nephew, because he was a long way from that, but there were signs of the old Leon that just weren't present when Eden wasn't around.

Everyone noticed it. The nursing staff commented on it to Gloria, which seemed to half offend, half make her proud. She was distraught, naturally, that her attendance seemed to have a minimal effect on Leon's progress, but if anyone was going to make a difference to Leon, then it might as well be her grandson.

So I agreed. I would take a few days away from the rehab unit.

As instructed by Juliana, I would rest, relax, see friends, eat.

Perhaps I might even get drunk.

13

'How about we do it here instead?' Erica suggested.

It was Saturday, 11 a.m., and I was still in my dressing gown. I'd not visited the unit and my mother was sitting opposite, vaping, flicking through the *Next Directory.* Erica was making herself useful, as usual, by washing up the dirty dishes in the sink. Upon seeing my car parked outside the house, Erica had come scuttling across to check all was well. I'd filled her in on Juliana's plan to return me to the land of the living, and Erica, liking nothing better than to plan a social gathering, was coming up with different suggestions.

I'd said no to the idea of attending a party at Erica and Charlie's house. I'd given the excuse of not wanting to be bothered with babysitters, which was true in part, but the real reason was because I couldn't face a crowd. I was a long way from being able to converse normally when Leon was receiving round-the-clock care and would be for the foreseeable future. 'Restaurant?' Erica suggested next, before catching herself. 'Oh, hang on, that still leaves the babysitting issue. How about we do it here instead?'

When she saw that I was dubious about the idea she added, 'I'll cook! In fact I'll do everything! I'll enjoy it. It'll give me something to do. We'll do it tomorrow night and you can invite whoever you please. Perhaps only those closest to you though, Jane, those that you don't mind crying in front of . . . if that's what's worrying you. Does that sound doable? I think it does. I think it would be good for you to be around the people who love you and Leon but without any pressure. What do you say?'

What could I say?

I had to say yes.

My mother waved her e-cigarette around, saying, 'Don't worry about me. I don't need an invite. I've got my own stuff going on.'

She had begun dating a tax inspector named Cliff. Which was odd because he was not her type at all. My mother liked showmen. Charmers with commanding voices who told her she looked twenty years younger than she was, and that she still had the body of a dancer.

'Take yourself off shopping to Liverpool ONE,' she said. 'I'll look after the kids. You'll feel better when you've bought yourself a new dress. I know I always do.'

So I did. I washed my hair, put on a clean pair of jeans, and headed out. It was a bright, windy day and the salty tang of the Mersey was carried on the air. By the time I got to the shops the place was busy with bodies. Too busy for my liking, but almost straight away I found two outfits that would be suitable for a dinner party, which I thought Leon would like. He liked me to show a bit of leg – this was in spite of his comment about my awful milky-white skin at the hospital – and I'd selected each of the outfits with him in mind. He'd be looking at me in them one day, I hoped.

The sales assistant removed the security tag from the red dress and said, 'I've got this one in the black and I get *loads* of compliments. Is it for a special occasion?'

'Kind of,' I mumbled.

The assistant was at least eighteen years my junior and I now wondered if I was making an impulse mutton-purchase that I'd later regret. 'Do you think it's too young for me?' I asked, and she stopped what she was doing and looked directly at me.

'How old are you? Forty?'

'Thirty-eight.'

'Well,' she said, 'I had a woman in here last week bought this dress and she was sixty-two. An', honest to God, she looked really good in it. She didn't look like a dog's dinner or nothin'.'

'OK, then,' and I handed her my card.

After a moment she said, 'That's been declined. You got another?'

'It's what?'

'Declined. If you've got another, I can try that.'

'No, wait, hang on . . . wait,' I stammered. 'Can you try it again?'

She gave a tight smile and said, 'I *can* try it,' but I knew by her tone and expression that if a card was refused once, it was really not going to be accepted a second time.

'Same,' she said, handing it back. 'Do you want me to try another?'

'I don't have another.'

For a moment I stood there helpless, waiting, looking at the sales assistant as if she might know what to do. Embarrassed, she looked away.

'I don't understand,' I said. 'This has never happened to me before. I know for a fact there's money in there.' I stopped short of telling her that there was always money in the account and instead I apologized, saying, 'I don't know what's gone wrong here. I'm so sorry.'

'Phone your bank,' she said. 'Sometimes they put a stop on your card just because you're not buying the kinds of stuff you usually buy. My mum tried to book a cruise in June, she'd seen it online, gone to pay, and the bank blocked it. She lost out on the entire holiday, if you can believe it. Call your bank and have it out with them. I would.'

'That account is empty, Mrs Campbell.'

The information smacked me hard in the face.

'What?'

'The account is empty. Is there anything else I can assist you with today, Mrs Campbell?'

'It can't be empty.'

'The balance of your account, Mrs Campbell, is minus one hundred and eighty-eight pounds, fifteen pence . . . Is there anything else I can assist you with today?'

'That's impossible,' I said. 'It's gone into the overdraft. I never use the overdraft. How can it be—'

'Can I ask for you to speak a little more slowly please, Mrs Campbell?'

Usually I didn't mind talking to India. I got it. I understood this was the way the world was now and there was no use fighting market forces. If the banks needed to outsource their labour to another continent, another time zone, requesting their employees work throughout the night to answer our banking queries, then OK. I could live with it. But today, today I needed someone who understood. I needed a friendly regional accent, someone who would say, 'Let's see what the problem is, love.'

I took a steadying breath. I was outside Harvey Nichols. Women were exiting laden with bags and giddy expressions. I let my forehead rest on the cool glass.

There was no money.

Where was all the money?

My heart was striking my ribcage in a series of unsteady beats. I swallowed.

'I don't see how the account is empty,' I said, slowly, as the operator had requested. 'Has the standing order payment not gone in? Is there a problem with the standing order payment?'

'Which standing order payment are you referring to, Mrs Campbell? I will need clarification of the amount and—'

'From my husband's account.'

'His full name, please.'

'Leon Campbell.'

'There has been no deposit from that account since July, Mrs Campbell.'

'Why not?'

But I could guess what was coming next.

'We would need to speak to your husband, Mrs Campbell, to find out that information. He would need to call back. If he is with you now he can do this right away. It will only take a couple of minutes for you to have your answer.'

'My husband is in hospital,' I said weakly. 'He's been in a coma.'

'That is very bad news indeed.'

'How do I access his account? I have no money. How do I find out what the problem is?'

'Well, Mr Campbell himself can call this number, and go through the security checks. He can call any time to speak to one of my colleagues and then we'll be able to assist him fully when—'

'Never mind.'

I called Juliana. I asked her to find out if Leon could by chance remember his online banking security number. And without hesitation he said he most certainly could. He was annoyed actually that I'd doubted his recall abilities.

He then proceeded to recite our old telephone number.

So I headed straight to the branch on Lord Street. The chances of Leon eventually remembering his security number, and the answers to all those silly questions, were less than slim. *Name of your best friend's first pet? A favourite meal? The car you learned to drive in?* So the branch was my only option. I'd explain my problem face to face. The last time I'd been here was to arrange the mortgage. Shit. The mortgage. We'd have missed a payment. And the gas, electric and the phone. And—

'We'd need proof that you have power of attorney,' the clerk said.

I'd had to wait an hour to see someone.

'You're kidding,' I said.

She wasn't.

'Can't you just look at his account,' I said, 'and tell me if it has funds in it? Then I'd know if this is a technical issue or . . .' I paused. '. . . if it's something more complicated that I need to deal with.'

Leon's publisher paid his earnings directly to his agent. His agent then removed his 15 per cent and sent the money to Leon's business account, from which Leon removed a sum each month and placed it into our joint account.

'I understand your plight, Mrs Campbell, and I know it seems unfair, but these are the rules of the Data Protection Act. If we're seen to go against that we could be prosecuted.'

'So, what do I do?'

'You need to speak to a solicitor.'

'But it's Saturday. No one will be at work until Monday. And I have no money. And no access to any money. I have children to look after. What am I supposed to do?'

The clerk shrugged as though she was all out of ideas.

14

We were never exactly awash with money. Even though Leon now earned a substantial wage, we lived as most people did, and cut our cloth accordingly. Each month after the mortgage payment was deducted, my car payment, and all the other sundry payments necessary to keep the show on the road, there might be a bit left over for emergencies, though we didn't have a proper savings pot to speak of. But there should have been *something* in the account. We'd never been in the red.

Regardless of this alarming development, I decided to still go ahead with the dinner party. These were our friends, after all. I needed them, needed their advice. And there would only be five of us.

Erica covered everything, as she said she would. She didn't even use my kitchen. She prepared the three courses over at her place and commanded her husband Charlie to carry it across the street in batches. Leon's writer friend Frankie Ridonikis and his wife Oona would be bringing the wine. Both couples were eager to see me away from the hospital, they said. It went without saying that they'd all done their bit, visiting Leon fairly regularly, but I knew Leon's state of mind was beginning to wear on them, as they, too, found conversation difficult with someone they no longer had a lot in common with.

Naturally none of this was voiced, but I could sense by their eagerness to attend the dinner, by their enthusiasm to show me a good night away from the rehab unit, that they were finding Leon's situation draining.

Oona made a big fuss of the children, bringing marshmallows and a Pixar DVD that she hoped they'd not yet seen. And Frankie, as was customary for him, flat out ignored the kids, instead making a beeline for me, thrusting one of the bottles of wine my way, a Beaune. 'You tried this yet? No . . . ? Excellent. Can't wait to hear what you think.'

Frankie got real pleasure from introducing something new, but was never at all pompous about it. You know the way it can get some people's backs up when you tell them you already have a cellar full of whatever it is that they're peddling as their latest discovery? Never Frankie. His eyes would come alive and he'd say, conspiratorially, 'You've found this one too? How absolutely wonderful! We're both drawn to the *very* best.'

Leon met Frankie when they did an MA in creative writing together at Liverpool University and they had remained close ever since. They were both published within two years of finishing the course, a huge rarity, and were often invited back to be lauded, to talk to students, and to give the benefit of their experience. Leon considered it a duty to pass on knowledge. He said other writers had been incredibly generous with their time and wisdom when he was studying the craft, and it was part of a writer's responsibility to mentor those who wanted it.

Frankie Ridonikis wrote the kind of books that Leon

termed 'upmarket commercial fiction', but Frankie would have described himself as a literary writer.

He wasn't, Leon said.

Never would be, Leon said. He was a storyteller, plain and simple. They would never let Frankie Ridonikis on to their prize lists. He would never be up for one of the big literary awards. And I said: Who gives a shit so long as he gets to write books for a living? But people did, apparently.

'And if it's not in poor taste,' Frankie was saying now, 'I have a couple of bottles of fizz in the car as well.'

'Frankie!' admonished Oona. 'You said you wouldn't.'

Frankie gave Oona a withering look. 'No, Oona, *you* said I wouldn't. I didn't say anything of the sort.'

Minutes later, he was sorting out the contents of the fridge to accommodate the wine. 'There are a few nice reds there as well,' he said to me, gesturing to the countertop. 'Be sure to grab one, keep it for yourself for later in the week, when you fancy something decadent. The Malbec would be my personal choice.'

It felt good to have some adult conversation that didn't revolve around Leon's progress, or the police investigation, or the perpetual question hanging over all of our lives: Who attacked Leon?

I smiled at Frankie. 'Thanks for coming.'

He rose and hugged me to him. 'We're here for you. We're always here for you. We want to do more. Let us.'

Frankie and Oona weren't friends as such with Charlie and Erica, but they'd met one another on numerous occasions, always through us, and seemed to get on well enough. Though sometimes I did sense, for all Frankie's bonhomie and charm, he could feel threatened by Charlie, as, quite simply, Charlie earned more money than him. I'd read once that women check each other out when walking into a room to see who is the prettiest, whereas men try to gauge who would win in a fight. But I'm not sure that's true. I've certainly witnessed more than a number of men being thrown off balance by Charlie's wealth. It was surprising. They became quite unlike themselves: defensive, mildly malicious, as if Charlie was compromising their masculinity in some way.

In between courses Oona wanted to know about Leon's progress. 'The Tate's been maddeningly busy, Jane, and I've not managed to visit Leon for a couple of weeks now. How is he? As in, how is he *really*?'

'Much the same. He seems OK.'

'Is he scared?'

'You mean scared of the future?' I asked.

'I don't know what I mean. I'm just trying to imagine what he must be feeling, and I think my overriding reaction to what happened would be fear.'

I thought about this.

'Do you know what,' I said, after a moment, 'I don't think he is scared. It's such a strange thing, but it's like he doesn't know what he was like before, so he has nothing to compare it to. He gets frustrated and angry when he can't do things, when he can't remember, but I wouldn't say he's afraid. He just seems to accept that this is what he's like now. He doesn't know how bad he is, if that makes sense.'

Halfway through the sea bass I broke the other news.

'So, we have no money,' I said bluntly. 'There's no money left in our account.'

Erica, first to react, put down her cutlery. 'How on earth can that be?'

I shook my head. 'I don't know. I can't get access to Leon's own account without power of attorney, and I don't know what to do in the interim. Please don't think I'm begging for money, that's not what this is, I have a credit card with some credit available on it, and I can borrow a little from my mother until I see a solicitor. Really, what I'm looking for right now is advice . . . if you have any.'

I felt foolish. Embarrassed. But if Leon's brain injury had taught me nothing else it was that people really did want to help. You just had to swallow your pride and ask them.

Oona reached across the table and covered my hand in hers. 'Don't worry, sweetie,' she whispered. And she looked at her husband, Frankie, as if he should say something comforting too.

'Why on earth is there no money?' Frankie boomed. 'Surely Leon is being paid by HarperCollins? The money doesn't just stop coming regardless of what his current situation is.'

'I don't know,' I said. 'It's possible that there's some glitch on the account, some reason why the money hasn't been transferred from Leon's business account into our joint one. That's what I'm hoping. Obviously, if that's what the problem is then it's easily sorted out. If not . . .' I shrugged helplessly. 'If not, then . . .'

Frankie wiped his mouth on his napkin. 'Jane,' he said firmly, 'here's what you need to do. Get on to Jon Grayling first thing tomorrow morning and demand he tell you what the score is. This just doesn't happen. It has to be the bank's fault.'

Jon Grayling was Leon's agent.

In all the years Leon had been with Jon Grayling I'd

never met or spoken to him. His offices were in London and he didn't come north unless he had to. He was close to seventy, a wizened, humourless man, people said, and I could think of nothing worse than calling him and admitting I had no money for groceries or nappies.

'Any other options?' I said feebly.

'It's the fastest way to get yourself some answers,' Frankie said. 'And his bark is way worse than his bite. He likes to portray himself as some kind of forbidding gatekeeper, but he's just an old fool, if you ask me. Leon should switch to someone who actually looks like he's alive. I'm sure he'd do better with someone younger. Anyway, that's beside the point, he's Leon's agent and he will know *to the penny* how much Leon has been paid and when and what monies are due to him. Call him, Jane. Call him tomorrow.'

'Is he allowed to tell me the details of Leon's earnings?' I asked.

'Officially, probably not,' Frankie said. 'But I'd say there are extenuating circumstances.'

Erica smiled my way. 'In the meantime you only need to ask and we'll help out,' she said softly. 'You know that, don't you? I'd hate to see you and the kids going short after what you've been through.'

'Thank you,' I said. 'Thank you. All of you. I didn't want to put this on you tonight but with Leon incapacitated it's made me realize how bloody vulnerable I am without him. In every aspect.'

Everyone nodded. Everyone except Charlie. He was quiet. Noticeably quiet.

In fact, he'd not said one word since we'd started eating. Did he think I was begging? Did he think I was expecting him to come to my aid because he was the most affluent member of our gathering and should therefore put his hand in his pocket?

God. I hoped not.

He had his eyes lowered and was spending an inordinate amount of time chewing each mouthful.

'Charlie,' I said carefully. 'I do hope you don't think I was insinuating that you should help me out with—'

'What?' he said, his face confused. 'Sorry? What?' As if he'd not been listening. As if he'd been lost in a reverie and I'd just snapped him back.

'I hope you don't feel I was hinting that—'

'He doesn't think that,' cut in Erica. 'Do you, Charlie?'

Charlie looked mildly stunned and took a gulp of wine. We waited. He didn't look like Charlie. He looked troubled.

He took another mouthful.

'Jane . . .' he began finally, 'I don't know how to say this . . .'

Erica put down her glass and frowned at her husband. Whatever Charlie was about to say Erica was not privy to it.

'I'm so sorry to be the bearer of bad news but there *is* no money,' Charlie said softly.

'What do you mean?' asked Oona.

'There's no money in Leon's business account,' he said.

The news hit me at the back of the head.

'How could you possibly know that?' said Erica crossly. 'How on earth could you possibly know the details of his—'

'Because . . .' Charlie paused, took a breath. 'Because Leon came to me for a loan.'

Silence.

'A loan for how much?' I asked carefully.

'That's not important,' said Charlie.

'I think it is.' My tone was measured, belying the fact I was utterly floored by Charlie's divulgence.

'Eighteen thousand,' Charlie said.

I felt a cold sweat spring up between my shoulder blades. My scalp seemed to shrink on my skull.

'Eighteen thousand?' I replied. 'For what?'

'Leon wasn't specific. He came to me a few months ago and said he needed it to tide him over. He said some royalty payments, or perhaps it was the advance on the next book, had been delayed. Whatever it was, he was running low, and he didn't want to increase the mortgage again.'

'*Again?*'

At this Charlie's eyes widened. 'Look, I don't really know the ins and outs,' he bumbled. 'I was just trying to help. I assumed you knew about it.'

'But why did he come to you?' Frankie cut in. 'Why come to you, Charlie, and not me? I would have lent him the money.'

Frankie seemed quite put out about this and I'm sure would have pursued the matter further if Oona hadn't shot him a look and said, 'Sweetheart, let's try to help *Jane*, shall we?'

'Did you have any sort of repayment schedule?' I asked Charlie and he said he did. I wasn't surprised. Charlie was a good businessman. 'How much is left on the loan?'

'I'm sorry, Jane. All of it.'

My mouth fell open. 'He's paid back none of it?'

Charlie shook his head. 'No.'

'Nothing at all?'

'Not as yet. But he assured me it was coming,' he said quickly. 'He assured me he would have all of it very soon. He was naturally apologetic about missing the early repayments but said he would settle the debt in full just as soon as he received the next chunk of money from his agent.'

'Oh, Charlie,' I said, mortified. 'You've been keeping this to yourself all this time, the whole time Leon's been in hospital? I'm embarrassed.'

'Don't be,' he said.

I looked at Erica. 'Please tell me you knew nothing of this?'

Erica held up both palms. 'Don't look at me. He tells me absolutely nothing about his business affairs. Do you, Charlie?'

Charlie half smiled. 'It was between me and Leon,' he explained. 'No need for anyone else to know. And besides, Jane, Leon will soon be back to firing on all cylinders, churning books out like never before, and this monstrous trauma you've experienced will seem like a distant memory.'

The table fell silent.

They were all thinking the same thing: Leon would not be back to firing on all cylinders and writing books again any time soon.

Leon had trouble remembering what he'd had for breakfast and who his wife was. At the rehab unit, Leon needed a list of instructions simply to make a cup of tea. He would become distracted halfway through the process, putting the milk back inside the fridge before he'd poured it into the cup.

'That might not actually happen,' I said quietly. 'Leon may never write a novel again.'

'Oh, Jane!' cried out Frankie. 'You must be positive! You can't be beaten by this, it's—'

'Frankie,' I said, 'please, don't. Positivity is not what I need right now. What I need is help in finding a practical way through this. You've all seen enough of Leon by now to know he's not going to be coming home the same person. I need to make changes. If I start hanging on to the dream that Leon will pick up where he left off and everything will be OK then I'm being delusional.'

Erica reached for her napkin and dabbed at her left eye. 'I'm sorry,' she sniffled. 'Sorry, Jane. I don't mean to be emotional when you're managing to be so brave. Sorry.'

I glanced around the table and it was clear by their collective expressions, relief but marred by some guilt, that they'd discussed this subject in my absence. 'Do you think I should sell the house?'

'No,' said Charlie immediately. 'No, Jane, you mustn't. Forget about that money for now. I don't want you worrying about paying me back when—'

'Charlie,' I said, 'that's very kind, but I was meaning because of the bank. The mortgage hasn't been paid. The bank'll want their money, even if you're willing to wait for yours. How much do you think the house is worth?'

Everybody seemed reluctant to answer.

'Charlie?' I prompted.

'Hard to say,' he replied. 'I could get you an approximate valuation right now on my phone but . . .' He paused, stalling for time. 'Well, the thing is, the house is probably not worth a lot more than you paid for it. So, yes, you could sell it and come out with . . . how much did you put down?'

'Close to forty thousand.'

'Forty would buy you some time. You could find

something smaller or even rent. But if Leon has remortgaged, which I'm pretty certain he has, then you may find yourself with not very much left at all.'

'Oh,' I said.

Why the hell had Leon remortgaged? *How* the hell had Leon remortgaged without my knowing?

'Oh,' I said again.

'Here's what I would do,' Charlie said. 'I would make an appointment with your mortgage advisor as soon as you can and explain the situation. The banks are not sympathetic to people missing their payments without good reason, but if you go in and tell them what's happened to Leon, tell them that he's the breadwinner and that he's out of action, they will give you a break on the mortgage without turfing you out of here straight away.'

'They would do that?' I asked, surprised.

'They would!' Erica chimed in excitedly. 'I heard of a family who were given more than a year's grace after the husband was made redundant from Unilever over at Port Sunlight.'

That was something.

'OK,' I said. 'I can do that tomorrow. I also need to get back to work. I'm going to find out if I can pick up more teaching hours. The programme at Walton Gaol is usually available. No one ever wants to do that.'

'Call Leon's agent first,' said Frankie. 'That's the priority. Call him and insist he send you a printout of what Leon's had recently, and then tell him you need to know when the next payments are due and how much they're for. Ask him to chase any outstanding money owed. Publishers can be bastards, Jane. They hold on to it until you're practically claiming income support.'

I told him I would.

Then he said, 'I can't believe Leon has no money. Why didn't he say something? Why pretend he was flush if he had nothing left at all?'

'If I knew that, Frankie,' I said, 'I wouldn't be—'

But Frankie interrupted, aghast, '*Christ . . . !* What if he owes money elsewhere? What if the attack was the result of Leon not paying *other* creditors?' He sat back in his chair, stunned. 'Christ,' he repeated. 'Jane, you really need to tell the police about this. What if he owes money all over the show . . . ? It's not safe for you here; you have to get out—'

'Frankie!' Oona said. 'Stop it. You're panicking her. Your mind is running away with itself. Ignore him, Jane, he has an overactive imagination.' She leaned in. 'I do have to ask though: did you really have no hint at all that Leon was in this financial predicament?'

I shook my head. 'None at all.'

'You didn't check statements?'

'We're paperless.'

'But you never even snooped on his computer, to see what you could find? Even after he was attacked?'

'It didn't occur to me. Why would it?'

'Well,' Oona said, her eyes sprung wide, 'perhaps it's high time you started.'

15

While the others were cleaning up the kitchen, I called Detective Inspector Ledecky. I told her about Leon's account and said that though it could simply be a screw-up at the bank, I thought it best she knew what was going on.

Because what if Leon did owe money to the wrong people? What if they came back? What if they'd *already* been back?

Ledecky admitted that one of the reasons the investigation was proving to be so tricky to solve was because it appeared motiveless. I had been asked, back at the start, if Leon had any enemies, and I'd said no. Because with the exception of Alistair Armitage, heckling Leon at literary events, and someone keying his car earlier in the summer – which we'd put down to bored kids – I'd never known anyone to have a go at Leon. I'd also been asked if we had any financial problems, and I'd answered honestly at the time: 'No, we're secure. We certainly don't owe anyone money.'

That looked as if it was no longer true, and Inspector Ledecky assured me they would investigate this development thoroughly. She didn't say whether she was still investigating *me* thoroughly, and I didn't ask.

Now I was at Leon's computer. It was the first and only time I'd switched it on without his knowledge.

Leon's computer was sacrosanct, the place where he created his masterpieces, and so no one was allowed near it except him. He wouldn't even let me clean the thing in case I deleted an essential piece of information, so the screen was covered in finger marks, and there were biscuit crumbs and grains of sugar wedged between the keys.

Throughout the rest of dinner, I'd been eager to get up to his attic office to have a look at it. Impatient for the guests to leave so that I could do as Oona had suggested and snoop. Also, DI Ledecky had mentioned that they might want to look at Leon's computer again, in light of the current financial development, so I didn't know how much time I had.

Once everyone had left, I quickly checked on the children: Jack had wriggled down the bed and Bonita was curled up on his pillow. I popped her underneath my arm and deposited her outside the door before looking in on Martha. Martha was lying on her back in her crib, arms flung up high on the pillow, as if she'd been told to drop her weapon. I leaned over and stroked her hair. I touched her cheek and, reflexively, she made a slow, sucking action – something she'd continued to do since being weaned. She was still so small. So innocent. What if there was no money now to take care of her and her brother?

Once I was in the attic, at the computer, I cursed myself for not doing this sooner. For remaining blind to what was going on inside our household. After Charlie's loan revelation, I was not holding out much hope that the lack of funds in our joint account was down to a mere banking error. Leon had been worrying about money for months.

I thought back to the days, weeks, before the attack, trying to come up with something I might have missed.

Why would Leon keep the fact that we had no money to himself? I had heard about this. Men who remortgaged secretly rather than tell their wives that the money had dried up. Men who pretended to go to work rather than come clean and say there was no longer a job to go to. I'd always dismissed the wives of these men as head-in-the-sand types who must have had *some* clue. How could you not?

And yet, here I was. That woman. The woman who, after the arrival of her children, had handed over responsibility of everything financial to her husband. A woman who didn't ever think to question that what he was telling her was the truth. A woman who was now left high and dry because she didn't open her eyes.

Had Leon been attacked by loan sharks? Was that even possible?

The style of his assault certainly bore the hallmarks of an authorized attack: fast, violent, cold-blooded.

But Ledecky had always maintained it was more likely to have been an opportunistic attempt on Leon's life because the weapon belonged to us. 'We're working on the assumption that this was largely unplanned,' she'd said just after the nail gun was discovered. Someone came upon Leon, spoke to him, saw the open garage door right in front of the car, the nail gun on show, and took his moment.

But who? And, more importantly, why? I could only assume Leon owed money elsewhere.

A cold sensation spread through me. Had Leon asked Charlie for money to pay his other debtors?

But this still didn't answer the question of why we were in debt in the first place.

The computer prompted me for a password.

I'd seen Leon type in this password hundreds of times when I'd been up here delivering tea, coffee and – if it was after five o'clock, and he'd had a long day – whisky. But I'd never asked him what it was.

I typed: 'DS Clement'.

Leon's fictional detective was the password he used for most things. He stayed away from the kids' names, birthdays, our anniversary.

It was incorrect.

I tried: 'Detective Sergeant Clement'.

Wrong again.

Shit, Leon. What is it?

It occurred to me that I might never get into his computer.

I cast around the room for inspiration, something that might help with the password problem. Leon kept his workspace orderly; it was pretty spartan. He liked things in their place and said his mind couldn't work out complicated plots if there was clutter in his immediate environment.

I looked to my right. The bookshelves. Leon didn't keep his own novels up here because they paralysed him, he said. He was always in fear of repeating himself and found them an unwanted distraction. But he did keep a small selection of his writerly heroes close by for motivation: Stephen King, Ian Rankin, Lee Child.

Lee.

I typed in: 'Lee Clement'.

Lee Clement was the full name of Leon's fictional

detective but he never ever used it in his books. I think he hoped the books might become big enough one day that the name itself would take on mythical status, and readers would ask the question: But do you know Clement's *Christian* name? (And yes, that's what Colin Dexter did with Inspector Morse, held back his name so it piqued everyone's interest. Hardly original on that score, Leon.)

I hit enter.

I was in.

A giddy feeling descended and for a moment I was too jittery to type. I moved the cursor around his home screen not quite knowing where to begin.

I started with his emails. It seemed as good a place as any.

One thousand and forty-one unanswered messages. I scrolled through them. There was a lot of junk: promotional messages from Dirty Tinder; Hot Russian girls who wanted to please, and, one assumed, to be paid in return. There was some relentless dickhead who couldn't spell, sending daily emails, assuring Leon that HMRC was offering a substantial tax rebate, so long as he provided his full bank details.

I really had no idea what I was looking for. So, short of a better idea, I tried searching Leon's emails for the name Alistair Armitage, the budding author who accused Leon of stealing his work, since he was the only person I could think of with a real grudge against Leon.

Nothing.

This didn't really surprise me. Leon had always tried to put as much distance as he could between himself and Alistair and as far as I knew he never corresponded with him online.

What else?

I searched his emails using the words 'debt' and 'repay' and 'loan' but, aside from the usual nonsense from Nigeria, nothing jumped out.

I searched for 'Lawrence Williams', again because I had no clue what I was really looking for, and again, nothing came up.

I closed Leon's Microsoft account and opened up his documents.

All his novels were on there, the various drafts of each one saved as a separate file. And there were also a number of video files.

This got my attention as Leon did not shoot videos. It wasn't his thing.

We weren't the kind of parents who were organized enough to record their kids' big milestones. We enjoyed Jack's nativity rather than capturing the moment on our phones. We didn't think to document their first steps, their first words; we were just so busy being excited.

I clicked on the first video file and there was nothing.

A blank grey screen. Nothing to see.

At least, at first, I *thought* it was nothing. A grey screen, yes. Then, raindrops on glass. The clouds behind the glass moving slowly.

Where was this?

I heard Leon clear his throat, and there followed a high-pitched creaking sound which I realized was Leon opening the Velux window.

He was recording from the very spot just to the left of where I was sitting now. He was filming out of the window.

He angled the camera down on to the street until it

came to rest on Lawrence Williams opposite and Leon zoomed in.

'What the . . .' I said aloud.

Lawrence was cleaning his car. He was seated on a small stool, polishing his alloy wheels. He had a range of brushes and cloths at his feet. He wore a set of safety goggles to protect his eyes.

This was standard Lawrence behaviour. The question was: Why had Leon filmed it?

I clicked on another video file.

Again, the other side of the street. He panned up and down the houses as if he was looking for something. He zoomed in, then out. I could hear his breathing. Hear him exhale, trying to keep the camera steady.

Jesus, Leon, this is creepy.

Then there was a break in the film and when we returned he was on Rose's VW Polo: Rose, pulling out of her driveway with great care, as was her way. Rose had almost killed a cyclist outside the Everyman Theatre a few years back by opening her car door without checking her wing mirror first. She'd confided that the horror of that day had always stayed with her and so she was now overcautious. This was before I left my car outside her house for three weeks, back when we were still what you'd call neighbourly.

Why the hell was he filming Rose?

'What are you doing, Leon?' I whispered.

I sat back in my chair and frowned at the screen. What made Leon document the street? It made no sense.

I opened another file and then another. Same deal: grey sky, occasionally blue; a long, low screech as Leon opened the window, before he began filming the street.

Was this what he did up here all day?

When he was supposed to be writing?

I hardly dared open any more. It was disturbing. I clicked on another and another. All the same. All filming the street, sometimes Rose and Lawrence going about their daily chores. Occasionally, there'd be a clip of Glyn Williams, entering or exiting his parents' house. A close-up on Glyn's shifty gaze, his odd, uneven, stiffened gait, as he walked to and from his car.

The clips seemed obsessive, compulsive. What was going through Leon's head to make him do this day after day?

I opened one more. This time we were back on Lawrence. He was carrying the detachable bin from his lawn mower and was walking away from his house. The camera zoomed out so we got the wider angle, to show Lawrence's position, and then back in again as Lawrence looked around furtively, first across the street, then next over his shoulder. He then proceeded to dump his grass cuttings into the recycling bin of the house next door but one to his. It was the student house. I'd seen Lawrence do this too. I didn't see the harm in it. Those kids weren't in the habit of recycling their green waste.

Lawrence made his way back and the camera panned out just as a car rolled slowly into shot. It was a black saloon.

The car stopped in the middle of the road just outside our house.

It was a BMW. A Volvo perhaps.

The car idled for a while and Lawrence, his interest piqued, placed the grass bin by his gate and ambled over. Once by the driver's window, Lawrence started nodding.

'Yes,' he seemed to be saying, 'yes, that's right,' and he was laughing a little.

I increased the volume.

I heard Leon's breathing quicken.

Lawrence was now pointing across to our house and nodding his head in agreement.

When was this?

I checked the date of the file. August. Two weeks before Leon's attack.

Lawrence was still talking. Did he know who was in the car? He lifted his head and gazed upwards, towards the camera, and Leon must have taken a sudden step backwards in response.

The screen now showed the wall.

'Go back!' I shouted out in desperation.

But the screen went black.

16

I couldn't sleep.

My mind was reeling from Charlie's disclosure, from Leon's extensive surveillance . . . the black saloon car. Had the person driving that car attacked Leon? Leon had backed away from the window. Did he know the driver of the car?

I got up and paced. I couldn't understand how Leon had this almost other life that I'd not been privy to.

As dawn broke, I decided I couldn't undo what had happened to Leon, and I couldn't sit in the attic going through video clips all day in the hope of finding answers. I dropped Jack at school and Martha at nursery, and by 9 a.m. I was outside the bank, and ten minutes later I was in the private office of the mortgage advisor – begging her for more time. She agreed. She put a hold on the mortgage payments and said we would meet again in February to reassess. She informed me that Leon had *not* remortgaged the house, as Charlie had theorized, but he had instead taken out a long-term loan *against* the house, to the tune of fifteen thousand pounds – which was all but the same thing. He'd told the bank it was needed to go towards a new kitchen. And at least this explained how he could gain such a sum of money without my signature.

Where this money had gone to, I had no idea. I racked

my brain trying to think of what he could have needed it for, but nothing came to me.

What were you doing, Leon?

When I returned, and I called Leon's agent, I got my answer.

I was put through to Jon Grayling, after being placed on hold, and when I asked about Leon's recent payments, asked when the next instalment would be due from the book that was to be published in March next year, Jon Grayling coughed loudly, before saying, 'Book? What book? There is no bloody book.'

'I'm sorry?'

'Leon has not delivered his latest book,' he said. 'As in he's not *finished* his latest book.'

'Hang on,' I said, quite sure that Jon Grayling was confused, 'we are talking about the same book, aren't we? *Red City*? Leon told me this novel was done and dusted.'

'Then I'm afraid you've been misled, my dear. That book is only two-thirds done,' he said. 'And those two-thirds are nothing to write home about.'

This, Jon Grayling said, was why we had stopped receiving payments.

I felt as if I'd been slapped hard across the face.

'I think Leon's been living on fresh air for the past eight months,' he went on. 'He was calling me every day in quite a state . . . Shocking really, because Leon has always been so reliable story-wise . . . But I suppose everyone dries up eventually. Leon said he was blocked. Just completely blocked.'

'Leon told me he'd been working on a new book,' I said. 'He told me *Red City* was finished and he was working on a new one.'

'There is no such book,' Jon Grayling said bluntly. 'Leon was nowhere near done with *Red City* . . . and I have to tell you that HarperCollins are happy to give you *some* grace, my dear, on account of Leon's health, but I must warn you that if that book never arrives on my desk, then you'll be liable to pay back the advance in full – which Leon received last year. I wish I had better news for you.'

I could feel fury building in my chest. A loud rushing in my ears.

Why had Leon not *told* me?

'Did he explain to you *why* he was blocked?' I asked, trying not to think about how much we now owed HarperCollins. 'Did he explain why he couldn't write any longer?'

Jon Grayling sighed, long and hard. 'I think if writers knew the answer to that then they wouldn't get stuck in the first place. So, no, I can't help you there. But he did seem . . . what's the right word . . . he seemed rather *angry* about something. He never confided as to what, so I can't say whether that's what was holding him up . . . You really didn't notice this yourself?'

'No,' I said. 'I really didn't.'

'Ah, well, writers are an odd bunch. I'll never fully understand them.'

We finished it there and I was left staring at the phone trying to make sense of it all.

No book.

And no money.

And no way of Leon generating any money.

And he was angry? Angry about *what* exactly? What did he have to be angry about?

Christ, I felt as though I was going round in circles.

My next call was to Teresa Graham, the adult learning coordinator. I'd last spoken to Teresa just after Leon's attack when I informed her that I wouldn't be able to resume my creative writing classes after the summer break as usual. She understood, naturally, and she tried her very best to sound empathetic, but I could hear in her voice the panic at losing another teacher at such short notice. So when I called her today and said I was coming back, and that I in fact needed more hours – *a lot more hours* – she sounded as if she might burst into tears.

'Oh, Jane. Really? One of my full-timers has been signed off sick for eight weeks, and I'm at my wits' end. Can you cover her classes? It will involve the programme at Walton Gaol . . . I know you probably won't want to do that one but—'

'I'll do it.'

I told her I had to or we wouldn't eat.

I put the phone down and made a list of all the other things I'd need to sort out: Martha's nursery hours would need extending, and I'd have to call the family credit helpline to check if I'd be reimbursed for the costs; I'd also need to—

My mobile was ringing.

Gloria.

I wasn't expecting her to call this morning as Juliana had said she was barring her mother from the unit for a few days as well as me. Usually, Gloria called each day. She'd arrive at the rehab unit before me, and would then call to dictate a list of things Leon would require – items for me to collect from home, or else pick up from the shops on my way in: clean socks, nail clippers, apples, a nice prawn salad.

I put the phone to my ear and Gloria said, 'Jane, he remembers. Leon remembers.'

Thrown, at first I didn't answer.

Then I said, 'What does he remember?'

And Gloria paused. Not for dramatic effect, but because she was so overcome that the words literally disintegrated in her throat.

'You,' she said eventually. 'He remembers you.'

I was numb. Speechless.

Was this real?

'What does he remember about me?' and she said I needed to come.

'Come quickly and see for yourself. He has new memories. Lots of them.'

I took a breath. My legs felt as though they would give out. I sat down heavily on the sofa.

I hadn't expected this. I really hadn't expected this. Even though we had had glimmers of change, they were just that – glimmers. Juliana had devoted hours to going over shared childhood memories, hoping to find the key to unlocking her brother's subconscious. They'd had limited success; nothing that you could put your finger on. But there was definitely something marginally different about Leon: a change in his expression, a peacefulness, I suppose, that made you stop what you were doing and regard him differently. *Was he in there?* I'd found myself thinking more and more of late. Was Leon in there, just waiting, waiting for the right moment to emerge?

Could it be possible that Juliana and Eden, between them, had now finally managed to unlock Leon's mind?

I got my coat.

17

What was I expecting?

Perhaps I'd envisaged a kind of grand reunion, whereby Leon leaped up and embraced me, as if we'd been held apart for months on end. At last, we were back together and everything that we'd been through would fall away in the moment; nothing mattered any more because we were one again.

The reality was somewhat less dramatic.

Leon remembered me all right, and he knew that he was no longer married to Gina, so that was a colossal step forward. But it was as if he'd not missed me at all, and to rub salt in my wound, he didn't even remember *not knowing* me for the time he'd been in hospital. It was as if Leon had picked up exactly where he'd left off.

He regarded me, when I walked on to the unit, as he might have done had I walked in on him watching TV at home. He was mildly interested, but he was busily engaged in doing something else, so I didn't get my reunion, and Leon seemed neither happy nor unhappy that I was there. He just accepted that I was, and probably always had been. 'Hey, honey,' he said simply.

I had to stop myself from interrogating him. From asking about the unfinished book, the hours of video footage, all that bloody debt. Dr Letts warned us not to excite him. 'You'll have many questions,' she told us. 'For now, though, you must let him be.'

There were other changes too that were noticeable. Other improvements. Now, it was apparent that Leon could understand that he didn't always understand, if that makes sense. His self-awareness was returning. He was also aware that there were glitches in his reasoning, and he was getting used to the idea that the person he was presenting to the world was not the person he once was.

Trouble was, Leon didn't know *which* parts of himself were the real Leon. He was unsure which parts of himself he could trust. And all of this was making him more frustrated than he had been back in the beginning, when he'd had no awareness at all. He became more distressed without warning, the erratic violence would still show itself at times too, and now, on top of all this, we had another problem.

Leon had been heard yelling in his room. He was shouting, 'Get out! Get the fuck out of here!' repeatedly. Over and over.

When this had happened to me, I'd knocked. Because I always knocked. But Leon hadn't been aware of my knocking, and so I'd gone ahead and pushed the door open without invitation. What I was faced with made my stomach drop through the floor.

Leon was masturbating. Publicly. Well, perhaps 'publicly' was unfair: he was inside his own room, granted, but the doors were without locks, and it didn't seem to perturb Leon that someone could walk in on him at any moment.

That was, until Gloria did.

On the couple of occasions that I'd walked in on him, he was unembarrassed and did not think to stop. And so I'd had to leave the room until he'd seen the act through to completion. I was too mortified to ask the nursing staff or Dr Letts about it, so I'd gone online, only to find, surprise, surprise, that increased sexual appetite was often part and parcel of traumatic brain injury, along with inappropriate sexual behaviour and frequent masturbation.

Great.

I didn't mention it to anyone. I just added it to the list of things-to-be-concerned-about-when-Leon-leaves-the-unit, but in hindsight, I should probably have mentioned it to Gloria.

'Get out!' Leon shouted at his mother. 'Get the fuck out!'

When I reached Gloria, it was as if she was glued to her spot in the doorway and *couldn't* get out. She couldn't move. I rushed to her side, closing the door to Leon's room, before guiding her gently by the elbow to a row of chairs further along the corridor.

She was shaking.

I settled her into the chair. She was silent. Too shocked, too overwhelmed by what she'd just seen, to speak.

Finally, she asked, 'Where has my son gone?' and her eyes were glazed and empty.

'Let me get some tea, Gloria,' I said, but she reached out and clutched hold of my wrist, stopping me.

'No . . . don't go.' Then she fixed her stare on the blank wall opposite before whispering, 'That person in there is *not* my son. I don't know who he is, but he is not my son.'

This was the first time I'd seen Gloria crack. Up until

now she'd remained unwavering in her resolve. She'd cared for Leon without complaint, never once giving a hint that she was concerned about his behaviour, or worried for his future. It was as if she'd had complete confidence that we would all come out of this unscathed, as long as we kept going, as long as we put one foot in front of the other.

'I'm frightened,' she said.

'I'm frightened too.'

'What if he stays like this? What if . . . what if I've lost my beautiful son and we're stuck with this stand-in from hell?'

It was as if this was the first time she had actually allowed herself to think this way.

'You've not lost him,' I told her. 'Leon will be back.'

'When?' she demanded. '*When* will he be back?'

I wished I had an answer. Wished I could comfort her, but I knew, *she knew*, that there *was* no answer.

She turned to face me. 'I can't take him.'

There was alarm in her expression and terror in her voice.

'I can't take him,' she said again. 'And I thought I could . . . I really thought I could. I'd decided that if you didn't want him, then I would take him home with me and care for him. But . . .' She began to tremble. '. . . I don't think that's going to be possible.'

'No one expects you to take him, Gloria.'

'But he's my *son*,' she cried. 'I should at least *want* to take him. I always said I would walk through fire for that boy. Husbands, lovers, you can tire of . . . that kind of love can wither with time, but your own flesh and blood? I always thought I would die for my children.'

'No one knows how they're going to feel when something like this happens. It's easy to pass judgement until it's actually you that's facing such uncertainty.'

She nodded but I sensed she didn't feel at all soothed by my words.

'Jane,' she said, dropping her voice, 'I've not told this to anyone, but I've begun questioning my faith.' I went to interrupt but she hushed me. 'I've questioned if God really does have a better plan for Leon. Because, right now, that's hard to believe. I look at Leon in that room, doing that thing, and I feel . . . I feel abandoned by God.

'I don't know what to do,' she said. She was still clinging to my wrist, but I wasn't sure she was even aware of it. Finally, she whispered, 'I'm in despair.'

The following day, Dr Letts said, 'I'd like to be able to tell you that despair is an uncommon reaction amongst caregivers, but that would be untrue.' And then she gave us and Inspector Ledecky the go-ahead to revisit the day of the assault with Leon. It was sickeningly disappointing though: Leon did not recall anything of what had happened that day, and the only thing he seemed certain about was that I did not do it. I was not involved, he said, and seemed most perplexed when Inspector Ledecky raised the issue, saying he couldn't understand why he would have said such a thing in the first place.

'She's my *wife*,' he said to Ledecky, affronted.

He also had no memory of the weeks preceding the attack itself. This was common, Dr Letts told us, and as much as Inspector Ledecky gave it her all, as much as she tried to take Leon back in time, in an attempt to get him to recover anything – *Anything, no matter how insignificant* – it was clear she was flogging a dead horse. So a very dispirited Ledecky told Gloria and me that instead she'd concentrate on analysing Leon's computer for clues, and I thanked her, told her I appreciated her continued hard work on the case, and in that moment there seemed to be a kind of thawing of the ice between us, a loosening of the mutual agitation. And then, just when I thought there couldn't be anything else thrown at us for the time being, we were told, seemingly out of nowhere, that Leon would be coming home.

Dr Letts gathered us for a meeting and said she deemed Leon ready for *re-entry*, as she happily referred to it, and none of us were quite sure if she was serious. He wasn't ready. *We* weren't ready. My job would be starting again shortly, and I didn't know how I would cope.

Leon was coming home, and we would receive no help. None whatsoever.

I didn't feel capable of taking care of him and I hoped Dr Letts would throw me some sort of lifeline.

'What do other families do?' I asked her. 'How on earth do they cope?'

'I'm not sure everyone *does* cope,' she replied honestly. 'But there comes a time when we feel the patient is more suited to a home environment, rather than continue to stay at the unit. And that's where we find ourselves with Leon. He's ready, Jane.'

She went on to tell me that, shockingly, brain injuries were more common than breast cancer in the UK, but that the families of brain-injured patients were left virtually to their own devices once the patients left hospital. 'It's not how we want it to be,' she said, 'but I'm afraid it's how it is. Some illnesses and conditions get far more attention, far more resources. And, sadly, it seems as if neurological conditions are left right at the bottom of the heap.'

'You've done so much for him,' I said quietly.

I didn't want to complain to this brilliantly minded woman who had given my husband the very best care possible. But I was terror-stricken. How *would* I cope? How would Leon cope around the children day in, day out? He found noise and distraction difficult. He could only handle one stimulus at a time – if he was concentrating on a task, such as lacing up his shoes, practising his writing, he couldn't bear to have music playing, or anyone conversing nearby.

Sharing space with two children under the age of five was going to be a living hell.

After the masturbation incident, Gloria had given me a brochure. There was a residential care home near Southport called Magellan House, which specialized in treating young people with head injuries. She told me to hold on to it. She'd been to visit it and said it was a good place. She said Leon could be happy there, if that's what it came to. I thought of it now as I spoke with Dr Letts.

'He hasn't been left alone yet,' I said to Dr Letts. 'I'm not sure he's OK to be left alone.'

'It'll be tricky to start with. You may not feel confident leaving Leon, but there comes a time when you just have to take the plunge.'

'Is he safe?'

'We believe so, yes. Safe to take care of your children? No.'

I felt as if I was stepping into an abyss. Like that trip home from the hospital with your newborn when you find yourself stunned to be entrusted with caring for something you know you are in no way prepared to care for. Except this wasn't an infant you could tuck under your arm.

Leon was a six-foot-two, fifteen-stone, angry slab of tightly packed muscle. And he had an irrational mind and frightening temper.

'I'm sure it will all work out fine,' Dr Letts said weakly.

18

We were now into autumn, Martha's third birthday passed without fanfare, and Leon was home.

He was asleep; he slept a lot. A full eleven hours each night and two to three hours each afternoon, though this morning he'd felt more woozy than usual and had gone back to bed at 11 a.m.

Dr Letts had told us at our last meeting that 'Sleep is the one thing he *must* be allowed to do. It's how his brain repairs itself. Without it, his confusion and agitation will be much, much worse.'

'But for how long?' Gloria had asked.

'Allow him to rest each day for as long as he needs.'

'I mean,' Gloria had said, her jaw tightening, 'how long before he doesn't need all this extra sleep? How long before he can function without it?'

And Dr Letts had given one of her that's-a-question-I-don't-have-an-answer-to smiles that we'd become very accustomed to.

I knew why Gloria was asking. She wanted to know how long before Leon could get back to work. I'd told her about the money situation, about Leon not delivering his manuscript to his publisher, and she'd become quietly stricken. Gloria's generation didn't do debt. It's not how they were brought up. It was the one thing they'd been taught to fear most as kids – along with the Cold War and poliomyelitis.

I'd not told her about the video footage. Not yet anyhow.

For the time being, Leon was sleeping in the spare room. I hadn't been sure how to approach the conversation of our sharing a bed. Sex, intimacy, had not been broached by either of us, nor by any of his carers. No one had given me the tools to cope with any given situation, and I'd been too embarrassed to bring up the subject with his clinical team. I really didn't know how I felt about it. It was too soon for any kind of intimacy with Leon. I knew him, and yet I didn't know him at all. I knew his naked body almost as well as my own, and yet *change* the mind that's in charge of that naked body, and the body becomes that of a perfect stranger.

As it turned out, Leon solved the problem as soon as he arrived home. Five minutes after walking through the door, he took hold of his bag and asked me where he would be staying.

He followed me up the stairs, and sat himself down on the end of the double bed in the guest room. Leon patted the mattress a few times and for a second I thought he was gesturing for me to sit beside him. 'Nice,' he said pleasantly, testing the mattress again by rocking his hips from side to side. 'The bed seems firm enough.'

'Hope it's OK.'

I said this even though he'd slept here countless times: when we'd argued; when I was nursing the kids, and Leon's writing was suffering from the broken nights; in the height of summer when our room was like a furnace and neither of us could stand the heat coming off the other's skin.

'There's plenty of space for your clothes,' I said, 'but of course you're welcome to leave them in our . . . you're welcome to leave them in my room if you prefer.'

Leon spread his hands wide. 'I'm easy.'

'Well, I'm only just down the hallway if you need anything . . . Is there anything you want right now? Would you like me to show you how to work the shower? It can be kind of temperamental; you have to fiddle with the hot tap until the—'

'Jane,' Leon said, smiling, 'I'm going to be fine. Thanks again for having me. Thanks for . . . well, you know . . . thanks for all of it.'

'It's OK,' I said, and I tried to hold his gaze. Then I looked away and bit down on my lower lip.

I needed to say something.

And because he was being so genial, because he was being so accommodating, I was finding it hard to come straight out with it.

'Leon,' I began carefully, 'there's something we need to talk about.'

He looked at me in anticipation.

I laughed a little to try to mask my self-consciousness. 'It's kind of awkward actually.'

At this, Leon's expression did not change. He still regarded me with polite interest, as if what I was about to say might turn out to be some kind of pleasant surprise. A day out perhaps. Or a present I'd been withholding.

Leon missed the cues others picked up on. 'Kind of

awkward' would make a normal person, and I hate to use the phrase 'normal person', because it's so bloody unkind, but those words would make a normal person sit up.

Leon remained relaxed. Happy.

'You see this lock,' I said to him, turning, gesturing to the bedroom door. 'I had it fitted for you.'

'So . . .' He paused, unsure what the relevance was. 'So you could lock me in?' He was perplexed, but not really put out by the notion.

'No, sorry, you misunderstand. It's there for you to lock *yourself* in.'

He dropped his head at this but I could tell he still didn't know what I was getting at.

I moved towards the bed and sat down beside him. 'It's the masturbating, Leon,' I said bluntly. 'We can't let the kids see it.'

'Oh.'

'You do understand that, don't you?'

He nodded.

'Sorry,' I said. 'I know you've just arrived home, but I need to know you're going to do certain things in private. They're so very young, Leon, and they don't understand what's happened to you. Not really. They're not old enough to understand what makes you behave so differently to before.'

'Am I really so different?' he asked earnestly, and as I looked at his expression – worried, shame-faced, almost – my heart broke for him.

'Not so different, no,' I said, trying to back-pedal. 'You're not so different to *me*. But to them you're not quite who you were. They get confused and I really need to protect them from—'

'Protect?'

Leon's spine straightened, and he shifted away from me. 'What do you mean protect?' he said.

I swallowed. I'd told myself I'd be firm when I did this. Told myself it was kinder to give Leon the ground rules straight away. Let him know what he was and wasn't allowed to do and then there'd be no ambiguity. 'Yes,' I said, 'protect.'

He didn't speak.

I watched him carefully.

You never knew what would set him off. There was a fine line to tread between getting him to behave in the way that I needed to, and having him totally lose his shit.

'It's as serious as that, Leon,' I pressed. 'They're so small. I must protect them from you sometimes. You're not always OK. You do understand what I'm saying, don't you?'

I repositioned the mouse and sat back in the office chair. Rain was hitting the window as if someone was firing a hosepipe at it. Leon's computer had now been returned to us and I opened another one of Leon's video files, and watched as the camera panned along the street.

I'd yet to find a media file that *wasn't* filming the street, and when I'd mentioned this fact to the uniformed officer, who'd returned Leon's computer the day before yesterday, asking him what the forensics team had found on there, he'd seemed clueless as to what I was talking about.

'I'm just the delivery boy,' he said.

The camera panned left to right, left to right, along Lawrence's property, as if Leon was looking for something in particular, and then, like almost all the others, the film cut off.

I checked my watch.

I'd come up here to find out some information about teaching creative writing to offenders. Prisoners. I was scheduled to be at Walton Gaol this afternoon and I needed some tips. Of course, I could have used my own laptop. But Leon didn't know about that and using his computer gave me the excuse to snoop in his media files. My laptop was hidden beneath my bed.

I calculated how much time I had – was there enough to take a look at Leon's Word documents too?

Fifteen minutes.

I wagered I had enough time if—

'Here you are.'

I turned around fast in my seat and saw Leon standing in the doorway.

'You scared me.' I closed the file quickly.

'What are you doing up here?' he asked.

'Nothing.'

'Nothing?'

I studied his face before replying. Was he challenging me? Was he becoming riled because he realized I was poking around in his personal effects and he knew there was something to hide in there?

'I was looking for some stuff on creative writing exercises for prisoners,' I stammered. 'You know, for the class this afternoon?'

Leon made a face to suggest that that particular memory sadly hadn't been committed to his hard drive, and he gave me a rueful smile.

I exhaled.

'Well, you'd better come down,' he said, 'because Frankie Ridonikis is here.'

'Tips?' answered Frankie, a few minutes later.

We were in the kitchen. 'Yes, tips,' I said, 'pearls of wisdom that I can pass on to the inmates.'

'Quit while you're ahead,' Frankie said. 'That would be my tip.'

Frankie was like this a lot of late – down on writing. I think it was since literary heavyweight Philip Roth told a newly published author that writing was torture and he should stop now while he still had the chance. I suspected Frankie had adopted the same stance as Roth because he thought it made him look like a better writer.

'Frankie,' I said, 'these people aren't wanting to be novelists. They're in prison. They'll just want a few pointers. What can you give me? You must have something useful to pass along. You've been doing it for long enough.'

'Don't do this to yourself,' he said dramatically. 'Tell them that. A writer's life is so full of woe.'

Frankie had come armed with his laptop, on the understanding he was here to babysit Leon while I went to work. He'd been pressured into it by Oona, who had phoned just after Leon had been discharged from the rehab unit, asking if she could do anything to help, and I'd said, 'Well, there is one thing . . .' and because she was required to be at Tate Liverpool practically every minute of every day, she passed the job on to Frankie.

'He's always claiming he can write absolutely anywhere,' she said, 'so let him.'

It was probably just as well she'd passed the job on to

Frankie because, pre-brain injury, Leon hadn't liked modern art at all. 'I don't want to see anything in formaldehyde, and I don't want to see Tracey Emin's knickers,' he used to say. Without his filter, he was now liable to air his opinions straight to Oona's face.

Frankie began arranging his stuff on the kitchen table. Laptop, memory stick, a spiral-bound notepad, two different-coloured pens.

'What are you working on?' I asked.

'Can't say, I'm afraid. One word about the new novel,' he said, wiggling his fingers like a conjurer, 'and *poof* . . . the magic is gone. I simply cannot write the bloody thing.'

Frankie hadn't always been so secretive.

When I first met him, he could talk for hours and hours about his work-in-progress. Now, though still always good company, always ready for a drink and a laugh, I sensed that the writing no longer energized him as it once had. Frankie was like Leon in that some of the magic *had* gone out of the process.

I would yell at the two of them: 'Do you know how lucky you are to be able to do this? Day after day? To get paid to do the one thing that you love?'

And Leon would try to explain to me: 'You think, Jane,' he would say, 'that once you're published all of your problems evaporate. You think your life will be complete, that you'll have finally *arrived* at the point you've been trying to get to for so long. But that's not how it works. Success is a slippery fucker. Every time you think: *That's what success looks like,* whether it's a publishing deal, work optioned for TV or film, a spot on the *Sunday Times* bestsellers list, by the time you've achieved it, the goal posts have moved. You've already set your sights on something else. Something bigger. Something further away, so you can never feel satisfied. Not ever.' Then he added, 'I think that's why writers drink so much.'

When Frankie got his first publishing deal he started to dress in a suit for every occasion. Always a black suit, and always with a white shirt, open at the collar, and no tie. He wore it no matter what the activity, and secretly Leon used to poke fun at him. Said it all went to creating this image he had of himself as a *serious writer.* When Frankie appeared in his suit today and failed to remove his jacket, Leon had looked him over and asked, earnestly, 'Frankie, have you had to appear in court?' and Frankie had looked really quite wounded.

I let the cat out, showed Frankie how to operate the espresso machine, and told him I'd be back in around three hours' time.

'No rush,' he said. 'I've got to get this edit done by the end of the week, so it suits me to be trapped here with no distractions.' Then he lowered his voice, checked Leon was out of earshot, and said, 'Did you find anything?' And when I looked at him blankly, he added, 'On Leon's computer? Did you find anything? Oona told you to snoop. Did you snoop?'

'Oh,' I said, understanding now. 'I didn't find much. Just a lot of short films of the street. I can't really make sense of them.'

Frankie was frowning. 'Leon was filming the street?' he said.

'Yes.'

Frankie shook his head as though he couldn't make sense of it either. 'What did Jon Grayling say?' he asked.

I closed my eyes briefly. Then I checked behind to make

sure Leon was still out of the room. 'He said there was no book,' I whispered. 'He said the reason we've not been paid is because Leon didn't deliver his last book.'

Frankie's mouth dropped open. 'Jesus,' he said.

'Did he ever say anything to you?' I asked. 'Did you have any inkling that Leon was having trouble with—'

'No,' shot Frankie. 'No, of course not. I would have said. Are you really quite sure about all this, Jane? It just seems so out of character; I can't understand why Leon didn't talk to anyone about it.'

I shrugged helplessly. 'I can only assume that Leon was so blocked in his writing that he borrowed money to get by, and then when he got to the stage of borrowing from Peter to pay Paul, it all got out of hand . . . Whoever came here that day must have shot him because he couldn't pay them back and—'

There was the sound of footsteps in the hallway. The slap of feet on the pine floor.

'Thanks so much for doing this,' I said in an over-loud voice, so Leon wouldn't know we'd been talking about him. 'It's really good of you.'

'Jane,' Frankie said, 'it's nothing,' and he furnished me with a sad, sympathetic smile. 'Least I can do . . . Now go and show Her Majesty's detainees exactly how it's done.'

19

I had nine classes to teach in total, all within the Liverpool area. I would teach two per day, except today, when I had just one: Walton Gaol. The security checks in and out of the prison were pretty time-consuming, I was told, so it was impossible to fit another class in beforehand.

'Anything I need to know?' I'd asked Teresa, the course coordinator, with regards to dealing with offenders.

'They'll all tell you they're innocent,' she replied dryly. 'As soon as the prison officer's out of earshot, they'll tell you they didn't do it. They'll tell you they're being held there against their will. Just smile and nod,' she said. 'Smile and nod.'

Walton Gaol – no one ever used its correct name: HM Prison Liverpool – was practically falling down. It was an ageing Victorian building, sinister-looking from every angle, sound echoing madly within its walls. I'd arrived there early, as instructed, and I now had twenty minutes to kill until the start of the class. I'd been left alone, deemed trustworthy enough, it seemed, not to start a prison riot by pulling the television from its wall mounting, or setting the fire extinguisher off. I felt uneasy. I had the same feeling I'd get as a kid when left alone in an empty classroom: eight years old, skipping in from the playground to retrieve something from my bag, the classroom an empty, alien space without a teacher in it.

I glanced at my watch. Ten minutes to go.

The prison officer who delivered me to this room seemed to assume I was completely relaxed about standing up in front of a group of prisoners – not to be referred to as inmates. I was advised of this earlier when my bag was searched thoroughly and a packet of soluble paracetamol was confiscated. (Walton had a big drug problem. Drugs were easy to come by and had been found inside tennis balls thrown over perimeter fences, inside the carcasses of dead pigeons and, more recently, dropped from the sky by drones.) The prison officer spoke to me as if I was a professional delivering a much sought-after service, and even though I was apprehensive, at least being here was proving to be a good distraction from the myriad problems awaiting me at home. 'They need a bit of culture now and again,' the prison officer said when he showed me the classroom.

'So, you think the programme's beneficial?'

He shrugged. 'No one seems to have a clue what's beneficial any more. Changes every year. But they seem to like it,' he said, meaning the prisoners. 'And it doesn't do them any harm as far as I can tell, so give it your best. You'll find them a very captive audience.'

'What . . . what are they like? Not what they've done,' I added quickly. 'I don't want to know that.'

I'd decided it was best not to know. Walton Gaol is a closed, category B/C prison, housing males who do not require maximum security, but who do pose a threat to members of the community. I'd decided that, as with any student, they deserved to not be pre-judged, deserved to be evaluated only on their work and what they brought to each of the sessions.

That's what I told myself anyway.

The truth was probably closer to the fact that I'd possibly have a full-blown panic attack if I were aware of just what these gentlemen had done.

No one in here has murdered anybody, I told myself.

The prison officer said, 'There's a few odd bods, but mostly you'll find they're your standard prisoners ... Keep 'em busy,' he said. 'They have short attention spans, so you'll want to keep them doing something. Other than that, I can't see you having any problems. This lot are very well behaved, all things considered. And keep that personal alarm on you. Don't leave it out of reach.'

There would be no prison officer present during the sessions. All I had was the small push-button pocket-sized alarm. I thanked him, and he told me he'd be back shortly.

I tapped my pen on the desk again and moments later the door opened and they began to filter in.

I stood up.

Dressed mostly in sweat pants and T-shirts, this all-white group was ranged in age from their early twenties to their late sixties. Immediately, I began to make judgements. A slow-moving, tired-looking soul of pension age, who wore his sentence with an air of resignation, shuffled past. I was wondering what he could have done to land him in here when a guy with a green ink tattoo on his neck asked what had happened to their usual teacher.

'I'm not sure,' I lied. (She'd been signed off with stress.)

When they were seated I introduced myself. 'I'm Jane Campbell, your replacement teacher. It's good to meet you. I hope I'll be of some use in the weeks ahead and, as an amateur writer myself, I'd say we're all in this together. I'm optimistic that we'll learn from one another and I'm excited to get started.'

No one looked particularly enthusiastic.

'We were told you were published,' said the tattoo guy. And then he looked around him at the other prisoners, who began nodding in unison. They seemed disappointed. 'Our last teacher was published,' he said. 'We were told our new teacher would be published too.'

I frowned. By the looks on their faces I think they'd been expecting James Patterson himself to walk in.

I didn't know their previous teacher was published. 'What was her name?' I asked.

'Valerie Dowling.'

I was too embarrassed to say I'd not heard of her.

'So, you're really not published?' someone else asked, his tone suggesting he was quite put out.

'I'm not, I'm afraid. But I have received lots of very positive comments from agents, and the opening chapters from one of my books won a competition in the *Mail on Sunday*. I'm yet to see my work in print though.'

I delivered this news with a modest smile, expecting at least one of them to be marginally impressed, but instead there was a lot of shuffling of papers and exchanging of nervous glances.

Why had I not been told about Valerie Dowling?

And who was this altruistic author?

Whoever she was I was wary of her. Who in their right mind does this job when they have a publishing contract? When they can stay at home all day in their pyjamas and make up stories for a living?

I realized I was holding my breath.

'Her books are really good,' the neck tattoo went on. 'We've all read her. She has five books published. All by Amazon . . . And you really can't get better than that.'

Ah.

Valerie Dowling must have been using Amazon's CreateSpace platform to self-publish her books. So she was not a published author in the traditional sense at all.

'They're really good books,' said a dead-eyed guy on the table to the right. 'She's a pro. She said she had no trouble getting published. I wonder why you've been finding it so difficult?'

I really didn't want to start slagging off Valerie Dowling for misleading them so outrageously, but then I didn't particularly want to defend myself either. They thought I was a bad writer. That I wasn't good enough to teach them. They thought—

There were raised voices from over by the door. The beginnings of an altercation.

'You're not even supposed to be in here!'

'Since when do you decide what I do?'

There were two guys. Both were late twenties, both with thick Scouse accents. The first was thin, scrawny as a pre-teen, and the second, stocky – and more sure of himself. He wore a red Liverpool Football Club cap pulled down low on his forehead.

'He's not allowed to join halfway through,' said the first, vaguely in my direction. He had stringy hair and acne scarring around his neck.

'Fuck off,' replied the other. This guy had more swagger. He had a mean, irreverent look that suggested he was further up the pecking order. I went very still.

I watched.

The two prisoners were standing behind their chairs, unwilling, it seemed, to sit next to each other. The room was arranged into six areas; rectangular, melamine-topped tables were bolted to the floor and each had room for four prisoners.

I gave a quick cast about the room, but every chair was filled. There were no empty spaces.

The two surveyed each other with a simmering hostility and I got a feeling in my belly like I'd eaten something rotten.

Could this turn nasty?

In the outside world, a disagreement over seating would come to, at worst, some passive-aggressive exchanges and a bit of hurt pride. In here? I had no idea how far things could escalate.

'Gentlemen,' I said, addressing the entire room, 'is anyone prepared to switch?'

Everyone looked down.

The scrawny prisoner said, 'No one's allowed to start courses halfway through. It's against the rules. He's not supposed to be in here.'

'I want to write a letter to my son,' said the stocky guy. 'Miss, you'd be able to help me with that, wouldn't you? I don't write so well. It's his birthday and I want to write him a proper letter. He's only eight.'

The other prisoner was shaking his head as if I shouldn't even dignify this with a response.

I said, 'Of course I can help you with that. Why don't you both sit down and we'll get started.'

'I'm not sitting next to him.'

'Suit yourself,' said the other, and took his seat.

I looked around the room. It didn't appear as if anyone was willing to switch.

'How about,' I said, 'if you sit there just for today and next session I'll randomly assign seats from the list of names? That seems a fair way to do it.'

The prisoner with the neck tattoo who was now sitting at the table closest to my desk said, 'No reason we should all have to move for the sake of them. These are our seats. We always sit in these seats.'

I sighed. My instinct was to say, 'What are you – children?' but no one was finding this behaviour at all unreasonable.

I held my breath. Then: 'I don't know what to do,' I admitted.

I sat down, giving them my best *I'm beaten* expression, hoping they'd have the good sense to sort it out between themselves. There followed a general shuffling in seats, clearing of throats, everyone suddenly interested in the one strip light that had a faint flicker in the corner of the room, and then the cause of our problem, the Liverpool FC cap-wearer, the would-be letter-writer, stood up and said, 'What if I move my chair over to your desk instead then, miss?'

And I said yes.

Because what else could I say?

This was the first time I'd led a class where no one wanted to give me their elevator pitch, or tell me the unique selling point of their novel, or tell me why their novel was so much better than (fill in bestselling novelist's name here) and that said bestselling novelist didn't deserve their success, because their books were truly awful, and it was just that they'd had a good marketing machine behind them.

It was the first group I'd worked with who wanted to write for the sole purpose of writing. I asked them what they got out of it, because they'd been at this for six weeks or so now, under the tutelage of Valerie Dowling, and they were remarkably candid with their answers.

Most didn't really know why they'd signed up in the first place. One admitted thinking that creative writing was something akin to graphic design. He thought he'd be working on different types of lettering and was hoping to relive some of the vandalism days of his youth. Another thought it would come in useful when filling out forms – something he'd always struggled with, as he'd left formal education at the age of thirteen.

This was a running theme: their disconnection with the education system. Their experience of finding learning difficult, boring, humiliating. Education had always been something to rail against, and you had to wonder how much that had affected their ability to cope with the normal day-to-day challenges of adult life.

I found adult life hard. And I was a person who'd had every privilege. The average person found life hard: working at a job they didn't like, bringing children up responsibly, keeping an eye on their weight, their alcohol consumption, avoiding getting into debt, managing their relationships, caring for elderly parents, keeping the house maintained. Most people needed a little something just to get them through the day. Leon and I relied on alcohol. Frankie and Oona on cocaine, apparently. Erica pushed away her troubles with frequent trips to Waterfields bakers in Huyton to buy cream doughnuts and vanilla slices. My mother swallowed opiates.

As I walked around the room, it wasn't so difficult to

see how, without the best of starts, one could end up here without very much effort at all. When you listened to their stories it was clear that being born into poverty meant you couldn't make a mistake. Make one and there was no back-up, no one to help you out. Life could slide away from you astonishingly fast and you could end up here.

No one, it turned out, wanted to write about their crimes. 'This is where we come to forget our crimes! This is one of the only places we don't have to relive them,' they chorused.

I was quietly relieved.

Moving about and observing what the men were working on, I was struck by how autobiographical it was: letters written to parents, expressing their sorrow at the way they'd let them down. Parents who were long since dead. There were stories from their youth, moments that changed the course of their lives forever. There was a raw intensity to the work that you just didn't see in the usual creative writing class. Truths that professional writers would have sold their own mothers to have come up with.

Reading their work was both thrilling and heartbreaking. I honestly felt that I had little to offer in the way of teaching – aside from some guidance in spelling and grammar. And I was just about to announce to the class as much, tell them how impressed I was with what I was reading, when the man seated at my desk beckoned me over. The man who'd joined the class late.

Leaning over his left shoulder, my eyes came to rest on the letter he was composing for his son's birthday.

On the page he'd written one sentence:

'Are you Leon Campbell's wife?'

20

My first reaction was to smile, nod, say the thing I usually said when asked that same question: *That's right. Do you read Leon's books? Are you a fan of crime fiction?*

But as I examined the man's face it was instantly clear that we were not about to chat about Leon's tough-guy cop DS Clement. Or how, rightly or wrongly, the city of Liverpool was portrayed in the books. Or where Leon got his ideas from. Or if there was a TV drama in the pipeline. And who would play Clement? Idris Elba? Wouldn't that be nice.

'Yes, Leon is my husband,' I told him.

A cold draught hit the skin of my arms and turned them to gooseflesh.

'What did you say your son's name was again?' I said. 'Why don't you write that down and we'll get started on the letter? Have you thought about what you want to say?'

'Le-on . . . Camp-bell,' he said, enunciating each syllable.

His voice was like thick treacle and my stomach folded in on itself in response. I watched him carefully.

His jaw had begun to tighten. The small group of muscles in his cheek contracting, standing proud of the flesh.

He kept his eyes front.

Then he said, 'Leon Campbell,' again.

I waited for him to elaborate. It was starting to dawn that it was no fluke this person had opted to join the class midway through the term. And that the earlier argument over seating was perhaps not just childish behaviour. The other prisoners didn't want to be near him. They didn't trust him. He was trouble.

'Do you know Leon?' I asked quietly.

'Maybe. Maybe not.' He turned his Liverpool cap the other way round, so he was wearing it back to front.

I fingered the alarm in my pocket. Took a small step back. 'Do you want help with this letter for your son?' I asked carefully.

He laughed. 'There is no son.'

'Then you're scaring me.'

'No need to be scared of me, love.'

The 'love' was uttered sarcastically and nasty-sounding. The way middle-aged women of Liverpool would do when arguing: 'Don't be coming round this way again, *love*.' 'P'raps you'll keep better hold of your husband next time . . . *love*.'

'What do you want?' I whispered.

He turned his head. He looked at me for a long time. 'Who do you think you are?' he said. He held my gaze. 'You've a couple o' kids yourself, haven't you?'

I swallowed. My breath quickened.

And when I didn't reply he got up. He turned around slowly, straddling his seat, facing me. Then he sat down again, placing his elbows on the back of the chair. 'Two little 'uns,' he said.

'I don't want to talk about that.' There was a quiver in my voice and he noticed it.

Smiling, he said, 'I told you there's no need to be frightened of me, love.' Then he addressed the entire room. 'I'm just telling Miss here that there's no need to be scared of me. Isn't that right, fellas?'

No one answered.

In fact, as I glanced to my left, it was as if the others were going to great pains to maintain eye contact with the desks in front of them. As if they couldn't look anywhere else but there.

'It's the quiet ones you want to watch out for,' he added, laughing a little. 'Still waters and all that . . . Take Roger over there. Never speaks. Never makes a sound. Do you, Roger?'

The older prisoner lifted his head. He was writing about his childhood in Maghull. His father worked at Aintree, the racecourse. He was a groundsman of some sort, and Roger would accompany him to the course on the day of the National each year, spellbound by the spectacle.

Roger averted his eyes quickly. He did not want to be involved.

'Do you want to know what Roger did?'

I shook my head.

'You won't like it.'

I started edging away. I maintained eye contact. I did not want to turn my back.

'Hey!' he said. 'Where d'you think you're going?'

'I have other students,' I replied, shakily. 'There are others here who require my help . . . not just you.'

In a silly, sing-song, lady's voice, he mirrored, '*Others here who require my help. Others here who require my help . . . not just you.*

'Don't waste your breath,' he said. 'That'd be my advice . . . You're not going to get this lot to learn anything. They're all soft in the head.' He tapped his index finger to his temple by way of illustration.

He was enjoying himself immensely.

He seemed to be gaining sustenance directly from my fear. He was one of those who thrived on chaos, on causing disruption. The most dangerous type of prisoner. I should have sent him out at the start. I should have read the cues from the others and called the prison officer back and asked that he be removed.

'You look frightened, miss. Are you frightened now?'

'I already told you I was.'

'Aw, you don't have to be. What can I do to you? One press of that alarm in your pocket and the room'll be running with people. I couldn't get to you even if I wanted. And I don't. I'm a nice guy. We're all nice guys here. Didn't they tell you that?'

'What do you want?' I whispered.

Sweat had begun to bead on my skin. I couldn't tell if he was playing me for the fun of it or if he had a real agenda. Was I the fly, and he was pulling off my wings, my legs, one by one?

We were around three feet away from one another and I took another step to increase the distance.

'Careful walking backwards there, miss. You never know what's behind you in a place like this. Have to have eyes in the back of your head.'

I wished he'd stop.

I'd been told to use the alarm in an emergency. I'd asked if the alarm was silent and the prison officer had looked perplexed.

'What use would that be?' he'd said, and it was then I'd realized that what I'd thought was a high-tech piece of kit, sending silent radio signals to officers in a control room somewhere, was nothing more than a high-volume rape alarm, designed to attract the attentions of a concerned passer-by.

'We've never had any trouble with civilians,' the prison officer had told me.

The man in front of me looked at his hands now and began drumming his fingers on the back of the chair, tapping out a rhythm.

Then he stopped and raised his head. 'Fuck off,' he whispered. 'Fuck off, fuck off, fuck off.' Over and over.

'Leave her alone, Toonen,' someone said.

So that was his name. Toonen. Did I recognize it? Had Leon mentioned it?

Almost lazily, Toonen looked over to his right. 'Or what?' The other voice didn't answer, and I didn't dare take my eyes off Toonen. 'I'm not doing nothin',' he said. 'She knows that. Don't you, miss?'

I nodded vigorously.

If I pressed the alarm how long would it take for help to get here? Five seconds? Thirty seconds? Three minutes?

My mind volleyed through what he could do to me in three minutes. I needed to get nearer to the door.

'Don't you move,' he mouthed silently.

I shook my head to say I wasn't planning to.

'You can go soon,' he said.

Then he started drumming his fingers again. 'How's Leon doing now?' he asked.

'He's fine.'

'Really? 'Cause I heard he was *not* in good shape. Heard

he lost his mind. That he's some kind of vegetable. That's what people are sayin'.'

'He's doing OK.'

'Can he still get it up?'

I didn't answer.

He rose from his chair. 'Aw, come on, miss, don't be shy with me.'

I took another step back.

He closed the gap between us. He said, 'Can he still make you squeal?'

I pressed the alarm in my pocket.

I pressed it again.

And again.

'What's wrong?' Toonen asked. 'You seem a bit panicked.'

By now I had my back against the door and he was almost upon me.

I pressed it again. Nothing.

'Please don't hurt me.'

He moved in. His face was inches from mine. 'I have a message for you.' His breath was inside my nose, inside my mouth. It was sour and foul. 'You make sure you listen to what I have to say.'

He paused.

Now we were forehead to forehead.

With one hand he reached up around my throat and began to apply pressure. With the other, he stroked the outer side of my right breast. Lightly, carefully, as though it was his intent to try to turn me on.

No one in the room moved. They were aware what was happening but not one person moved.

He leaned in to my left ear. 'You stay away from playing Miss Marple, Jane.'

I tried to tell him I didn't know what he meant but he squeezed my throat harder. It started to burn.

'You stop all this nonsense. No more trying to find out who hurt Leon.'

He squeezed my throat harder still until I gagged. Then he began clawing at my breast. I was paralysed to get away.

'The people who hurt your husband really don't want to hurt you too. Or those little kids . . . Now, nod your head for me, sweetheart, tell me you understand. Tell me you'll stay out of this.'

I tried to nod.

'That's right,' he said. 'That's right. There's a good girl.'

21

I bolted out of there. I could still feel his hand around my neck, his breath inside my mouth.

I was gagging and retching as I ran. I gulped for air. My breathing had stalled. No oxygen reached my brain and I felt my legs would dissolve beneath me. I could go no further. I was bent at the waist, heaving, wheezing, my lungs begging, when I felt a hand on my shoulder.

Panic coursed through me.

'Easy,' said the voice.

I looked up.

A prison officer. He told me to calm down. His manner was firm. 'You need to calm down or you won't breathe.'

I tried. But it was as if Toonen had compressed my larynx to the point that it wouldn't open. Fleetingly, I wondered if he'd snapped my hyoid – the small bone shattered in strangulation victims.

I put my fingers to it. The skin was hot to the touch.

'Breathe,' he said. 'Can you stand?'

I tried to straighten. He put his arm around my shoulder and held me up. I still hadn't seen his face clearly; my vision was blurred.

'I'm going to take you into that room,' he said, pointing.

There was a door, a few feet away on the right. 'You'll be safe there. D'you think you can walk?'

I nodded.

Slowly, slowly, he guided me and, once inside, he asked me if I was OK. He was a bearded, blond, great big bear of a man with flushed cheeks. A Viking. I tried to speak. I was still breathing hard.

'Apart from your neck, are you injured?' he asked.

'No.' My voice came out cracked and strangled-sounding.

The room was an office-type space. Except that the desks were without computers. It must have been some sort of break room. There was a kettle in one corner and a sink unit. A row of mugs upside down on the drainer.

'Sit down for a minute.'

'My bag's still in there.'

He nodded grimly.

Moments later, he returned with the bag and handed it to me. I opened it and the contents appeared untouched.

'It was Toonen,' I told him. 'He forced me up against the door.'

'Ryan Toonen. Troublemaker,' he said.

'He knew things about my husband. He knew things about me . . . he threatened me.'

The prison officer made a cup of sugary tea that turned my stomach, but he insisted I drink it; then he told me I'd need to make a statement. 'You'll have to do so before you'll be granted permission to leave,' he explained. He was apologetic. Told me he was very sorry this had happened, but that it was unusual. In fact, he said, he'd never known this to happen to a civilian, never mind a woman, in the whole time he'd been at Walton.

He escorted me to another wing where I gave an account to a jaded female officer who documented the incident in full. She was probably quite a looker two marriages ago, and when I told her I was worried there would be repercussions from people Ryan Toonen knew on the outside, she gave a shrug and said, 'Toonen's a lot of hot air.'

'But he knew my husband,' I argued. 'He knew *me*.'

'So talk to the police,' she said tonelessly before asking me to sign and date the statement and telling me I could go.

Were they watching the house? The people who attacked Leon? Were they watching me? The kids?

Did Leon owe them money? Would they keep coming until they got what they needed?

I felt sick at the thought.

I didn't remember driving home.

Didn't remember making my way across the city, stopping at red lights, changing lanes. I wasn't aware of where I was going until I found myself signalling to turn into my street.

I pulled up to the kerb. Lawrence, Rose and Glyn Williams were in their front garden. They were taking down the hanging baskets from either side of the front door. Glyn was up a ladder and, on seeing my car, he smiled my way. He went to raise his hand, but then he dropped it again suddenly when Lawrence appeared to castigate him.

I turned away. And it was only then that I realized I'd not switched my mobile back from silent.

I reached into my bag and looked at the screen and my heart stopped.

Twenty-six missed calls.

Twenty-six missed calls from Frankie Ridonikis.

22

I found Frankie in the lounge nursing a glass of Scotch. Christ knew where he'd found it because I didn't know we had any. It wasn't something either Leon or I drank, so it must have been at the back of the cupboard, along with the half-bottle of Advocaat that came out at Christmas.

Frankie was ashen. 'I'm so sorry, Jane.'

He stared straight ahead as he continued to sip his Scotch as though he was too rattled to do a lot else.

I went into the kitchen and poured myself a finger of Scotch. Downed it. And placed my hands flat on the counter top while I tried to get a handle on my breathing. My throat still throbbed from where Ryan Toonen had held me fast. I looked at the bottle of Scotch, contemplated having another, and instead went back to the lounge. I needed to collect the kids from school and nursery shortly.

'There was a scuffle,' Frankie admitted.

'What do you mean, scuffle?' Frankie Ridonikis was not a big man. Nor was he a fighter. Though he was wiry, and sometimes wiry people can surprise you with their strength. From the look of Frankie, though, I'd say he must have come off worst; he didn't appear beaten up but, rather, roughed up. As if Leon had zipped Frankie inside his gym bag and swung him around his head a few times – the way psychopathic adolescents liked to do with cats.

Leon had then escaped.

I put my fingers to my neck. It was throbbing. My mouth felt as though I'd been drinking lighter fluid. I was trembling, but Frankie was too shaken up himself to notice.

'Are those scratches?' I asked him.

He nodded.

'From what?'

'That bush by the back door.'

'The rose bush?' I asked.

'If you say so, yes.'

Fearing for his life, he said, Frankie had rushed upstairs and locked himself inside the bathroom – Leon hammering on the door for a full half-hour demanding he come out and face him.

'How did things escalate to that?' I asked.

Frankie didn't know. 'It came out of nowhere,' he explained. 'He got up from resting, came downstairs, and I suppose he was mildly surprised to see me. He couldn't recollect my being here earlier; it was as if his memory had been—'

'Wiped clean?'

'Exactly that.'

'It happens. But he remembered *you*, right? He knew who *you* were?'

'Oh yes, he remembered me. We even chatted about work. He was interested in how I was going about editing my new book, so we talked shop for a bit. To be honest, for a while it was like I was speaking to the old Leon. He even cracked a couple of funnies . . . They weren't actually funny, but that's a step in the right direction, yes?'

I agreed. Jokes were a new thing. A good thing.

'Go on,' I said.

'Well, then he just totally fucking lost it. He grabbed me by my neck and lifted me from the chair. He said I was spying on him. That I'd been sent here to take his material. He said that I was nothing but a second-rate writer who bored everyone to tears and was incapable of original thought.'

'You know he doesn't mean that.'

(He did.)

'I know, but, Jesus, Jane . . . he was frightening. I'm not sure you're OK to be here with him. I mean, is he even ready to be out of that place yet? I don't think he is. Was he properly assessed?'

When it looked as if Leon was not going to give up and Frankie was worried he was going to knock the bathroom door right off its hinges, Frankie had made the decision to climb out of the window. He did not have his phone on him, so effectively he was held prisoner. He lowered himself on to the ridge tiles of the utility room's roof, before dropping over the side of the building, getting tangled in the roses on his way down.

When he had tried to sneak around the side of the house Leon was there waiting, shaking his head, bemused by Frankie's attempt at escape.

'I'm off,' Leon had said to Frankie calmly.

'Where are you going?' Frankie had said, but Leon told him it was none of his business.

'So, you have absolutely no idea where he headed?' I asked Frankie.

'None.'

I exhaled. This was the last thing I needed. What I needed

was to get rid of Frankie, call Inspector Ledecky and tell her about Ryan Toonen.

'What was he wearing?' I asked.

'Jogging bottoms and a T-shirt.'

'No coat?'

'No coat.'

'Well, I suppose he's not going to freeze to death.' It was a mild day. Damp but mild. 'What did he have on his feet?'

Frankie shrugged. 'I'm sorry, Jane, I can't remember.'

Leon had taken to wearing flip-flops most of the time. He'd also done away with the need for underwear, something we'd talked about at length. I'd pleaded the case for wearing it but Leon simply saw no need. 'Like wearing gloves inside the house,' he'd explained.

Frankie threw back the rest of his drink.

'How many of those have you had?' I asked.

'Three,' he said. 'But I'm absolutely fine to drive.'

He wasn't, so I dropped Frankie at home. He lived not far from us in one of those three-storey, once grotty, now decadent, Georgian townhouses on Upper Parliament Street. The place was furnished and decorated white on white, like a Copenhagen apartment, and this was done to showcase Oona's art. Her stuff was all a bit GCSE textiles for my liking: hemp cloth stuck on to jagged bits of green patina, Celtic designs bordering large hangings of parchment. There was no actual drawing involved.

Some time ago, at a dinner party at Frankie and Oona's (when Leon had had a drink too many), Leon had picked up a pen and paper and challenged Oona to sketch a man riding a bicycle – to prove that she could draw. She'd laughed it off, but when Leon wouldn't let it drop, she ended up smoking and crying outside, telling me what a cruel fucker he could be.

And she was right. He could.

Oona had become a skeletal version of herself in these last months. None of us knew what was at the back of it, but it seemed to have been done wilfully: she had begun exercising to extremes and choosing the vegan option whenever we ate out. We knew she'd gone too far. Her head looked too big, her eyes abnormally large inside her face, and when finally she gained back some of the weight, it was as if her features couldn't quite recover from the lengthy assault. *What's done is done,* they seemed to say, and she was left looking like an older, shrivelled version of the person she once was. She had, before that, been very good-looking, but now no one could quite remember, so her beauty no longer held much relevance.

When Frankie was out of the car, I picked up the children from school and nursery and began searching for Leon. He was alone. He couldn't look after himself. I had to find him.

I doubled back towards our house, reasoning that because Leon was on foot, and without money, he couldn't have got very far. I told the kids to look out for him too, but every time I spoke, it sounded as if the ends of my words had been scraped away. Jack looked at me suspiciously and I told him I thought I was coming down with a cold. I scanned the pavement and thought of Leon. He must have known he was in danger. He must have known Toonen's associates on the outside would eventually come to collect, and when he couldn't pay them, he'd pay with his life. Was that what the videos were all about? He'd tried to get them on camera as some sort of insurance?

'Why is Daddy out all on his own?' asked Jack now from the back seat.

My first instinct was to lie: *He just wanted to go for a nice walk*. But the way in which Jack asked, his voice full of worry, his little eyebrows knitted together, a crease I'd never seen before forming across his forehead, made me think he needed the truth.

Jack knew that the person who had come home from hospital was not the person who'd gone in. I'd catch him looking at Leon, sceptically, when Leon said something out of context, or did something slightly off. Such as when Leon covered the whole of his chicken leg in ketchup before eating. Or smothered Jack in kisses before he went up to bed, because, after all that time of being unable to recognize the children, Leon had now done a complete one-eighty, and was embracing them with gusto. Particularly Jack. He would spontaneously squeeze him – too hard. Which I could see was making Jack uncomfortable.

Jack was now frightened of Leon, but he was also frightened of pulling *away* from Leon, lest it hurt his feelings. Because if Jack did pull away, the hurt would register instantly on Leon's face, and I could see this tore Jack up. He didn't know what to do.

Two people who had always had such an easy warmth with one another were now practically strangers and it was agonizing to watch.

I'd tried to talk to Jack about it. Tried to explain as best I could that he should not feel bad if he didn't always like being held so tightly by his daddy. It was going to take a bit of time for all of us to adjust to one another. But I also told him he might find it easier if he *pretended* to be having fun with Leon sometimes. He didn't always have to be having fun for real.

I could try to rein in Leon's sudden displays of affection, but it wasn't fair to tell him to stop altogether. Nor did I think it was healthy for Jack in the long term to pull away from Leon completely. We all had to find ways of being able to be around him, and the fake-it-till-you-make-it approach was currently working out the best for me, so I hoped it might help Jack too.

Martha, by contrast, didn't care one bit what Leon did. I'm not sure she even remembered Leon properly. Of course, when he was in hospital, and then later in the rehab unit, the adults around her had talked of Leon incessantly. But I don't think she actually pieced together that this person who was taking up so much of our time was her father. Now that he was home, she seemed perfectly at ease and would squeal with happiness whenever Leon tickled her too hard, or hung her upside down by her ankles.

'Daddy's not really supposed to be out on his own, Jack,' I said in answer to his question. 'He left without telling Uncle Frankie where he was going and I'm a bit worried.'

'Do you think Daddy might get lost? Or someone might steal him?'

These were the warnings I'd given to Jack in the past. He was not allowed out of our front gate because he might get lost or stolen.

'I think so,' I said.

'Daddy won't get lost,' said Martha, giggling, as if the thought of Leon disappearing was truly hilarious. 'He's big.'

‘He’s big,’ said Jack crossly, ‘but he’s not clever any more, Martha.’

I looked in the rear-view mirror to see him turn away from his sister in disgust.

The light was starting to fade. I headed towards Sefton Park and drove slowly around the perimeter. Would Leon go for a run? I had no idea what the new Leon would do. I don’t think *Leon* knew what the new Leon would do.

I thought about reporting him missing. ‘Is your husband a vulnerable individual?’ I imagined them asking.

He was a six-foot-two man in good physical shape who had not lost his ability to fight mean.

But yes, he was vulnerable. Of course he was vulnerable. He had a brain injury. He was easily riled and he had no concern for his own safety. Add to that he had no coat, no money, no phone and no keys.

Which was why I’d had to leave the back door unlocked – just in case he came back.

23

The sky was now black.

The house, too, was in total darkness; the porch dark like the inside of a sack – which meant Leon had not yet found his way home.

We'd been looking for nearly two hours and the kids were tired, fractious and needed a meal. I'd stopped to ask at the shop on Lark Lane, where Leon sometimes bought his beer; enquired at Keith's Wine Bar, where Leon would grab a coffee when the writing was getting on top; I went to his gym; I drove to the Albert Dock, the Salthouse Dock, the Queen's Dock. The docks were one of the first places the people of Liverpool were drawn to when someone went missing. But there was no sign of Leon anywhere and eventually I had to give up and return home.

I opened the front door. 'Leon?' I shouted from the foot of the stairs.

Nothing.

I should ring the hospitals. Find out if he'd been brought in injured. I should call Gloria too. She should know.

But something stopped me. Should I worry her with this? So soon?

I turned on the table lamps in the hallway and flicked

off the stark ceiling light overhead. I got the kids out of their coats and shoes. Martha was demanding a chocolate biscuit and was using a new habit she'd adopted when I wouldn't give in to her demands. She would repeat the same word over and over, woefully, until she was finally able to make herself cry, and her tears, she intimated, were evidence of how wrong I was in denying her whatever she so clearly needed. *Biscuit. Biscuit . . . Biscuit.*

'You can have half,' I said to her, and she quit the tears, skipping off to the kitchen to help herself.

I turned on the kitchen light for her, hung up my coat, and took out my phone from my bag. Then I googled 'the Royal', pressed 'call', and waited for an answer.

'The Royal Liverpool Hospital.'

'I wonder if you can help . . . my husband's missing and—'

'Missing persons are dealt with by the police.'

'Well, he's not . . . The thing is he might not actually *be* missing. I don't know yet.'

Silence from the woman receptionist at the other end.

'He has a brain injury,' I explained. 'And he's wandered off. And I'm not sure he's really able to look after himself. Not yet anyhow. He's not been out of hospital very long and I'm just trying to find out if he's been hurt. If not, then I should probably wait a bit longer before contacting the police . . . He's only been gone a few hours.'

'His name?'

'Leon Campbell.'

A pause, and then she said, her voice softer now, 'We haven't had anyone brought in with that name today, love.'

'He has no ID on him. What if he's injured and no one knows who he is?'

I could hear her typing.

'We've not had any unidentified men through these doors today at all. Have you tried Aintree? There's the A&E there as well.'

'I'll call them next. I was hoping he couldn't have got that far. He was on foot.'

I walked through to the kitchen to check on Martha. She was sitting at the table; her chubby legs, encased in flowery leggings, were swinging backwards and forwards, and she was sucking the chocolate from a KitKat. Her fingers were covered, as were her cheeks, and her chin.

I stopped dead.

Behind her, the kitchen door was wide open.

'Did you open that door?' I whispered.

Martha shook her head.

A shudder passed down the length of my spine.

'You're quite sure you didn't open that door?' I said, the alarm clear in my voice.

And Martha looked up at me, her eyes rounded and fearful, now quite aware there was something very wrong.

'Did you?' I repeated.

'I didn't,' she said. 'Mummy, I didn't.'

'Mrs Campbell? Are you still there, Mrs Campbell?' I could hear the receptionist's voice coming from the phone in my hand.

I cut off the call.

I walked over to the back door and stuck my head out. There was a motion-sensor security light that came on whenever anything came within a few yards of the house. But everything was in darkness, meaning it hadn't been triggered in the last five minutes.

Did that mean someone was already *inside* the house?

Had the person who attacked Leon come back?

I closed the back door, gently, so as not to make any noise, and I stood with my back against the wall, my breath catching with fear.

I motioned to Martha to keep quiet.

'Fingers on lips?' she whispered.

I nodded.

I considered my options. If there was someone inside, then I'd need to be able to get out fast. Need to get the kids out fast. I wondered if it was a mistake to have closed the back door.

I opened it again.

I could take the kids across to Erica's. Deposit them with her and then get Charlie to return with me to check the house.

Charlie kept guns. Shotguns. Up until this moment I'd always considered them to be a monstrous liability. Why keep guns in the house when the statistics said that rather than defending your own property successfully, you were far more likely to die from your own weapon?

Suddenly guns didn't seem such a bad idea after all.

'Don't move,' I said to Martha. 'I'm getting your brother.'

'Can I have another biscuit?'

'Don't *move*.'

Jack was in the living room. He was watching TV. Or else he was supposed to be watching TV. That's where he'd headed earlier, but the TV was on and he wasn't in there.

I walked into the room, stood in the centre, and did a full three-sixty. Then I did it again just to be sure.

No Jack.

He must have gone up to his room.

I stood at the foot of the stairs and listened for any sounds coming from above. Was Jack up there? Had someone *taken* him up there? I cursed myself for not spotting the open back door immediately on my return. If I had, I could have got straight out of the house and called the police.

Children make you astonishingly vulnerable. You can't run and you can't fight.

Did I get Martha out now and come back for Jack?

No. I couldn't leave him.

I took the stairs carefully, one at a time, planting my feet silently, still listening. There was no light filtering from beneath Jack's door. None from Martha's either.

'Jack?' I whispered. 'Jack, are you up here?'

My house didn't feel like my house. I loved this house. This was the place I wanted to be when the outside world was chaotic, when things got too much. This house restored me.

Now my house was a stranger in an alleyway. It was threatening, wanting me to feel afraid of it.

'Jack?'

Again, my voice came out strangled-sounding and hoarse.

There was a little light pooling around the top of the stairs from the lamps I'd lit previously in the hallway beneath. But other than that, the rest of the first floor was in shadow.

I moved into the darkness and stopped.

There was a sound.

From above.

Someone was on the second floor. Someone with a heavy tread, too heavy to be Jack's.

The steep attic stairs elbowed round to the right half-way up. Meaning the top of the flight was invisible from where I stood. I placed my foot on the first step and then retracted it quickly. *Think, you idiot!* Think about what you're about to do. People met their deaths by not considering the facts, not weighing up the risks.

I punched out a quick text to Erica. *Someone in my house. In attic. Send Charlie.*

I would wait for Charlie.

That was the sensible option. Safety in numbers. Charlie would help. He would know what to do.

I checked my phone. No reply.

But what if he didn't come? What if Charlie wasn't home and someone had my son up there and—

I scaled the stairs fast.

I saw a strip of light beneath the door. Moving closer, I could hear nothing. No voices from within. I nudged open the door enough to see inside.

What greeted me was carnage.

Absolute devastation.

And sitting amongst it all was Leon. Leon, his head between his knees, his fingers laced around the back of his neck, rocking forwards and backwards.

Jack was over in the corner, his back to the room, and he was on Leon's computer. I let out a gasp of relief. He was here. He was OK.

Images I was familiar with bounced across the screen in front of Jack. It was a children's programme – some low-budget, ten-minute, BBC thing that I would sit Jack in front of periodically, whenever I needed to complete a task that required concentration.

'Leon?' I ventured cautiously.

He lifted his head. His corneas were bloodshot, his lids swollen and heavy. He looked like a wounded animal. Get too close and you could get killed. I could see he'd been crying. Was still crying, in fact.

'Jack,' I said, 'leave that alone for a minute and go and check on Martha for me, will you? She's in the kitchen. You can help yourself to a biscuit.' My words were delivered unusually brightly and Jack was instantly suspicious.

He climbed down from the office chair, turning to glance at the screen, unsure if he should plead his case for remaining.

'Jack,' I repeated levelly, my voice firm. 'Go.'

'Bye, Daddy,' he said.

'Bye, son.' Leon didn't look up as Jack left the room.

There was stuff strewn everywhere: hundreds of loose pages of what appeared to be Leon's old manuscripts; also there were bills and receipts scattered about. The whole place looked as though it had been tossed by looters.

The two chest-height filing cabinets, in which we housed old accounting records, birth certificates, as well as Leon's research material and work-related stuff, had been emptied. Each of their drawers had been pulled open, the contents strewn across the room. The cabinets looked ravaged, almost.

My gaze moved to the floor. There was a hole. A proper, great, gaping hole. The floorboard was splintered and it stuck up at a wild angle.

My first thought was that someone had broken in.

And then Leon lifted his head and whispered, 'Thanks.'

I looked at him, uncomprehending. 'Leon, has someone been up here?'

He gave a lazy kind of laugh before saying, 'You well and truly fucked me, didn't you, Jane?'

'Fucked you?'

This was not something Leon would say. Not to me.

'Are you OK?' I asked. 'How's your head? Frankie said—'

I stopped. It was now dawning on me that this was not the work of some crazed intruder, but Leon himself.

Which meant he was confused. Which meant he was upset.

He'd clearly been searching for something. Something that might make sense of his new situation? Something to shed light on how he ended up with a brain injury? Or was he simply trying to figure out who the real Leon Campbell was before all of this happened?

Christ, I thought suddenly, he'd not come up to try to *write*, had he?

Surely he'd not set to, trying to pick up where he left off with *Red City*, and this chaos was the result?

He wasn't ready to tackle something of that magnitude. He needed baby steps. That's what Dr Letts said. 'Try to get him reading. Short things to begin with. Shopping lists, the sides of cereal boxes, the *Daily Mirror*.'

'Aw, Leon,' I said, making my voice soft now, encouraging. 'What's happened here?'

I spread my arms wide to indicate the room's disorder but he didn't respond and it struck me, looking at the contents of what were once meticulously organized files, now dropped haphazardly, or flung far from where they should be housed, that the files themselves resembled Leon's brain. What was once an ordered system, containing a multiplicity of information, easily accessed, was now more like a dumping ground for useless facts and memorabilia.

I moved towards him. My intent was to comfort him. But as I approached he reared up.

He flew from the floor to his full height in a split second.

'Leon,' I said, my heart beginning to thud hard inside my chest, 'what's going on?'

I reached out to him, but he slapped my hand away hard and left it there, stinging. Memories of being slapped as a child crowded my thoughts. Humiliation. The shock of the strike slackening my insides. My face beginning to burn with quiet rage.

'Leon,' I said, quietly, and he glared at me. His eyes were locked on mine and he looked at me with a wildness that was something close to hatred.

'Please,' I said. 'Explain this. What happened?'

He shook his head in defiance. The thick muscles of his forearms began to twitch.

'You can't tip this place upside down and let Jack witness whatever it is that's sending you off like this,' I said. 'It's not fair.'

Leon turned away.

'He's beginning to change, Leon,' I pressed. 'He's not the same little boy any more.'

Leon didn't speak and at first I thought he might apologize, ask for help. But instead he sighed out long and hard before setting his jaw. 'Two sets of prints,' he said simply.

What?

'Your prints were on that nail gun, Jane,' he said.

I opened my mouth to speak and then closed it again.

Where was he going with this?

He'd known this information since regaining consciousness. Why was he bringing it up now?

I regarded him levelly. 'And so were yours, Leon,' I said. 'Two sets of prints.'

He widened his eyes and then he laughed. 'Well, I sure as hell didn't shoot my*self* in the head.'

I held his gaze.

'What?' he said, challenging. 'Oh, don't be ridiculous. You're not really suggesting I would do that? Why would I do it?'

'I've no idea.'

'Don't fuck with me, Jane,' he said. 'Don't fucking joke about this.'

His voice had taken on a warning quality. His *don't you dare* tone.

'I'm not joking,' I said quietly. 'But if you feel you have the right to accuse me of doing that to you, after all we've been through these last few weeks, then you should know it's crossed my mind that you could have done it to yourself.'

This was true. In my quieter moments, I had thought about it. When nothing else seemed to make sense, and I'd questioned Leon's sanity before the brain injury, I had wondered if it was possible. Had he wanted a way out? Had he thought about ending it so he didn't have to face up to things?

'Again,' he said, but through his teeth this time, 'why would I want to do it?'

Leon didn't know about the loan from Charlie. On a couple of occasions, I'd mentioned money, mentioned how Charlie could be generous-to-people-who-found-themselves-in-difficulties, but I was met with a bewildered look. He also didn't know about the videos I'd found. And, of course, he didn't know about what had just happened with Ryan Toonen.

Could he have shot himself as a way out of whatever shit he'd got himself into?

I cleared my throat. 'I don't think you were altogether clear-headed in the weeks preceding the attack.'

He laughed. 'Maybe I wasn't.'

I was about to say that he was in trouble. That he was being threatened. But he pulled a folded piece of paper, a brochure of some sort, from his pocket and without warning he threw it at me.

The corner hit just below my right eye.

Too frightened now to move, to pick it up, I whispered: 'What is it?'

'Read it.'

'I don't know what it—'

'Read it! In fact,' he added nastily, 'why don't you read it out loud, you bitch? Read it so we both get to hear.'

I unfolded the brochure and stared at it. I began to shake. 'Jesus Christ,' I whispered.

Not this.

'Read it!' Leon yelled again, and he slammed his fist into the wall next to my head.

I cried out in fear. My legs turned to liquid as I slid down the wall.

Leon had never hit me. Never shown violence around me.

'Read it!'

I pleaded with him to quieten. 'The kids will hear . . . They're not used to this, Leon . . . they'll be scared. Please . . .'

He punched the wall over and over until the plaster broke through. He punched until his knuckles were bloody and he was breathless with exertion.

Then he took the brochure from my shaking hand.

He read from it, his words coming out like bullets, purposely meant to wound. '"Magellan House",' he said. '"A modern care facility that includes ten bedrooms. Magellan provides skilled and loving care. The level of service is besp . . . The level of service is bes . . ."' He began to stammer. He didn't know how to pronounce the word 'bespoke' any more. 'Who was he, Jane?' he yelled again instead. 'Who the fuck was he?'

'Who was who?'

'The shit you've been screwing all this time!'

'He wasn't anyone.'

'You're lying. You're lying to me.'

'I'm not. I'm not. There is no one else. How could there be?'

He had it in his head that I'd planned this. That I'd planned his incapacitation because I'd been having *an affair* with another man. He yelled that I'd wanted him out of the picture, but was too afraid to leave him. So I shot him in the head instead, and now look at him. Look at *us*.

I couldn't tell him it was his mother who had given me that brochure. That she'd handed it to me and told me to keep it safe. That I might need it one day.

He pushed the brochure into my face. He was smothering me. Hurting me as he moved the flat of his hand backwards and forwards as if rubbing it in, as if trying to somehow screw the thing into me.

'Leon,' I said, my speech stifled. 'Stop, I'll call the police.'

He pulled away and I sank to the floor.

'You won't call the police. You're too scared to call the police. Because then they'll know. They'll know what you've done. That detective was right. She told me you'd done this. She said I remembered you doing this.'

'Leon, I—'

He towered above me. His chest was a huge slab of muscle. His thighs, visible through the thin cotton of the joggers, taut and massive. They were like a sprinter's. Overdeveloped, powerful. Unnatural.

'You wanted me gone,' he said.

'I didn't. Why would I?'

He had evidence, he said. Proof. 'And,' he said, 'didn't that detective say that no one was seen at the front of the house that day but you? Didn't she say that, Jane? Didn't she? Answer me!'

'I didn't try to kill you, Leon.'

I was trying to make myself small, edging along the floor towards the sofa, my knees pulled in tight to protect my chest.

But he caught hold of my hair.

'Tell me,' he said, pulling my head back. 'Tell me, Jane.' His eyes were bulging, his face inches from mine. 'Who were you sleeping with?'

'You!' I cried out. 'It was always you . . . Jesus, Leon, listen to yourself. You can't remember anything. You can't remember *anything* about our life from before. You're not being fair. We loved each other.'

'When?' he said sceptically. 'When did we love each other?'

'All the time.'

He seemed to find this fact incredible. Unfathomable.

And I could see how it could be a stretch – the two of us entwined, naked. This, when there had been no physical contact beyond a few awkward hugs since he was brought out of the coma.

Right now it seemed an impossible feat to try to persuade him of what we were like before. What we had. Who we were. The love between us that was at times fierce, frightening, brutal, but then could also be astonishingly tender, and so, so easy.

I felt beaten, crushed.

I had nothing left.

'I loved you, Leon,' I whimpered quietly. 'Only you.'

And then I sat, curled up, my breath coming out as quiet, raggedy gasps, my head buried low, waiting for this to all be over.

Eventually Leon gave up trying to get the 'truth' out of me and went downstairs.

I lay on my side, my face turned to the wall, and stared at the knots in the wooden skirting board.

I ran my finger over them. I was too shattered now to cry. Too worn out. There was no emotion left. It was all so bloody sad. It was all so sad and there was nothing anyone could do to make it better.

I had to ride this out and see how long I could last. *For better for worse.*

I'd vowed to love Leon. Vowed to stay with Leon. But this wasn't Leon. As his mother said, this wasn't her son, this was some stand-in from hell, and I was supposed to stay and look after him. Help him get better. Rehabilitate him somehow.

I couldn't do it.

'Jane?'

Leon was calling out my name from the first-floor landing.

'Jane, are you up there?'

'What is it?' I said weakly.

Would he apologize? Did I even *want* him to apologize?

I rubbed at my eyes. An apology wouldn't cut it. I would have him readmitted to the rehab unit. Or admitted to Magellan House. That, or else have him arrested. We couldn't go on like this. I couldn't risk the kids being in the same house as him. There was no—

'Jane,' he called out, 'where's the bread?'

I crawled towards the door. 'What?'

'The bread?'

'What do you mean?'

'Jack's hungry,' he explained, 'and I can't find any bread. I'm going to make beans on toast for everyone. Where do you keep it?'

'The freezer.'

A pause, and then: 'Why the freezer?' There was no trace of anger in his voice.

'It stays fresher.'

'Oh,' he said brightly. 'Oh yeah. Makes good sense. Do you want some?'

'No . . . no, thank you.'

I heard his footsteps retreat down the stairs and my weight fell heavily against the wall.

Leon was like a dog now. He lived only in the moment. He would have no real memory of causing the destruction of the past hour. And I could go downstairs, rub his nose in the mess, yell at him, and he would look at me sorrowfully, but confused nonetheless, and he wouldn't understand my actions, wouldn't grasp the reason why I was being so mean. And he would cower at my raised voice, my raised hand.

My phone pinged. A text from Erica. *Charlie on his way.*

I sent a reply. *No need. Sorted.*

For a time, I remained amongst the detritus, amongst the double-spaced typed manuscript pages that had once held such meaning for Leon, thinking: We can't go on like this. *We can't go on like this.*

I looked at the hole in the wall, at the hole in the floor, and thought: What if he'd hit me instead?

What if it had been my head?

What if he'd hit *my* head against the wall?

And I curled myself up and wished to be someone else.

24

All night I thought about leaving.

After Leon had gone to bed, and I was in the shower, the water scalding my skin, I thought about nothing but leaving. As I scrubbed the traces of Ryan Toonen away from my body, not stepping out of the shower until the water ran cold, I thought of leaving Leon.

But I had nowhere to go.

I considered the notion of turning up at my mother's: kids at my feet, suitcase in each hand, telling her that I simply couldn't take it any more, but I knew it wasn't the answer.

My mother wouldn't have me for more than a couple of nights, and, when it came down to it, I *couldn't* leave Leon.

Not yet, anyway.

Not until I'd at least tried to find a way through this. Exhausted every available avenue. That's what I'd vowed to do when we married; I'd vowed to stick it out until the end.

I went to call Hazel Ledecky, tell her about what happened at Walton Gaol, but then I cut the call off before it connected.

What if whoever had done this to Leon found out I'd

gone to the police? What if they found out I'd ratted out Ryan Toonen, and there were repercussions?

Toonen had given me a warning: *No more trying to find out who hurt Leon. The people who hurt your husband really don't want to hurt you too. Or those little kids.*

Of course, on paper, it seemed so simple. I absolutely *should* report it to the police. They could find the connection between Ryan Toonen and Leon – some lowlife who was known to both of them – and the police could make an arrest.

But as I pictured Jack and Martha's faces, terrified, because there was a man in the house, a lunatic they'd sent to frighten us, I wasn't sure I could go through with it.

So I didn't. I didn't call. Instead I contacted the rehab unit in the morning and I told them I needed help. I called and said I was not equipped to care for Leon alone. But though exceedingly sympathetic, I sensed they were not unused to these pleas from desperate family members, and it took some real imploring on my part before eventually they agreed to send someone over to assess Leon. Someone would come by tomorrow, they said. There might be the chance of a part-time carer, they said. But it was clear they weren't promising anything.

Now it was ten thirty at night and I was propped up in bed. Bonita was curled up on my lap and I was trying to think of ways to keep Leon calm. I needed to prove to him that I did not put that gun to his head. That I was not responsible for the state he now found himself in, lest he became violent again whenever he remembered. Did I have anything that would prove I had nothing to do with this? Perhaps showing him the correspondence between himself and his agent Jon Grayling might persuade him that he'd not been altogether equable. That he was not quite himself in the weeks leading up to the attack. Perhaps if he knew about his unfinished book, the debt he'd accrued, he might then begin to better understand—

'Who's Alistair Armitage?'

Leon was standing in the doorway, fully naked.

He was piggy-eyed and did not appear completely awake. Was he sleepwalking?

But then he saw my eyes drift southwards, and he became embarrassed – covering himself with his hands.

'I just woke up,' he said, frowning, 'and I can't get the name out of my head. Alistair Armitage. Do I know him? Do I know anyone by that name?'

Bonita uncurled herself and angled her small head towards Leon.

'Kind of,' I said carefully.

Alistair Armitage was the author who heckled Leon at events. The one who accused him of taking his ideas.

'How do I know him?' he asked.

'He's a writer . . . you just sort of know him through work.'

'Oh,' he said, and he seemed relieved. 'Good. Thought I was going mad there for a minute.' And he took himself back to his room.

I watched him go.

What had prompted that particular memory? I puzzled. Seemed like an odd thing to suddenly pop into Leon's head. Sure, his recollection of things returned with no real orderliness – memories from thirty years ago resurfaced mixed up with things that had happened back in July. But there had been a kind of running theme so far. Most of what Leon remembered were events that had elicited heightened emotions: births, deaths, feeling afraid as a child . . . that sort of thing.

Where had he plucked Alistair Armitage from?

I frowned. I grabbed my laptop from beneath the bed and typed 'Alistair Armitage' into Google.

Who was this guy and why had Leon suddenly remembered him?

I scrolled through the results. It seemed 'Alistair Armitage Author' was big into social media. He was a mustard-keen blogger. He'd self-published a couple of novels, but without the weight and money of a big publishing house behind him, it looked as if he'd had to rely on social media to get his products out there. This could be an uphill battle, I knew, because I had friends who'd self-published and it required a lot of hard work to get the books noticed.

I read a couple of Alistair's recent blog posts and decided I needed to talk to him.

Up until now, I'd always taken Leon at his word that *of course* Alistair Armitage was a hanger-on, a jealous wannabe, someone who had taken to stalking Leon because his own work had yet to resonate with publishers. And he was desperate to blame his lack of success on something, *anything*, rather than admit his own lack of talent.

But what if that wasn't entirely true?

What if Alistair Armitage was not a misguided hapless failure and there was actually some truth to the story of Leon sabotaging his work?

Was that possible?

I didn't want to believe it, and – granted – it was unlikely, but then again, it was also unlikely that a successful author such as Leon should lie about his financial situation to everyone he knew. And also keep hidden the fact that he was unable to finish his latest novel.

I sent Alistair a quick email.

Dear Alistair

You don't know me. I'm Jane Campbell. Leon Campbell's wife. I know you two have a 'history'. Would you be willing to talk to me? I have some questions. I'm sure you heard about Leon's brain injury and things are quite difficult for us at the moment. I'd appreciate a moment or two of your time if you could spare it.

Kind regards
Jane Campbell

Immediately, I got a response.

Dear Jane

I have been interviewed by the police three times. I have nothing further to say.

Sincerely
Alistair Armitage

Interviewed three times? I'd got the impression that Hazel Ledecky had dismissed my information on Alistair Armitage. That she hadn't taken it seriously at all. Perhaps she was doing more behind the scenes than we were giving her credit for.

I sent a reply.

Dear Alistair

I appreciate that. And I really wouldn't ask if it wasn't important. I feel like you could be the missing link in finding out what happened to Leon. Do think about it. Please.

Jane

And then I got this:

Dear Jane

I find it hard to talk about this without it having a deleterious effect on my health. I have spent a small fortune on medications, supplements, counselling, meditation retreats, osteopathy, acupuncture . . . I could go on. I am currently experimenting with CBD oil for anxiety-related problems (it's extracted from the cannabis plant, now legal in the UK) and this, finally, seems to be working. My point is this: I've come a long way since your husband's actions ruined my life. My health is everything. I value it more than my writing.

I understand that you are looking for answers but I am not the person to supply them. In my experience, someone like Leon Campbell, who I have been consistently disappointed in because of his inability to tell the truth, does not oppress the little people to further his own career in isolation. There will be others he has hurt.

Please do not contact me again. Just the mere fact of writing this email has caused the tremor in my right forearm to return. Something that I thought I'd seen the back of.

Alistair

OK, so he was a little more upset and affected by his quarrel with Leon than I'd first anticipated.

But that kind of reaction to failure wasn't exactly unheard of amongst the writing community. I had online writing friends who'd had to have therapy when one member of our writers' group got a publishing deal and they didn't. Suddenly, people who'd at one time been chatting on Twitter almost hourly, supporting one another, championing one another, could now not even bring themselves to type an emoticon.

Writers are a sensitive bunch. We feel more intensely, sulk more readily. I've heard it said that to be a writer you must be thin-skinned enough to feel the pain of others deeply, and as thick-skinned as a rhinoceros to be able to withstand all the rejection.

Alistair Armitage was obviously pretty thin-skinned. But I found it hard to believe that Leon was responsible for *all* his health issues. He seemed like the kind of guy who just couldn't let go of the past. One who blamed his current situation on everyone but himself. A common enough affliction.

But that line about Leon oppressing people to get what he wanted? That made me pause. Was there any truth to it?

Pre-brain injury, Leon would have described himself as a bleeding-heart liberal. He *fought* against injustice. He was outspoken on the rights of minorities. But when push came to shove, like many an outspoken socialist, would Leon feather his own nest before helping out a neighbour in need?

Undoubtedly, yes.

I needed to find out the truth of what happened with Alistair even if it all came to nothing. There was certainly more traction to the idea that Leon was targeted because of unpaid debts. But there was more I needed to know about Leon's state of mind before the attack.

Perhaps that was the answer.

Perhaps the key to all of this lay within Leon himself.

I got up and used the loo. On my way back to the lounge, I looked in on Leon. He was asleep again, sprawled diagonally across the bed: one leg was thrown wide, out of the duvet, and he was snoring softly. A slice of amber light illuminated the breadth of his chest and I watched as it rose through a number of inhalations. Like this, he looked like the old Leon. My Leon. And the cold stone of loneliness I'd been carrying around inside my stomach since the day of his attack felt heavier than ever.

The next morning, Wednesday, I sat across the breakfast table from Leon, watching him carefully.

He was joking around with the kids, going cross-eyed every time he put his spoon to his mouth, and Martha thought this was beyond funny. Jack, more reserved, and knowing that this behaviour would not have been tolerated in the past (as Leon would have been in his pre-writing, stressed-out state), spooned cereal into his mouth carefully and methodically.

I caught Jack's eye. *It's OK,* I tried to communicate, *go with it.* And he stopped eating, nodded at me almost imperceptibly, before asking Leon if he knew how to hang a spoon from his nose.

'Did I used to do that?' asked Leon.

'No,' said Jack.

'OK, son, then let's try it . . . Martha,' he said, 'you try it too.'

I reached forward to grab Martha's spoon. It was covered in Weetabix and the lot would end up inside her hair. Leon didn't think through these spur-of-the-moment ideas, had no recollection of how Martha would howl like a banshee when you tried to neaten her up. But then suddenly Martha laughed out loud, so uproariously, so delighted by Leon's attempt at hanging his spoon from his nose (unsuccessfully), that I sat back in my chair again.

Let them play. Play was the one thing they'd been short of, being ferried as they had been to my mother's all too often. My mother was the least playful person I knew when it came to little kids. Men, by contrast, she could act playful around for hours, without ever becoming tired of performing for their amusement.

'Leon,' I said casually, 'remember last night you asked about Alistair Armitage?'

'No.'

One thing about Leon's new personality was you always got a straight answer.

'Was he important to me?' he asked.

'Not important exactly,' I said. 'But he was . . .' I paused, searching for the right word. 'I think he was significant.'

'Significant.' He shook his head. 'Sorry, I've got nothing. What did he look like?'

'Kind of featureless. It doesn't really matter if you can't remember him. I just wanted to know.'

I sent the kids to brush their teeth. Martha tended to simply suck on the end of the toothbrush rather than endeavour for any kind of sideways action but I decided her attempt would have to do today. I needed to be at Lark Lane community centre for nine thirty, so would have to go straight there after dropping Jack at school and Martha at nursery. Creative writing was followed by a West African drumming session and the teacher purportedly became rather hostile if he was late in starting.

Leon stood and removed the breakfast dishes from the table, taking them over to the dishwasher and beginning to place them inside with great care. He'd been taught how to stack the dishwasher correctly by Matt, the occupational therapist at the rehab unit, and Matt was pretty anal about what went where. 'Leon,' I said gently, 'I usually just rinse the breakfast stuff in the sink. It only takes a minute. Leave the things on the worktop and I'll do it if you like.'

He turned. 'Do I know this already?'

I smiled. 'Kind of,' I answered, because I mentioned it each day. It was one of my secret tests to assess how his short-term memory was doing.

Leon deposited the rest of the dishes next to the sink before sitting at the table with a pen and his stack of yellow Post-it notes. Then, taking an extraordinary amount of time over each word, he wrote out, in a cursive, decorative hand: 'Breakfast bowls to be washed in sink.'

One of the oddities of the brain injury was that Leon had reverted to the joined-up handwriting that he'd learned as a child. For as long as I'd known him, and I'm sure for all of his adult life, Leon had written in boxy capitals. The handwriting was a nice throwback, one of those few pleasant anomalies that sometimes happened with brain-injured patients. Like those people who woke from a coma speaking fluent Spanish. Or the ability to balance quadratic equations.

The Post-it notes were everywhere.

I gestured to the one on the wall by the light switch. 'Can you remember what that says?'

Leon rose from the table. Clearly he couldn't remember as he moved closer to the small yellow square. He read, 'Nurse, Wednesday 10 a.m.'

He frowned and then turned around to face me. 'For me?' he asked.

I nodded.

'Is today Wednesday?'

I nodded again.

'Why would I need a nurse?'

'She's coming to chat to you. It's part of the follow-up care you receive from the rehab unit. They keep a close eye on all their discharged patients to check they're coping and to assess what sort of support they might need.'

Not true.

They'd only agreed to send someone round because I'd begged.

'What do you mean, what sort of support I might need?' Leon said. 'I don't need any support. I'm OK as I am.'

'Maybe someone to talk to about how you're feeling so you don't get so anxious and irritable? That would be OK, wouldn't it? Someone to help you work stuff out that you might be struggling with?'

'I don't feel anxious and irritable,' he said simply.

Conscious of the time, I let it go. I got the kids into their coats and shoes and took the car keys from their hiding place within a pocket of one of Martha's old coats. It would be at least six months until Leon would be allowed to get behind the wheel again but that had not stopped him from trying. The sensible thing would've been to get rid of Leon's car. It couldn't be used. But when I'd raised the subject with him he'd reacted as though I'd suggested the removal of his penis. So for now, the car stayed. It was parked on the street. Which of course would be driving Lawrence insane but he'd not said a word. Not one word.

Halfway out of the door, I shouted to Leon to stay away from the toaster and the oven, and told him I'd be back by eleven. I pulled the door closed and in the past this would have been the moment that I'd have shouted out one last 'I love you!' the kids chiming in: 'Love you too, Daddy!'

But we didn't really do that any more.

25

Returning home, after class, I saw there were no spaces left on the street except for one outside Lawrence and Rose's house. I'd not parked on their side since Leon had backed into their wall, as it seemed as though I was crossing a line of some sort. I almost drove on. Almost did another circuit in the hope of something becoming available, but then I was very firm with myself. This was my street too.

I pulled into the gap and then tried to act blasé as I retrieved my handbag and the small bag of groceries from the passenger-side footwell. *No big deal. Nothing to make a fuss about.*

And it was when I was closing the car door that I saw her.

Rose was standing in her front window watching me. Glaring at me. She was very still. Like the time just before she aimed her missile at Bonita.

Her face seemed smooth, completely without expression, and if I hadn't known better, I might have thought her unreal.

I swallowed. Busied myself with my keys.

And then I thought: *No. Enough of this.*

So I turned to face her. I didn't gesture. Didn't smile. I

simply stood my ground and stared back at her, willing her to lose her nerve and move away.

She didn't.

She stuck it out. Seconds felt like minutes and I could feel my heart thumping in every one of my muscles as I wondered what motivated this woman to behave as she did.

I can stay here all day, Rose, I was trying to convey with my eyes. *You're not going to creep me out with your weirdness,* when suddenly I heard the pip-pip of a car horn behind me.

I turned and saw Erica slow her car, lower her window.

'You all right, honey?' she sang. 'Leon behaving himself?'

And I smiled. Nodded. Told her I'd be across later for a cuppa and some adult conversation if she fancied.

When I turned around again I saw Rose had closed her curtains. But I knew she was still watching. I could feel it. I could feel her eye on me from the gap in between the drapes.

I crossed the street angrily.

I put my key in the lock, vowing to have a word with Lawrence about Rose, sod what Ledecky said about keeping away. She was becoming unnerving. And I really didn't need to feel any more uneasy than I already did when—

On the tinted glass of the front door was a yellow Post-it note. 'I don't want to talk to you. Go away', it said, in Leon's careful, cursive script.

My heart sank. Jesus Christ, Leon. Not today.

He'd left this for the assessor. He'd sent the assessor away before she'd even had the chance to talk to him.

I slammed open the door and dumped my bag in the hallway, shouting, 'Leon!' ready for a fight.

He couldn't do this. I'd pleaded with the rehab unit for this evaluation. He couldn't just say he didn't want it and pretend he wasn't in. I needed this carer. I needed some back-up. I couldn't carry on doing this on my own.

'Leon! Where the hell are you?'

I heard sounds from upstairs. I stopped in my tracks and listened.

'Leon?'

'Yoohoo!' called out a cheerful voice.

There were footsteps at the top of the stairs.

'Up here. Leon's giving me the guided tour.'

It was a woman's voice. Pleasant. Accommodating. She wasn't visible from where I was standing but she sounded around sixty.

'We're almost done!' she sang. 'Be down in a minute.'

I could see her in my mind's eye as a rounded woman with soft white flesh, a woman who radiated a floral aroma when she moved.

I exhaled. Calm down, I told myself. Make a good impression. I was still rattled after Rose but she didn't need to think I was a loose cannon as well.

I went through to the kitchen and put the kettle on. Opening the fridge to retrieve the milk, I saw that Leon had added a Post-it to a jar of apricot jam. 'Not nice', he'd written.

I smiled.

He wasn't a fan of it before the brain injury either. He preferred raspberry.

Leon had read somewhere once that children needed to be presented with new foods as often as twelve times before they would accept and develop a liking for them. Something he'd put into practice with his own children, and something that I could find pretty draining after a long day alone with them (especially when one of them was either whimpering or gagging over whatever was on the end of their fork). But Leon would persist. And when I tried to intervene, saying that they were still so little, and I was certain they would be eating Brussels sprouts by the time they were seventeen, he would say that that laissez-faire attitude was exactly the reason teenagers today only ate boneless chicken. His new change of policy amused me. One taste and the apricot jam was deemed too unpleasant for a second try.

I could hear Leon and the woman making their way downstairs. She was telling him that her knees were not what they once were, and she found going downstairs more difficult than going up. 'Ageing,' she declared, 'is no fun at all, Leon. And the thing about it is, you never think it's going to happen to you! I used to roll my eyes when my mother complained about her poor old bones. Now I wish I'd been more sympathetic because—

'Mrs Campbell!' she exclaimed when she saw me. 'How absolutely wonderful to meet you. You have a beautiful home here. And your children – Leon has been showing me their photographs. Well, they're just little poppets. What a lucky lady you are.'

I stepped forward. 'Call me Jane.'

We shook hands.

'I'm Miriam Price. We've had a very fruitful morning.'

Leon was nodding along with her enthusiastically.

'When I saw the note on the front door,' I said, 'I wasn't sure if this meeting had actually gone ahead.'

Miriam Price batted my words away with her hand. 'Oh, we soon got past that. Didn't we, Leon?'

I glanced at Leon. He was looking at his feet.

'I think he was worried I was here to interfere,' she said. 'But once we'd had a nice little chat through the letterbox it was all sorted out . . . Leon says you're a creative writing teacher? That sounds like such a lovely job.'

Ryan Toonen's lascivious smile flashed into my head. I felt his hand around my throat, the smell of his breath inside my nose. 'It has its moments.'

'I've always wanted to write a book,' she went on. 'The stories I could tell! Honestly, you wouldn't believe. It'd be a bestseller.'

I looked at Leon. In the past he would have groaned audibly at this statement. 'Everyone thinks they have a book in them,' he used to say, 'and that's exactly where it should stay.' But he was smiling at Miriam encouragingly, as if he could think of nothing better than to read her life story retold as fiction.

'Not that there'd be a lot of sex in my book,' Miriam confided. 'And that's the one thing you need for a bestseller, isn't it? Sex *sells*, as they say.'

'Sex doesn't sell,' Leon cut in unexpectedly. 'World War Two *sells*.'

'Really, Leon?' she said, quite astonished. 'Never would have thought that.'

'Readers can never get enough of Hitler,' he added, and I wondered where on earth he'd plucked that information from (though it was true).

'Hmm,' Miriam Price replied. 'I suppose he was a rather excellent villain. Anyway, enough about him. We're here to talk about you, Leon.'

She was exactly as I'd pictured her: a soft-fleshed woman, no sharp edges. There was a hint of Zoflora about her person and I could imagine her happily using it to disinfect her surfaces as that's what her mother, and her mother before her, had done. She had high colour in her cheeks and, taking in the whole package, I thought she was rather a good foil. No wonder Leon had let her in. She wasn't the type to get your back up. She was the grandmother you missed being hugged by, the dinner lady who gave you extra custard. 'What's your professional opinion?' I enquired, with regards to Leon.

It occurred to me that I didn't know what her profession actually was. Was she a clinical psychologist? A community psychiatric nurse? To be honest, I was past caring what people's official roles were. After months of dealing with health professionals their titles and job descriptions had become meaningless to me. *Can you help?* was all I wanted to know. And something about this woman told me that she could.

'I'm going to recommend that Leon—'

Her phone began to ring.

'Excuse me a moment.' She raised her eyes skyward in a gesture of *never a minute's peace* as she put the phone to her ear. 'No, I'm still at work. You know you're not supposed to ring me until after three . . . No, it's not after three . . . I don't know, you'll just have to ask them yourself . . . Well, I can't do everything . . . I thought you valued your independence.' Then she sighed out wearily. 'No,' she said, seemingly beaten, 'I've *told* you I won't put you in a home . . . We've been through this how many times? I won't put you in a home.' I sneaked a look at Leon to see if her care home reference pushed his buttons about Magellan House all over again, but he remained passive. 'Call you later,' she said. 'No, I won't forget.'

She closed her eyes for an extended moment as if trying to regain her equilibrium. 'Where were we?'

'Leon,' I said. 'You were going to recommend . . .'

'Ah, yes. Sorry about that. My mother over in Old Swan can't seem to get her head around the fact that I'm not at her beck and call twenty-four hours a day. I'm off to Goa next week, but I daren't tell her till I'm *actually on the plane*, or she'll be struck down with something life-threatening. Or else throw herself down the stairs – she's done that twice . . . Anyway, Leon . . .' and she glanced sideways to where Leon was standing before smiling at me conspiratorially, as if she had something up her sleeve. 'I've gone through the assessment process fully and I'll be honest with you, Mrs Campbell, Leon is not someone we can provide carers for at this time.'

My face must have dropped to the floor because she reached out and placed her hand on my upper arm reassuringly. She gave it a small squeeze.

'But you saw the state of the attic?' I said. 'You saw our bedroom ceiling? Leon put his foot right through that. And when he gets mad I just don't know if he's—'

'If it was only up to me then *of course* I would authorize some supervision for Leon. It would make all your lives easier, anyone can see that. But sadly, right now, we have far more needy cases than Leon, and we always have the problem of a limited pot of money.'

'You know he physically attacked a friend of ours too?' I said, arguing the point. 'Frankie was looking after him and he had to lock himself in the bathroom because Leon was so violent. And you know Leon wandered off and I didn't know where he'd got to?' My voice was shrill-sounding and desperate. 'I know none of this sounds particularly life-threatening, but I'm alone here. With a job. And two small children. I'm not sure I can cope with the unpredictability of it all.'

'I'm not sure I could either, but when I discussed the problem with Leon, told him that you were finding the situation untenable, he came up with rather a good suggestion.'

I turned to Leon. He was looking at his feet again.

'He mentioned a nephew,' she said. 'Edwin?'

I paused.

'Eden?' I said. 'You mean Eden? What can Eden do?'

'Leon says that when he chatted to him recently, Eden mentioned he wasn't doing very much right now.'

This was true. Eden had failed his GCSEs. Everything apart from art and product design, so he was scheduled to retake maths and English in January. Leon and Eden had been Skyping every few days and their conversations seemed to perk Leon up considerably.

Miriam Price said, 'He could hang around here not doing very much – I believe teenagers are rather good at that – but he would be keeping an eye on Leon for you at the same time. Stop him wandering off and so forth.'

'Leon suggested this?'

'He did.'

I glanced at Leon. He still had his eyes glued to the floor. He looked like a child in the headmaster's office waiting to hear the outcome of his misdemeanour.

'And he *promised*,' Miriam Price said, raising her voice now so that Leon was included in the conversation, 'he promised that if we could arrange this, then he would behave himself properly this time. Didn't you, Leon?'

Leon lifted his head and nodded vigorously.

'You won't let me down now, will you, Leon?' she said.

'No.'

'Because I'm counting on you. It's going to require some sorting out and we don't all want to waste our time, do we?'

'I won't let you down,' Leon said.

Miriam Price turned back to me and winked. Her behaviour was completely improper, treating Leon as a child in this way. She was probably breaching all sorts of rules of professional conduct.

But Leon was behaving like a lamb and I could have kissed her for it.

'Eden,' I said to myself.

'Leon says he likes the lad's company,' she said. 'Says he finds him soothing and hc feels less frustrated when he's around.'

She smiled at me encouragingly.

'So, what do you think?' she said, waiting for my response. 'Do you think it's a goer or not?'

26

It was decided Eden would arrive the following week. Juliana was happy with the proposal as she didn't like the idea of Eden lying around the house all day doing nothing, and Eden told me he was eager to escape, as relations between Juliana and Meredith were, as he put it: 'Proper frosty at the minute, Auntie Jane.' He would sleep on the sofa bed in the attic as Leon was still in the spare room.

In the meantime, I had a further four days alone with Leon during which I tried to keep him calm and away from the subject of his attack. It wasn't easy, and I was still holding out hope that Inspector Ledecky would magically appear armed with news that she'd made an arrest after searching through Leon's computer and our financial records. Mercifully, Leon was at his best when the children were around, but when they weren't, he remained volatile, and I was counting down the hours until I had Eden here, who I hoped would occupy Leon, and stop him ruminating on the brochure for Magellan House – which he kept brandishing at me as proof that I'd wanted rid of him.

He carried the brochure around in the pocket of his jogging bottoms all the time and I was certain that if I could just get the bloody thing off him, then he'd quit with his accusations, and he would be a lot more settled. But he wouldn't part with it. I'd even sneaked into his room when he was asleep and emptied his pockets, only to find he'd removed the brochure and stashed it where I couldn't find it.

I was now beginning to feel pretty wrung-out and frayed, a skittish version of myself, and I wasn't sure how long I could keep going. I'd tried once more to contact Alistair Armitage, but that now looked like a dead end too, as he'd declined to reply, so I was back in Leon's documents folder, trawling through the files, hoping to find something, anything, to show Leon to convince him that I wasn't responsible for all of this.

The attic was still in mild disarray. I had done a perfunctory clean-up immediately after Leon wrecked the space: tidying papers into piles, vacuuming the plaster from where he'd punched the wall, but a joiner was needed to repair the hole in the attic floor and the corresponding hole in my bedroom ceiling, as well as the hole in the wall, before Eden arrived. I'd booked a guy in, but I'd had to make the call in secret as Leon kept assuring me he was capable of sorting out the damage himself, because *he may not be able to remember how to punctuate dialogue correctly, but he sure as shit knew how to fix a sodding wall.*

I didn't have the nerve to tell him he was shit at fixing walls *before* the brain injury. So I told him I was having difficulty sourcing materials. Then I was hoping his short-term memory would get on with its usual business of scrambling all recent incoming information, and he wouldn't bring it up again.

I sat at Leon's computer and scanned his documents, wondering which to open next. I'd already waded through a folder entitled 'BAD BOOK REVIEWS', hoping I might find something, but it had only served to depress me. Leon would not receive a book review – good or bad – for another new book, ever. He would never write another book. I knew that now, and I wondered what was worse for a person: never having had your dream realized, or having your dream realized and then having it all taken away again.

I scrolled down the list of files.

Nothing was jumping out.

I was about to start at the top of the list, wade through them all alphabetically, when something caught my eye.

At the bottom of the folder was a document entitled 013. Leon wasn't superstitious but there weren't any documents entitled 01 through to 012, so it looked out of place.

I clicked on it.

Microsoft Word began to load.

From the double-spaced lines, indented margins and the flowery prose, it was immediately evident that this was a piece of fiction. I glanced to the bottom of the screen. The document was 356 pages long. I read the first paragraph and it was a little over-written, too many adjectives for an opener, but it did have something.

Could this be one of Leon's early manuscripts?

Every writer has them. Unpublished books that are kept firmly in the bottom drawer, for no one to see.

When I moved in with Leon I'd begged him to let me read his early work. I wanted to see how much he'd progressed. I wanted to know that he didn't just arrive as this writer, fully formed and ready to go. I wanted to know that, like me, he was once quite crap.

But he wouldn't show me. He said he'd not held on to

his early novels as they embarrassed him. Much as an actor does not enjoy seeing himself on screen, Leon said he found the work unsatisfactory. He told me he never went back; looking ahead was the key in fiction writing. Then he assured me that my work was of a far superior quality to what he had produced in the early days, that my talent did not require the heavy lifting that his had, and the reason I was not receiving the breaks right now was nothing to do with my skill as a writer, it was all down to luck.

So I'd let it drop.

Now, reading this manuscript, it felt rather thrilling. As if I'd been allowed in a room that was kept locked. Or I'd found the key to a box placed on a high shelf.

I got past the first few pages and had to admit that if this was Leon's early work it wasn't half bad. You could tell it was the work of an amateur: there was too much exposition, too much back story about the main character, crammed into the opening. We were being told why he was the way he was, why he was a lone wolf. We were being knocked over the head with why he found human connection hard – naturally, it all came down to the hurts of his past: the woman he couldn't get over, the child he never saw, the sister that was murdered. A more skilled writer would let the reader try to work this out for themselves. Or else cause the reader to think: *Who is this character? He's holding something back. I have to keep reading! I need to know more!*

After giving us his main character's *raison d'être* pretty bluntly on the page, Leon then started to build up his story. And I could see the beginnings of how Leon liked to shape his novels emerging. But the prose was clunky and repetitive. The dialogue like bad movie dialogue.

I smiled as I read because I realized how far he'd come and, yes, I could understand why he'd want to hide this from me; it was immature and lacking in depth, but it was also quite endearing. This was who Leon was before I met him. This was Leon's best attempt. And it was not great.

At the bottom of page nine there was a sentence highlighted in yellow.

This was a habit of mine, and perhaps of many writers. You highlighted the stuff you needed to check, or edit, because you couldn't find the right words the first time around. Or you added notes in as you wrote, notes to come back to later.

The highlighted sentence read: 'Change AA's plot point here? Go for something more risky, less cliché.'

I read it again.

Change AA's plot point.

Who or what was AA?

I scrolled down the document fast.

Every ten pages or so there would be another of Leon's notes to himself highlighted in yellow:

'Increase tension here.'

'Another twist here?'

'Make main character do something FFS!'

Around halfway through the manuscript, across the bottom of the page, there was simply: 'Zzzzzzzzzzzzzzzzz.'

This row of Zs was something Leon used to text me if he was in the pub for the evening with a particularly boring person. Or sometimes he'd send a line of them if he was with Frankie Ridonikis and Frankie was droning on about the complicated interior lives of his characters.

I scrolled ahead again. For a while there was nothing.

And then, there on page 256, were the words: 'Lose AA's shitty romance stuff.'

AA.

My blood ran cold.

I stared at the file, realizing what I had in front of me.

This was not Leon's early work.

It was not his novel.

This novel belonged to Alistair Armitage.

27

I asked Frankie Ridonikis to meet at Otterspool Prom after I'd picked up Jack and Martha from school and nursery.

I didn't tell Leon who I was meeting and I took the kids along so they could blow off some steam. They rode their scooters back and forth, putting a foot down each time they came to make a turn, getting in the way of some serious-minded cyclists.

Frankie arrived looking like a real author: five-day stubble, mildly dishevelled, a once-expensive but now shabby overcoat worn over his black suit. He wore brown brogues that needed polishing, and he smelled faintly of yesterday's Jim Beam.

'Thanks for coming,' I said.

We rested our elbows on the railings, side by side, and looked out across the Mersey. The broken cloud gave the water a dappled look. It could be such an ugly body of water, and then, at other times, astonishingly beautiful. The salt tang in the air always made it feel like home.

Frankie coughed up some phlegm from his throat and then spent a moment deciding whether to shoot it into the water. I looked away.

'How's Leon doing?' he asked.

'That's why I asked you here.'

Frankie turned to me. 'Look, Jane, I'm so sorry about what happened when I came over. I should have handled it better, I should have calmed him down, stopped him from taking off like that.'

I held up my hand. 'Don't apologize. No one can control Leon when he gets like that. And you never know when it's going to happen. He trashed the attic when he got back. That's the scariest part; it always comes from nowhere.'

'Yes, but I let him go and I shouldn't have.' He turned back to face the river. 'It's been playing on my mind. I could've tried harder to stop him, spared you all the worry and . . .' Frankie paused. Sighed. Then he rubbed at the stubble of his neck as he tried to get his words together. 'Oona's had a massive go at me over this. We're still not really speaking, to be honest. She said I was catastrophically weak-willed and unforgivably selfish to leave you with the task of trying to track Leon down alone.' He seemed genuinely disgusted with himself.

'Frankie, I wasn't alone,' I said playfully. 'I had two small children to hinder my progress as well, remember?'

Frankie shot me a doleful look. 'I didn't tell Oona you had the kids. *Shit,*' he said emphatically. 'I don't think it occurred to her either that you'd have to bring them along too.'

I took a quick glance over my shoulder to check on Jack and Martha and saw that the scooters had been abandoned around fifty yards away and they were squatting down on their haunches. They were greatly absorbed in something on the ground, probably a dead worm. Martha had a knack for hunting them out.

'Forget it,' I said. 'Leon's OK. I'm OK. And I'm not about to tell Oona about the kids so just forget about it.'

Frankie smiled. 'You're too generous.'

'Anyway, did you really think I asked you here to berate you?'

He shrugged. 'I didn't know what to think.'

'I have a problem,' I said. 'I know, I know, you're thinking I have many problems . . . but this is serious, Frankie.'

Frankie arched an eyebrow. 'What is it?'

'Remember Alistair Armitage?'

Frankie looked blank.

'The writer?' I said. 'The aspiring writer who'd heckle Leon at events?'

'That dickhead?' he said. 'What does he want? He's not been bothering you, has he? Because, honestly, Jane, I know Leon was always reluctant to really frighten the guy, but if a lunatic like that was bothering me, I wouldn't hesitate. What's he done this time?'

'He's not done anything. It's the quite opposite really.'

Frankie looked at me questioningly.

'I found a manuscript,' I explained. 'What I thought at first was a very rough draft of one of Leon's early manuscripts. I thought it was what would later become *Dark River*, because there were some elements that seemed familiar—'

'God, I loved that novel,' Frankie cut in wistfully. 'It's still his best work, I think. D'you know, after all the years we spent struggling to be published, we finally got the news we were going to be published within less than three weeks of each other? Special time,' he said. 'Nothing gets anywhere near that feeling.'

'Anyway,' I said, 'it wasn't Leon's *Dark River*. Frankie,

the novel I found wasn't Leon's at all. It was Alistair Armitage's.'

Again, Frankie looked completely blank.

'He *copied* Alistair's work. He copied elements from his manuscript and turned it into *Dark River*.'

'No.' Frankie shook his head. 'No, that's not possible.'

'I know you don't want to think it's possible . . . but honestly, he'd marked the entire thing up with notes and edits, I saw it with my own eyes and—'

'No, Jane,' Frankie said again. 'I mean it's *not actually possible*, as in I was with him. I was with Leon for the entire time he was writing that book. We were together. We were writing buddies. We critiqued each other's work as it was being written. Christ,' he said, 'I *lived* that novel with him. It can't be someone else's work, Jane. It really can't.'

'Well, it is.'

He shook his head. 'You seem so certain.' Frankie examined my face in a way that suggested he couldn't quite believe what he was hearing.

'What?' I said.

'I just find it really hard to believe that you could doubt Leon so readily. He's not a plagiarist. You know that. He's one of the most original crime writers alive today. You know that too.'

I shifted uncomfortably. 'I know what I saw.'

Frankie looked across the water. He was frowning. He didn't buy it. He didn't think his friend was capable of such treachery.

'OK,' I said, 'you don't believe it, but what if it *is* true? And worse, what if someone finds out?' My words were coming out in a rush as I explained the real reason for my asking him here. 'Alistair's been calling him a liar and a thief for years. What if this somehow emerges now and, I don't know, Alistair Armitage sues us? Is that possible? Can someone sue an author for stealing their work? What am I saying – of course they can. I know that. I don't know why I'm asking . . . But would it mean we'd lose our assets? Can they take what's ours? Could we lose the house, Frankie? That's what I'm really worrying about. That's why I asked you here. I need your advice. What would you do if this was happening to you?'

Frankie turned and regarded me sadly. 'Jane,' he said, 'this is not you. This is not who you are.'

'No, stop. Answer me. I need to know. Are you a limited company? Leon's not. That means they could take our personal stuff. That means they could take the house, Frankie.'

'What's going on?' he said.

'I'm trying to explain—'

'No. What's really going on?' he said, only more softly this time. 'You need to talk to me.'

He held my gaze.

'Come on, Jane.'

Tears began to pool in my eyes and I had to look up and blink to stop them from running down my cheeks.

'It's this,' I said, gesturing helplessly, meaning the plagiarism situation.

'It's not,' he said.

'OK, then it's nothing.' I felt like a fool. 'There's nothing wrong. I don't even know why I'm bloody crying.'

He handed me a tissue from his inside pocket. 'How is it?' he asked.

'How's what?'

'How's your life? How's your life now with Leon?'

'Oh, Frankie, please don't ask me that,' I said, blowing my nose.

'Well, we can see you're trying to be brave and soldier on,' he said. 'But is that really the best thing for all of you in the long run?'

I stopped and looked at him wide-eyed. 'You're suggesting I leave him?'

'I'm suggesting that staying isn't the only option.'

'Well, it kind of is.'

He smiled. 'Are you lonely?' he asked.

And I nodded, suddenly unable to reply.

'You must be lonely,' he said.

'I am. I am incredibly lonely. I miss him. And I'm scared to death all the time. I'm scared in the house, scared when I go to bed, scared when I take the kids to school. And nobody seems to care! Everyone's so focused on Leon getting better, on Leon getting the help he needs. No one seems to care that I don't *have* Leon, that we don't have a life any more, and no one cares that the person who did this to him is still out there. What if he comes back, Frankie? What then? I'm virtually on my own in that house. Leon sleeps like he's dead now . . . and I just feel so bloody vulnerable.'

Frankie pulled another tissue from his pocket but instead of handing it to me he reached up and wiped the tears away himself.

'Don't,' I said, sniffling.

But he didn't pull away.

'I can't bear to be touched right now,' I said.

'You seem like you're starved of touch.'

'I am!' I cried out, and I took a step away from him. 'But I can't take it, OK?'

I dropped my head, embarrassed.

After a moment I leaned my back against the railing and turned to check on the kids. They were on their scooters again now and Martha was trailing behind Jack trying her best to keep up. Her little face was full of determination.

'So, what are you going to do?' asked Frankie.

'About the manuscript?'

'About all of it.'

'I don't know. I really don't know. So far in my life I've always known what to do. Life throws up options and I always know which way to head. This? This, I have no clue how to navigate. I wish someone would just tell me what to do, give me a set of instructions to follow, and I could get on with it.'

'Forget the manuscript.'

I did a double take. 'Really? That's your advice?'

'What's to be gained?'

'You mean bury it?'

'I mean forget you ever saw it. I still don't believe for one second that Leon copied that loser's work, but let's say for argument's sake that he did. What's to be gained by revealing it?'

I blew my nose again.

'Look,' he said, 'you've got enough shit on your plate. And Leon can't exactly defend his actions, so let it go. Honestly, you don't need this.'

It wasn't what I'd expected him to say.

I'd expected him to be shocked, yes. Disbelieving, yes. But then I'd expected he'd tell me to contact Leon's agent and come clean. Frankie, for all his minor vices, had a lot of integrity.

He smiled at me encouragingly and I moved towards him, leaning my weight against him heavily in a gesture of thanks.

He put his arm around me, pulling me in close. 'Keep putting one foot in front of the other, Jane,' he said. 'Keep waking up, keep tending to those kids, keep doing what needs to be done. Do that day after day and eventually your life will look different . . . When I don't know what to do, I do the basics, the essentials, and if you get through each day, sooner or later life will present you with more options. That's just how it all works.'

28

Eden arrived on Monday. I was supposed to pick him up from Lime Street, but he'd overslept, missed his train, and something to do with the tickets not being transferable meant that Juliana and Meredith ended up bringing him. I made dinner for everyone. Invited Gloria and my own mother too, as the busier I made myself, the less time there was to think about Leon's plagiarism.

I'd not slept since discovering the manuscript. And though I wanted to believe what Frankie had said, that Leon was incapable of such underhanded dishonesty, I couldn't shake the feeling that he could be.

I, of all people, knew the desperation involved when wanting to become a published author. Could it be possible that Leon had also felt that same desperation? Had he reached his aim by entirely fraudulent means? I knew I wouldn't be able to let it drop, knew I'd have to talk to Alistair Armitage and find out for sure.

The doorbell rang, and Gloria arrived in the kitchen wearing a platinum-blond wig and some sling-back, peep-toe stilettos that she could barely walk in. 'Jesus Christ, Mother!' exclaimed Juliana upon seeing her. 'Have some self-respect, will you?'

That Juliana was all riled up about something was

evident in her snippy manner, but when I enquired if she was OK, she replied, 'Why wouldn't I be?'

Later, I was ladling chilli into bowls when she began asking questions about the investigation.

'Why is nothing happening?'

'I'm not sure,' I replied.

'Well, don't the police tell you anything? Don't they talk to you, tell you why they haven't found out who did this yet?'

I shook my head. 'I don't know any more than the last time we spoke. They still don't have enough evidence to charge anyone, so there's not a lot we can do . . . Things move slower than they do on TV, Juliana.' I handed her two bowls to deliver to the table, but she stayed where she was.

She was frowning. Looking at me in a way that was both doubtful and accusatory. 'I can't help feeling that you're being remarkably uninvolved in all this, Jane,' she said, and she held my gaze, waiting for me to defend myself. 'Don't you *want* to know who attacked Leon? Couldn't you be doing more instead of being so . . . passive?'

Passive.

I wanted to laugh out loud.

Oh, Juliana, if only you knew where my enterprising pursuit of information had got me.

I wondered how *she* would cope: Toonen in her face, his hand around her throat. What would she make of the hours of video footage on Leon's computer? What would she do if she were to find out her beloved brother had stolen another man's work? That his career she so often boasted about was built on a lie?

I sprinkled some more chopped coriander on top of the chilli and stirred.

'Don't you ask the police what's going on?' she said. 'Don't you demand answers?'

Her voice was rising and the other guests were beginning to notice. There was a hush from the table.

Gloria tried to change the subject. 'I love your nail polish,' she said to my mother and my mother told her it was OPI's I'm Not Really A Waitress, which Gloria was totally charmed by.

Juliana set the bowls down hard on the counter top. 'Does anyone actually care about who did this to my brother?' she said loudly and motioned to Leon, who was happily forking chilli into his mouth. 'Am I the only person bothered about this? Because by the looks of things it seems as if the rest of you just don't give a shit.'

'Your language, Juliana,' said Gloria.

'Why are you all happily going about your lives as if none of this matters? Leon will *never* be the same. Ever. I've lost my brother. Just look at him, for Christ's sake! Look at what he's like now. Doesn't that upset you? Isn't it an issue for any of you?'

There was a moment of horrified silence as each of us considered Leon and wondered just how wounded he was going to be by Juliana's words. She made him sound imbecilic, and she knew better than that. She knew not to talk about Leon as if he wasn't there.

'Why do you always have to do this?' interrupted Eden.

'Do what?' replied Juliana.

'Why does it always have to be about you?'

'This is *not* about me! How can this be about me?'

'Well, why is it always you who has to cause a scene? It's not healthy,' Eden said.

Juliana was outraged. 'I'm not causing a scene. This is

my family! I'm allowed to express an opinion in front of my own family. That's what families do. Or would you prefer we all simmered away quietly?'

During this exchange I caught sight of Leon studying his mother in her blond wig, frowning a little, as if knowing there was something different about her, something off, but he couldn't quite put his finger on it.

'You look good today, Mum,' he said to her. And she reached out and squeezed his hand.

'Thank you, son,' she said.

Eden got up and took the two bowls that Juliana had slammed down in frustration and delivered them to my mother and Meredith, who were looking down at their laps, trying to stay invisible. This was my mother, who could usually be *counted* on to speak up and say exactly the wrong thing at the wrong time to the wrong person.

Juliana closed her eyes tightly and pinched the skin at the top of her nose. I thought for a moment she might be about to cry. 'What I'm trying to say,' she said evenly, 'and what I think I may have expressed incorrectly, is that I'm frustrated by the lack of progress. That's all. I'm not trying to upset anybody. Please tell me I'm not alone in being concerned.'

When no one said anything, she gave a long sigh and said, 'Raise your hand if you're with me.'

Cautiously, everyone's hand lifted.

Leon was still busy eating and didn't raise his until he realized he was the odd one out; then he went ahead and raised it, but not before asking my mother what it was we were voting on.

'You,' she said.

Which confused him even more and so he retracted it again.

Perhaps he thought we were voting on whether to get rid of him.

'Darling,' Gloria said to Juliana, 'I'm not sure what it is that you want us to do.'

'I want you to care!' she cried.

Gloria made a pfft sound. 'Aw,' she said, shaking her head back and forth as if to say Juliana was being unfair, 'you know very well that we all care very much about Leon.'

'So, do something!'

Gloria folded her hands neatly in her lap. 'Can't you see, darling?' she said. 'Can't you see? Nobody . . . not one of us here . . . *knows* what to do about Leon.'

They left around eight.

There was much hugging and apology. Eden acted as though it was nothing unusual, that this kind of acrimony was day-to-day life with his mother. I'd come within inches of telling Juliana what had happened at the prison. Telling her that I was frightened to be seen poking around in Leon's attack, that I'd been threatened to stay away. But she would have wanted to know more. She'd want to know everything and I couldn't take that chance.

'You're sure you don't mind doing this?' I asked Eden later with regards to his babysitting Leon, and he told me he had nothing better to do. He was retaking two GCSEs in January but, other than that, he was just killing time. 'Getting under her feet,' he said, referring to Juliana.

We hadn't come up with a suitable phrase for what he was about to undertake with Leon. 'Carer' sounded too weird, Eden said. 'I'm not his carer. That makes it sound like I'm wiping his arse and heating up canned soup.' 'Helper', he decided, wasn't appropriate either. 'Maybe I'll be his PA.'

Gloria wanted to give Eden fifty pounds a week to look after Leon. She offered to pay her grandson this wage, a wage that I could not afford to shell out, as she thought it would be good for both of them. I would provide Eden with his meals and any transportation costs incurred. After Leon had taken himself off to bed, we were standing on the front step, Eden smoking. I'd asked if he was allowed to smoke and he'd said not really but went on regardless. We were on the lookout for the cat.

Bonita hadn't come home for the third night running so I was standing on the front step calling out for her. Occasionally she did this. Disappeared for a day and then reappeared, mewing loudly, announcing her return.

She would breeze in through the kitchen window and the Leon of old would rush to her, serenading her, using his own made-up lyrics from the Peter Sarstedt song 'Where Do You Go To (My Lovely)'? Though he'd sing it in a Northern Irish accent: *Where do you go to, my lovely? . . . Yes I do . . . So you are . . . Am I right?*

I missed his singing.

Eden returned inside, but I stayed on, in my pyjamas, calling out the cat's name into the night. 'Bonit-ahh.'

The street was quiet. Eerily quiet, in fact.

A fog had settled and though I could make out Lawrence's house opposite, it was undefined; the rooftop and windows were occluded by murk.

'Bonit-ahhh!'

I heard an engine start further along the street.

Someone revving gently. I looked over. The car was parked on the opposite side, three houses along. A black saloon. Or was it grey? It was hard to tell in this light.

The driver switched on their headlights, turned them to full beam, and instantly I was blinded, the car itself disappearing behind the glare.

Then the engine revved again, loudly this time.

It pulled away from the kerb and crawled along, coming to a stop outside my house. My mouth went dry. I could see only the bonnet. The windows were obscured by the garden wall, but I felt sure it was the same car filmed by Leon.

The engine revved again. A warning. A threat.

And my heart stuttered in response.

I ran inside.

29

I lay with my eyes open, listening for the return of the car, until after 1 a.m.; it didn't come back. I tried to tell myself it was a coincidence. That the car had nothing to do with me. But I didn't believe it.

I reasoned that if the occupants had really wanted to scare me they'd have approached the house. They'd have got out and approached *me*. And I could only think that their reason for not doing so was that they were looking for Leon instead.

The following morning, I phoned Ledecky. I told her of the dark-coloured saloon on Leon's home videos and the appearance of a similar car in the street last night.

'Registration plate?' she asked.

I told her I didn't know it and she sighed heavily. She said she'd have someone take a look at the CCTV from both Aigburth Road and Ullet Road, at around 8.30 p.m., but: 'Dark saloons are remarkably common, so . . .' She let the words hang.

Afterwards, I called the vet's, and I was told that: 'No, a small tortoiseshell female has not been brought in . . . either alive or dead,' but I was asked to stay on the line as Bonita was microchipped. They would check the Petlog database. No luck. The receptionist said Bonita had not been handed in elsewhere – or they'd certainly be aware of it. 'She's probably locked in someone's shed,' she said, trying to be helpful. 'You know what cats are like.'

I told her I did.

'You might want to print out some leaflets . . . ask people to check their outbuildings.'

My morning class at Toxteth Library didn't start until eleven and so I headed up to the attic to put together some 'Have you seen our cat?' leaflets. I'd already promised the kids that if the vet didn't have Bonita then we could pin them around the neighbouring streets when they got in from school. They were looking forward to it – I think because they'd seen it done on American TV, so it was lodged in their minds as something little kids did. Like running a lemonade stand, or selling cookies to neighbours, both of which, I'd had to explain, wasn't something English children made a habit of doing. Probably because we didn't like our neighbours all that much.

While I was waiting for the leaflets to print, I gazed out of the window and watched for Bonita. I'd been doing this pretty much every time I passed a window. 'Where are you?' I'd whisper, before panic started to seize me as I thought through the possibilities: Was she lying dead somewhere? Would we still be waiting for her to come home in a week? A year?

Was she trapped, slowly starving to death?

Or could she be nearby? Practically right on the doorstep? And if only I'd looked a little harder, been more thorough, I'd have discovered her before it was too late?

I refocused and checked my emails.

At the top of my inbox was one from Teresa, the course coordinator, forwarded on from Walton Prison. The gist of it was that there would now be extra measures put in place to make sure there was no repeat of last time's session. Ryan Toonen would naturally not be in attendance and they had allocated a prison officer to supervise as the class had proved to be particularly popular, and they were reluctant to pull it from the schedule altogether. In a nutshell, they wanted me back. If I could bring myself to go back.

I fired off a quick reply saying I would have to think about it but would have an answer for them by the following day.

Would I return there?

Not likely.

It saddened me because of all the classes I'd conducted, Walton was the one where I felt I was being most useful to people who were not usually accustomed to receiving any help. The one where the students might actually benefit from committing their thoughts to paper. But no. I couldn't go back.

I scrolled down my emails. Junk. Junk.

More junk.

And then, at the bottom of the screen, a reply from Alistair Armitage, sent late last night.

My breathing quickened. I didn't think he'd respond. I'd constructed another quick message to him in one last-ditch attempt, telling him I'd come across a manuscript in Leon's files. A file that I thought might belong to him. The subtext of what I was saying was: *I believe you. I believe that you were wronged by Leon.*

I opened his response.

Jane,

I beg of you. Do not contact me. I am in fear for my safety now and cannot help you.

Alistair

I stared at the screen. His safety?

I read it again thinking he'd become terribly paranoid. I felt certain if I could just talk to him, if I could meet him in person, tell him I'd found the manuscript, that I really did *believe* him, then he could open up about what had actually happened. About how Leon came to have his manuscript in the first place.

I replied, telling him we could meet in secret, that we could keep this totally between us, but my message immediately bounced back.

Mail Delivery Failed: Returning Message to Sender.

I slammed the desk with my fist.

He'd deleted his account.

Why wouldn't he talk to me?

Every thread I followed seemed to lead nowhere. A dead end. I got up and paced. I glanced at the clock. Did I have enough time to have another poke around in Leon's stuff? I had forty-five minutes. I opened the first filing cabinet, pulling out the hard copy of *Red City*. I'd spent over an hour putting the pages of it back in the correct order after Leon had hurled the manuscript across the attic.

I sat back down in the office chair.

This was Leon's unfinished novel and up until now I'd not read any of it. I still had no clue as to why he'd not been able to finish the thing, so I speed-read it, stopping at the end of each chapter to read the last paragraph – 'the cliffs' as Leon called them, short for cliffhangers. They were certainly all there. They made you want to turn the page, made you want to keep reading. So where had it all gone wrong? I wondered. Why had his method stopped working? Why had he had to ask Charlie for a loan, just to keep the wolf from the door?

I flicked forward to page 261, to where the novel ended, and I put the manuscript face down on the desk. Leon's books ran close to 400 pages usually. What had happened on page 261 to give him writer's block? What had made him come up here each day to procrastinate, to fill his time with anything but writing?

When I first knew him, Leon used to claim that there was no such thing as writer's block. 'Bricklayers don't get bricklaying block,' he liked to say.

He did go on to revise this statement, though, in the years that followed, as he published one book after another, saying that he was running out of things to talk about, that he was afraid of repeating himself – and he later came to the conclusion that writers became blocked for two reasons:

Either they didn't know where they were going, as in they had no idea of the story they were trying to write, and the only remedy for this was to down tools and figure out the main plot points of the story before continuing. And the other, and probably more predominant reason for writers becoming depressed, despondent and full of self-loathing, when they couldn't produce good work, was fear. Fear of putting the words down wrong. Fear of writing total rubbish. Fear of people laughing at their attempts. Basically, that all-encompassing human fear of not being good enough.

I suffered from this fear myself from time to time. Just before I made my way to the keyboard to write I'd feel a huge swell of resistance inside my chest as if I needed to flee. As if I should be anywhere other than where I was about to go. This fear would be followed by an intense tired feeling: a heaviness across the shoulders, a dragging feeling in the legs, as if I might not make it to the keyboard.

I read once that Christopher Dean, of celebrity ice-dancing duo Torvill and Dean, experienced something similar as he was about to skate in major competitions. His legs would become so heavy and leaden he feared he wouldn't make it out on to the ice.

Did all artists suffer from this? And if they did, did that mean that I was in fact an artist and—

'What the fuck do you think you're doing?'

I froze.

Leon was in the doorway.

He'd returned from his daily run with Eden and his T-shirt was damp with sweat. There was anger in his eyes, and his face was set with fury.

'What are you doing, looking at my work?' he demanded.

One fast appraisal of his stance and I could sense his urge for violence. Could feel the charge in the air.

How fast, I almost said aloud in awe, *how fast you go from nothing to this, Leon. From zero to a hundred.*

Quickly, I ran through all the possible responses I could give that might best alleviate the situation. That might prevent his anger from escalating to the point of him smashing the place up again.

'Move away from the desk, Jane,' he warned.

I could smell the adrenaline on him. He didn't want me

up here. Something in his brain was telling him this was *not OK*. He needed me out of this room immediately. What I was doing was dangerous.

My email was still open. I eyed the manuscript. It was face down, the title page not visible. Did he know I'd been reading his work?

'Get out,' he hissed.

'I'm not doing anything.'

'GET OUT!'

He eyed the screen. He thought I was in his files. What did he not want me to see?

He began moving from one foot to the other, like a boxer first entering the ring. The energy inside him was building. I'd been around him enough times of late to know it needed to come out. That it *would* come out.

Did I feign innocence? Did I tell him not to be silly, that *of course* I wasn't looking at his work? That I would *never* look at his work?

'Go away, Leon,' I said firmly. 'I'm busy,' and I turned around to face the screen and began typing.

I typed like a concert pianist. It was all gibberish, but I made like what I was doing was extremely important and I was not to be disturbed.

I could feel the pulse in my neck. Could hear a mighty whooshing in my ears as I waited to see what he'd do next.

'I think I told you to leave,' he said.

'And I said I'm *busy*.'

Then I sighed out long and hard before turning back around towards him. 'I really don't need you in here interrupting,' I said. 'Where's Eden anyway? He's supposed to be keeping you out of my hair whilst I sort out this paperwork.'

'You're in my stuff.'

'I'm not.'

'Jane,' he said, his voice menacingly level. 'You need to step away from the computer right now,' and he advanced towards me.

'Jesus Christ, Leon!' I flared, and I stood up. 'Who is going to do this if I don't? You? Are you going to do it?'

He stopped dead in his tracks.

'Come on then,' I continued, 'be my guest. Come and log into your account and authorize a payment to United Utilities . . . What? You can't? Oh, I beg your pardon. For a minute there, I thought you'd suddenly remembered how to do ALL THE THINGS I HAVE TO DO BECAUSE YOU CAN'T DO THEM ANY MORE.'

I sat down again. Resumed typing.

'Anyway,' I said, after a second, 'what's so important that I'm not allowed to see? Another woman's naked photographs? Secret gambling habit?'

'Jane.'

'What, Leon?'

But he couldn't answer.

Or else he wouldn't.

He kept glancing at the screen and then back at me. He knew I knew something but was afraid to ask what.

Just how much are you remembering right now, Leon? I thought. Or is this muscle memory? You find your wife at your computer and your body tells you to eject her from the room, even if you don't fully understand why?

I waited.

I studied his face.

It was unreadable.

He advanced another step but I put my hand up. 'Here's

something you need to understand, Leon. You can be a hindrance. A total fucking hindrance sometimes. It's like having another toddler . . . But I'm trying here, honestly, I'm trying to keep our lives together. I'm trying to be mother *and* father. I'm trying to pick up the slack and bring money into the house . . . So, how about you let me get on with it, and stop making it so difficult?'

Leon just stared at me.

He left without speaking.

I put my hands to my face and exhaled. Was this how it was going to be now? Every time Leon got half a memory back he'd become hostile? Aggressive?

After he'd gone, I deleted all the gibberish I'd typed, and I turned over the manuscript of *Red City* and glared at it, willing it to relinquish its secrets.

'What happened to Leon whilst he was writing you?' I whispered to the pages. 'What made him lose his way, made him dry up?'

I couldn't work it out. The story was all there, ready to be finished. It made no sense, it—

'Jane.'

Leon was back. He was standing right behind me.

He'd mounted the stairs without my hearing and I held my breath.

I closed the email. 'What do you want, Leon?' I said carefully, bracing myself for another round.

I turned. Leon had changed his T-shirt and washed his face.

'I'm sorry,' he said simply.

I blinked at him.

Leon had not apologized for anything since sustaining the brain injury. It was as if that bunch of neurones had been severed and 'sorry' just didn't exist for him any more. I watched him. I had no idea if this was a genuine apology or not.

'I'm sorry I shouted at you,' he said.

'That's OK.'

He was shaking his head. 'No,' he said, 'no, it's not OK. I don't want to keep being like this, Jane. I don't know where it comes from . . . this anger. I don't know how to stop it from coming out.'

I cleared my throat. 'I don't think you always *can* stop it from coming out.'

He nodded.

He wanted to say more. He wanted to say something else, but he didn't know how. 'I'm sorry this has happened to you,' he said eventually. And I could see how hard it was for him. 'I keep thinking that this has ruined *my* life, that it's *me* who can't do anything any more, that I don't know who *I* am . . . but I hadn't really realized that this has affected you too. It's affected your life a lot, hasn't it?'

I told him it wasn't always easy.

'It must have been really shitty when I came out of the coma and I wanted Gina,' he said. 'When I wanted her instead of you.' He reached out his hand to me. 'Sorry,' he said, again.

'It's all right . . . It'll get better. Eventually, it'll get better. I know it will.'

And he brushed his fingertips across my cheek. I didn't flinch. I didn't pull away and he was examining me closely. He was looking at me intently, really looking into my eyes, as though trying to figure out if I would ever be able to love him again.

He threaded some stray strands of hair behind my ear. 'Red,' he said softly, not taking his hand away.

'Yes, red.'

'It's pretty,' he said.

And then: 'I've missed you, baby.'

Was it possible to experience the full gamut of human emotions in less than five minutes? It seemed as though it was.

Downstairs, I gathered up my work bag and headed to the kitchen to grab a bottle of water. Eden was in there pretending to look busy, avoiding eye contact. I opened the fridge. 'Thanks for doing that,' I said to him.

Eden tried to look blank. 'Doing what?'

I smiled. 'Eden, thank you for getting Leon to apologize. It's really good that you're here . . . You're helping.'

And he went sheepish before looking at his feet.

'You're welcome, Auntie Jane.'

30

The following afternoon, Leon and I walked to school together, posting missing cat leaflets through letterboxes along the way. Eden had gone into town to have his hair restyled and to meet up with a few lads he knew from playing *Call of Duty* online. He had Leon playing it now as well and I'd yet to decide if that was a good thing or not.

Leon and I held hands.

This was a new thing.

And I felt as I might have done had we been a couple in the early stages of a relationship: awkward, bashful, mildly embarrassed, but happy nonetheless. Leon strode along, chest out, gripping my hand hard as though I was a toddler, as though I might suddenly veer off, distracted by a bird, or a blowing leaf, throwing myself into the oncoming traffic.

He beamed at me. 'We should do this every day,' he said.

I agreed, not wanting to spoil the moment, as it would not be feasible to do this every day. I couldn't always get back from my classes in time to make the journey on foot.

We headed on to the playground and a number of parents greeted Leon by name.

'This is my wife, Jane,' he said proudly, and to their

credit they didn't say they already knew me, that they saw me at the morning drop-off; instead they smiled, saying, 'Lovely to see you out together,' which made Leon beam all the more, and squeeze my hand all the more tightly too.

Jack came rushing out, the first of his class, and thrust a huge sheet of paper at Leon which was covered in hand prints. He had blue paint around his collar and on the inside of his left ear. Leon bent to kiss his son's cheek as Jack fumbled in his book bag, saying it was very important that he gave us a letter about Knowsley Safari Park. If the money wasn't handed in straight away, then he wouldn't get to go.

'There are only thirty spaces,' he said worriedly.

I stood there silent. My breath had caught in my throat and I was struggling to breathe. All at once my whole body had started to quake as though I'd stepped directly from a warm pool straight into cold air.

Jack was wearing a cap. A red cap. A Liverpool Football Club cap. It was a small, child's version. Brand new. Never before worn.

Ryan Toonen had worn the same Liverpool cap when he attacked me in prison.

'I like your hat,' Leon said to Jack.

Leon was a lifelong blue. An Everton FC supporter. The sight of his son in a rival cap like this would have at one time made him lose his shit.

I spun around.

The faces were a blur. They melded into each other. Each face was the same.

Who had given the cap to Jack?

Leon plucked it from Jack's head and tried to wear it

himself. Jack responded by leaping up repeatedly, trying to reach it.

'That's mine!' he said, laughing, not really minding. Happy that Leon was more fun than the other dads who were pulling their kids along by their hands, eager to get home.

I took the cap from Leon.

Inside, scrawled in capital letters with a permanent marker, was a message: 'WATCHING YOU'. Then, below, there were a couple of badly drawn eyes.

'Who gave you this?' I screamed at Jack.

And Leon looked at me, horrified.

I shook the hat in Jack's face. 'Who gave you this, Jack? Answer me!'

'A man,' he said, frowning.

'What man?'

'A nice man.'

'When? Where? What did he say to you? It's really important that you tell me exactly what happened here, Jack. What did he say to you?'

Leon caught hold of my elbow and said, 'Jane, what the hell's wrong with you? You're scaring him.'

I shook him off. 'What did he look like?' I said to Jack. 'What was he wearing?'

Jack burst into tears. 'I don't know,' he whimpered.

He dropped his bag and threw himself at Leon's legs, clinging on to his father and burying his face in Leon's jeans.

I squatted down next to him. 'This is so important,' I said. 'What did the man say to you? Why do you have this hat?'

But Jack shook his head, his face still buried. He didn't want to tell me.

I touched his shoulder. 'Please, honey.'

Jack wiped his nose on his hand and looked at me out of the corner of his eye. 'He told me it was for me. He told me he had a present and I was special – that's why he was giving it to me and no one else.'

'He didn't try to hurt you? Didn't ask you to go anywhere with him?'

Jack shook his head. 'He was nice, Mummy. Honestly. He was a really nice man.'

We took a cab to get Martha. I called the nursery en route and yelled at the poor assistant who answered. 'Where's Martha? Where's my daughter?' She was there. And by the time we arrived the manager of the nursery was waiting for us at the front, a grave look on her face, not sure what all the madness was about.

'Did anyone come here?' I demanded. 'A man? Did you see anyone hanging around the play area? Anyone asking for Martha?' It wouldn't have been difficult to spot her. She was the only biracial child in the place.

The manager assured me that, no, no one had been near. No one suspicious. 'Just another ordinary day, Jane,' she said.

Back at home, Leon didn't understand why I hadn't told him about Ryan Toonen. He couldn't get his head around the fact that I would take this on alone without saying anything to him. He was mad at me leaving him out of the loop. 'You don't trust me,' he said.

'No, it's not that, it's—'

'You don't think I'm capable of knowing this stuff!'

'I do.'

'Then why didn't you *tell* me?'

'They threatened me. They threatened us, Leon.'

He was as mad at me as he was at them – whoever they were – for threatening his family. He paced the room, his hands clenched into fists, the tendons in his neck standing proud of the skin, corded like guy ropes.

He wanted to smash something up. Tear someone's face off.

'These are the same people who attacked you, Leon,' I said. 'I don't know what they want. I don't know why they won't leave us alone.' Then I added quietly, 'I don't know what you did to them.'

Leon stopped.

It was the first time I'd broached the subject to Leon himself that his brain injury could be the result of a revenge attack. That he might have actually done something to cause it.

Watching him, it was clear that this had not occurred to him until this moment.

He closed his eyes.

He pulled his brows together in concentration as he seemed to be willing the memory to return. His head rippled with tension. And I went very still. I could see he was close to a breakthrough.

Come on, Leon.

Remember.

It took everything I had to keep my mouth shut and let his brain do the work. *Why did they do this to you? Why did they want you dead?*

Leon opened his eyes.

'I can't remember,' he said.

31

Hazel Ledecky interviewed Jack.

She did it at home as she thought it would be less intimidating for him. I watched as she did her best impression of an approachable adult, a friendly person, a person a small four-year-old boy could place his trust in, open up to, and I realized she was a lousy actress.

Jack was ashen, scared to death of her.

'Jack,' she said, bending towards him, 'tell me as best you can what the man looked like.'

But as she leaned in, Jack leaned away from her in his chair and, realizing he had nowhere to go, lifted his knees up and hugged them tightly.

'Did he have white skin like your mummy . . . ? Or was his skin like your daddy's?' she asked.

'White,' Jack whispered.

Ledecky glanced at me. 'The playground is without CCTV,' she said. 'And can you tell me how tall he was?' she asked Jack. 'Was he tall like your daddy? Or was he a much smaller person like that police officer over there?' She pointed to DC Payne, who was by the back door, taking notes.

Jack looked at me. 'Mummy, I need to go to the bathroom.'

He didn't. He'd only just been.

'It's OK if you don't know the answer, sweetheart,' I told him. 'Just tell Inspector Ledecky that you don't know the answer. It's quite all right.'

'I don't know the answer,' he said. 'I think he was tall.'

'Did he know your name?' asked Ledecky.

Jack nodded.

'Did he call out to you?'

Jack nodded again.

'And why did you approach the man, Jack?'

Jack looked at me, lost.

'She means why did you go to the man,' I said.

'Because he shouted out my name.'

This went on for the next hour, Ledecky gaining very little in the way of actual intelligence from Jack, and Jack getting more and more rattled, more and more upset that he'd made a mistake, that he'd committed a grave error of judgement, by simply accepting a gift from a man who knew his name. It might have been easier if we could have explained to him the context: that he was being used to frighten us, that whoever had attacked Leon was using this incident as a warning. But of course that would have frightened him all the more, unjustifiably. And I could see he really couldn't get his head around why this austere, serious-looking woman was in our kitchen, going over the facts with him in minute detail.

Ledecky left the house armed with very little from Jack, but now at least she knew about Toonen and the prison incident. 'You really should have told us about that sooner, Jane,' she castigated; she was annoyed with me. 'We could have been working on it, we could've—'

'He told me someone would hurt my kids.'

'Yes, but—'

'He told me they'd *hurt* my kids,' I said again, seeing that she wasn't getting it.

And she nodded once and left. After that, I did what I could to ensure the children were safe. The staff at both Jack's school and Martha's nursery were all warned to be on high alert for anyone suspicious hanging around. I talked to classroom assistants, to the lunchtime supervisors; I made them understand just how serious it was and told them not to take chances. Anything out of the ordinary and they were to bring Jack and Martha inside immediately and call me. I kept my phone in my back pocket the whole time and, even though it was set to vibrate, I checked it unremittingly.

We also stopped walking to school. Images of cars mounting pavements, of runaway bin lorries plagued my dreams, and I kept the children away from open spaces, from busy shops, from anywhere I deemed unsafe.

Aside from going to work, I didn't go out alone. I checked my rear-view mirror constantly. We holed up inside and I just had to hope it was enough. Hoped that I was demonstrating to whoever was watching us that I was following orders. I quit my emails to Alistair Armitage, and I kept my head down. The cap was sent for forensic testing but came back clean. Jack had said the man had worn gloves, so it was a long shot, anyway. Inspector Ledecky interviewed Jack once more, trying to glean any further information, but she got nothing of use. A white man in dark clothing with gloves, that's all we knew. No other children in the playground could add anything further. 'I'm sorry, Jane,' Ledecky said, 'but whoever's doing this is making it very difficult for us.' Apparently the dark saloon car on the CCTV had been one of many dark saloon cars out that night apparently and when she'd interviewed Ryan Toonen in prison, naturally all she'd got was a string of no comments.

I thought about running away.

We could leave. Disappear. Run away in the middle of the night and go to the other end of the country. Start again where no one knew us.

I fantasized about this. I fantasized about it and came up with intricate plans in my head.

Indeed, I was fantasizing about it when I got the phone call.

'Am I speaking to Mrs Campbell?' a voice said.

And I said, 'You are.'

'Then I'm afraid I have some very bad news for you.'

32

I drove through the unfamiliar streets trying to hold it together. Widnes was not a place I visited. Fifteen miles from home, it was a town I saw the signs for every time I left Liverpool, and yet, in all of the times I'd *left* Liverpool, I'd never had cause to go. What did I know about it? Very little. A rugby league town and the place where ex-Spice Girl, Melanie C, had once gone to school.

The satnav sent me along Speke Boulevard but after forty minutes, I was beginning to regret my choice, thinking it would have been faster to take the M62.

The woman had very kindly tried to give me directions but I began losing her words after a moment or two and told her I'd look up the postcode instead. 'I'm not really able to concentrate,' and she said she understood. She told me she would be there all day – until around five thirty – so I was not to rush. 'Take your time,' she cautioned.

I found the place and parked badly. Reversing in and out of the space, I couldn't get it right even though it was something I usually did automatically. My nerves were shot. I left my car far too close to the car next to me. They wouldn't be able to open the driver's side door.

I wound my way between the other parked vehicles and headed for the area marked 'Reception'. A sign announced that visitors were welcome by appointment only, and so I pressed the bell and I waited. A young woman unlocked the door and beckoned me in.

Inside, the walls were covered in photographs. 'Happy in their new home', the captions read. There was a breakdown of the cost of rehoming an animal: neutering, vaccinations, food.

I felt nauseous. My insides swam.

I gathered myself and approached the woman behind the desk. 'You called me,' I said. 'I mean, I'm not sure if it was you exactly who called, but someone did . . . earlier.'

She altered her look. Consciously tried to soften her expression. 'Jane?'

I nodded.

'Follow me.'

As we made our way along a hallway, in a hushed, sympathetic voice she said, 'Like I said on the phone, the microchip numbers match so there's really not a lot of chance that this—'

'I need to check for myself,' I cut in, and I stopped walking. 'I need to know for sure . . . because of the distance. It's over twenty miles from our home.'

She blinked. She got it.

We went into a side room, a kind of storage room. There were bags of food on the floor. Cat baskets stacked against the far wall. On a table in the centre, wrapped in a pink, fleece blanket – a blanket with small paw prints printed on it – lay Bonita.

Dead Bonita.

I walked towards her and the woman held back.

'Is it her?' she asked quietly from behind me.

'She looks different. Bigger.'

The woman gave a helpless kind of shrug and looked at the floor. 'She's stiffened,' she said uneasily. 'It changes their features.'

I pulled the blanket from her neck a little. It was definitely her. It was Bonita. There was blood on her shoulder and her lips were pulled back, baring her teeth. Her left eye bulged madly. My pretty little fearless cat looked like a bad taxidermy project.

'I didn't think to bring a blanket,' I said quietly.

The woman told me I could keep the one she was wrapped in. 'It belonged to the gentleman who brought her in.'

'I don't understand how she got all the way to Widnes,' I said vaguely.

And the woman said she didn't either. 'Although they do sometimes climb inside work vans,' she added, talking, I think, just to fill the silence. 'We've heard of cats being found over three hundred miles away.'

'Alive though,' I said.

'Yes,' she conceded. 'The cats were found alive.'

'Do I have to fill out any forms?'

'No, you can just take her. Would you like a minute on your own with her first? I can give you some privacy if that would help.'

I shook my head. 'The man who brought her in?'

'He didn't run her over,' she said quickly, and she looked at me suddenly quite stricken.

'I'd like to thank him if possible.'

'Oh,' and she let out a small breath. 'Sometimes owners . . . sometimes they can get pretty angry, so we're not obliged to give out details.'

'I'm not angry,' I said. 'I'm grateful.'

Still she seemed unsure.

'I want to thank him,' I explained. 'This man took the trouble to bring Bonita to you. We could have spent weeks ... months ... years waiting for her to come home. And the kids wouldn't have understood. This' – I motioned to her lifeless, stiffened body – 'as distressing as it is, has to be better than thinking she was locked up somewhere, alone, dying.'

She held the door for me as I carried out Bonita's body and placed her carefully in the boot of the car. I pulled the blanket over her head and then changed my mind, tucking it around her neck instead to make her more cosy. For some reason, I'd elected to bring along her cat basket, but we wouldn't be needing it now so I took it back inside. A donation of sorts.

I handed it over and in return the woman passed me a strip of paper. On it was a phone number.

'Name's Rodney,' she said.

Rodney said he'd hoped I'd call.

He thought it was important that we meet.

As the woman at the shelter had implied, they had a policy of not giving out the numbers of people who'd brought in dead pets, but apparently Rodney had specifically asked that an exception be made in this instance. He gave me 'old person's' directions to his house: number 189, just around the bend, the one after the house with the peeling paint and the red truck in the driveway. If I found myself outside the house with the overgrown pampas grass and the yellow wheelbarrow in the garden, I'd gone too far.

I looked around as I got out of the car. It was a suburban estate, built, I guessed, sometime in the sixties. The houses were identical bungalows, row after row; the place had an Edward Scissorhands feel. Rodney was out of the house as soon as I pulled up to the kerb. He'd clearly been watching out for me.

He approached and shook my hand. 'Sorry for your loss,' he said formally, and he touched the peak of his flat cap.

Beneath a rainproof jacket, he wore a brushed-cotton shirt with a tie, and on his feet were rubber-soled, sensible shoes. At first glance he looked like your average busybody, but closer inspection revealed a kindness in his eyes. There was real warmth.

'It happened over there,' he said, pointing to a bungalow diagonally opposite. The house had vertical blinds in every window so you couldn't see inside.

'Did you see it?'

He shook his head. 'I'd been watching her though. One minute she was sat there, cleaning and primping herself, as cats do, and the next she was in the road. I'd say it was quick, if that helps. Instant in fact, because by the time I'd got my coat and cap on she was already gone . . . Driver didn't stop. They use this road as a rat run.'

'You were very kind to take her to the shelter.'

'I'm a cat person myself.'

'The lady at the shelter said it was your blanket. The pink one? Would you like me to return it when I've washed it?'

'You keep it, love,' he said. 'Bury her in it if you like. But . . . I suppose you probably have your own you'd like to use.'

I told him I'd like to use his blanket and he seemed pleased by this.

Then there wasn't a lot more to say. I'd thought about bringing something, a gift, a thank you for going above and beyond the call of duty, but when I'd stood in the Shell garage earlier, picking up objects – flowers, a bottle of wine, chocolates – nothing seemed particularly appropriate so I'd left empty-handed.

'I should have got her registration plate,' Rodney said absently.

'It doesn't matter,' I replied.

Then I said, 'Wait. You saw the driver? I didn't think you saw who did it.'

He shook his head to indicate I'd misunderstood. 'I *didn't* see the driver,' he explained, 'but I should have got the registration plate of the woman who left her there. It didn't occur to me at the time. I saw the woman pull up right over there, and I thought she needed something from her boot, or her boot wasn't shut properly, something like that. Then when she drove away I saw the little cat was on the kerb looking all bewildered. She stayed like that for a good hour. Not knowing what to do, I expect. I only put two and two together later that night – I realized that the woman had left her there on purpose. Dumped her. Anyway, the cat had gone by that time. She came back each day though and I'd look out for her. It was as if she was waiting . . . I don't know, maybe waiting to be picked up again?'

'Do you remember what kind of car this was?'

'Yes.'

'You remember the colour?'

'I remember everything that goes on around here,' he said.

33

'Rose!' I yelled through the letterbox. 'Rose, get out here!'

I banged on the door with my fist. 'Get out here right now!'

Then I held my finger on the bell so that it rang continuously. 'Rose!' I took my keys from my bag and rapped on the glass. 'I know you're in there! Get out here and see what you've done!'

Bonita was next to me on the floor of Rose and Lawrence's covered porch. Let her see exactly what she'd done.

I moved to the front window. Cupping my hands around my eyes I looked through the glass and there was a flash of movement, a wisp of clothing, as someone left the room.

Quickly, I ran back to the front door and looked through the letterbox again.

I could see the tips of Rose's slippers peeking out from the lounge doorway. She was hiding in between the two rooms, hoping she was invisible from my two vantage points.

'I can see you, Rose.'

She stayed perfectly still so I let the letterbox bang shut with a clatter and sprinted around the side of the house. I vaulted their small gate and ran to their back door. She would not hide from this. She wouldn't.

I grabbed the handle but she was already on the other side. Christ, she'd moved fast. She was furiously trying to lock the thing before I came through the glass. Her face was set and her tight grey curls were bobbing madly with the effort.

'Open it, Rose!'

'I'll call the police,' she said, eyes locked downwards, her fingers working furiously.

'*You'll* call the police?' I screamed. 'I'll call the police, you old witch! Do you know what you've done? Do you?'

'You have no proof of anything.'

'I don't need proof.'

'If you're going to come here accusing me of something then—'

'You killed her! You went and killed her!'

Rose flinched at my words but still she wouldn't make eye contact.

'Look at me!' I screamed and her head shot up. 'Is it not enough for you to see me struggling with Leon every day? Is it not enough so you have to go and kill our cat as well? I hope you're happy. I really hope—'

'I didn't mean for her to—'

'What? *Die?* Well, what *were* you expecting when you trapped her? When you drove twenty miles from her home? When you dumped her by the side of the road? What did you think might happen, Rose?'

Quite pathetically she said, 'I thought she'd wander off and go and live with someone else.'

I closed my eyes briefly at her stupidity. 'Cats don't do that, Rose. They try to get home.'

'Some do,' she said, and then she looked at me, fresh panic in her eyes.

'Oh, God,' I said, realizing. 'You've done this before. You've taken people's cats before, haven't you? So, what is this? You're going around the streets and rounding up *all* the cats now? That's your good turn for the gardeners of Liverpool? You CAN'T do that!'

'But we're part of Liverpool in Bloom!' she cried. 'We're showing our garden as part of the festival.'

'Oh, fuck off, Rose.'

She took a step back from the glass and fixed me with a defiant stare. Though she was trembling now, in quite a pronounced way. 'Please leave,' she said firmly.

'I'm leaving!'

I only took three steps though before doing a fast about-turn and rapping on the glass again. She was still standing there, shell-shocked.

'I'm leaving, Rose, but you know what? That husband of yours will be dead soon. He's pretty old, isn't he? And your weirdo son is no use. And when you need help, when you fall in the night and can't get up, when you can't drive that car of yours any longer, and you get totally cut off from life, I will pretend I have no idea who you are. In fact, I might drive *you* somewhere, Rose. Widnes, let's say. I'll drop *you* by the side of the road and leave you, and you'll have no idea where the hell you are. Goodbye, Rose. I'm calling the police.'

Faintly, I could hear her protesting through the glass as I walked away. 'Don't! Please don't call them! Please, Jane . . . don't . . .'

'Rose Williams killed my cat.'

'Jane,' answered Inspector Ledecky, her voice smooth with deliberate neutrality. 'How is Jack doing?'

'Rose Williams killed my cat,' I repeated.

I heard her exhale.

'I'm on my way,' she said resignedly.

Ledecky was with us within the hour and by that time I was no calmer than I had been whilst trying to rattle Rose's door off its hinges. By now Martha was sobbing quietly on the beanbag, thumb in her mouth, her cheeks pink as though they'd been slapped, and Jack was sitting on Eden's knee on the sofa, Eden tapping out a rhythm using Jack's hands that Jack appeared to find soothing.

They were distraught. They really thought Bonita would come home, full of adventures for them to speculate on, draw pictures about.

I paced the floor.

Fucking Rose.

What sort of person traps cats and releases them miles from home?

If Leon had been allowed to continue with his voyeurism he might have caught her in the act; we could have named and shamed, shown Rose forcing Bonita into a sack and put it on social media. We could have ruined her life just like that shuddersome Cat Bin Lady.

'Sit down, Auntie Jane,' said Eden, 'you're making me tense.'

'I can't sit down. I'm too angry to sit down.'

The doorbell went and I flew out of the room, pulling the front door open, almost panting. I didn't say hello. Just held the door wide for Inspector Ledecky, who executed a curt nod as she passed by me.

Ledecky glanced left and on seeing the children and Eden in the lounge, made her way along the hallway to the kitchen. Once there, she didn't wait for me to start yelling. 'You'd better sit down,' she said, as if this was her house.

'I'd rather stand,' I said defiantly.

Ledecky raised her eyes to the ceiling wearily. Her eye-bags were heavier than usual. 'Jane, do stop being stubborn and take a seat.'

I acquiesced. Muttering. I sat down at the head of the table so we were at ninety degrees to one another.

'Where's Leon today?' she asked.

'In the bath.'

'How's he doing?'

'Fine,' I snapped. 'Well, aside from the cat, he's fine.'

'No more visitors to Jack's school?'

I looked at her. 'Do you really think I would keep something like that to myself?' I said. 'No, there have been no more stalkers. No, for now no one has been threatening the children. Or us.' I shook my head at her in disbelief. 'Anyway, what are you going to do about Rose?' I said. 'She admitted it to me. She's not going to deny it.' I sat back in the chair and folded my arms across my chest. 'Rose is a nasty little bitch of a woman and I know you probably think she's all sweetness and light, but I can assure you she's not.'

Inspector Ledecky shifted in her seat. 'Of late,' she began, 'Lawrence Williams has noticed some changes in his wife.'

'Changes?' I spat. 'Killing cats, there's a change for you.'

'Rose is currently undergoing tests for dementia,' she said carefully.

'Whoa.' I held up my palms. 'You're not seriously going to try and pass off her behaviour with this excuse, are you? What? She's losing her mind? She didn't know what she was doing? I can tell you right now she knew *exactly* what she was doing. She's an evil, evil monster of a woman who—'

'Jane. Lawrence has been taking Rose to see their GP for close to eighteen months now. This is not a recent thing. And no, I'm not trying to excuse what she did to your cat.'

I rolled my eyes.

'They haven't received a definitive diagnosis as yet,' she said. 'Dementia is of course notoriously hard to diagnose without physical changes to the brain, evident on scans and so forth, but Rose has been exhibiting behaviour that Lawrence says is completely out of character for his wife.' She paused momentarily before adding, 'She has been exhibiting behaviour that would be classed as . . . xenophobic.'

'Xenophobic?'

She nodded.

'Racist?' I said. She'd completely thrown me. 'You're serious?'

'When I spoke to the Williamses, shortly after Leon's attack,' she said, 'this came up. Their son, Glyn, seemed particularly keen to get it off his chest. He was worried I would find out about Rose and jump to conclusions.'

'Did you jump to conclusions?'

'It was a lead that we felt needed pursuing fully, so we questioned Rose a number of times about how she felt about . . .' DI Ledecky hesitated.

'A black guy living opposite?' I offered.

She nodded.

It was now that I remembered Glyn's visit again. Shortly

after Leon's attack, he'd lingered outside the lounge window. He'd appeared tormented, as if he had something he needed to say, something crucial to impart.

'Glyn came here,' I said to Inspector Ledecky. 'He came here after Leon's attack. Do you remember?'

'I do. We were investigating Rose at that point, so I gave him strict instructions to stay away. I ordered all of them not to speak to you but, to be frank, he was in a terrible state. He thought if you found out what Rose had been doing, there would be repercussions, and he wanted to stave off any retaliation.'

'Why didn't you tell me this earlier?'

'Because I didn't have to.'

'You didn't think it was relevant? You didn't think it might have been useful for me to know?'

'What would you have done, Jane? Marched over there?'

'No.'

Ledecky held my gaze. I probably would have.

'So why *didn't* you arrest her?' I asked.

'Because she didn't try to murder your husband. Eventually, we tracked down CCTV of Rose driving out of Tesco on Allerton Road, at the exact time Leon was being attacked.'

I got up and poured myself a glass of water. I offered one to Inspector Ledecky but she declined. Sitting back down again, I said, 'OK, so what else did she do to Leon? And, really, should she even be driving?'

'She claims not to remember what she did to Leon, but Lawrence is pretty sure she keyed his car.'

'Oh,' I said, remembering. 'We'd put that down to kids.'

'And Lawrence thinks she might have thrown weed-killer on your camellia.'

I was nodding. 'Yes, that did die quite suddenly.'

'And positioned nails near Leon's wheels so he'd get a slow puncture.'

I'd forgotten he'd had a puncture. It had seemed like nothing at the time.

'Stupid stuff, really,' she said. 'Stuff that goes on between neighbours all the time. But it was the intent behind it that worried Lawrence. According to him, Rose's father had racist tendencies, and Rose has been peppering her sentences with phrases and terms her father used since the start of her mental decline . . . particularly when she's talking about Leon.'

'Leon had been filming them,' I told her. 'I found masses of video files, films showing their side of the street. I thought he had some problem with Lawrence, or else he was fearful of being attacked . . . to be honest at one point I thought he was losing his mind.'

'I found those files too, Jane. Leon wasn't losing his mind. I think he *was* fearful of being attacked. Don't you? Perhaps he started off wanting to document the street because he feared for his own safety, but then caught Rose in her acts of sabotage . . . accidentally.'

I closed my eyes. All at once I felt very tired. As if I could fall asleep right there in the chair.

Then I laughed. 'You know, there have been moments when I thought Rose could've attacked Leon.' I shook my head. Now I felt like I was losing *my* mind.

Ledecky smiled. 'Have faith, Jane,' she said. 'We *will* get whoever did this.' And she stood and made to leave.

At the front door she turned. 'We're so close,' she said. 'We're so close I can feel it. I'm going back to Walton Gaol to re-question Ryan Toonen. I plan to put the wind up him a bit more, tell him his uncooperative behaviour won't go down well when his parole comes around . . . Let's see how he reacts to that. Who knows, he might decide to talk after all.'

34

Leon and Eden buried Bonita in the garden.

I instructed them to put her over by the rhubarb patch, a spot she'd liked because it got a lot of warmth in the summer, a spot she'd spend hours sitting in, grooming herself, angling her small face up towards the sun. It being November, the garden was a grim, bleak, unwelcoming place right now, and as they dug, and the children stood in their mackintoshes and wellingtons, sombre-faced, with poems ready to read out loud in memory of their beloved cat, summer seemed like decades away.

For the next few days Lawrence kept a low profile. Every time I came out of the house he'd shoot back inside. And there had been a noticeable decrease in activity over there. The car washing, pavement sweeping, gutter clearing, soil tilling, had all taken a back seat. He clearly didn't want to face what had happened to the cat.

I told both Leon and Eden what Rose had done to Bonita with instructions to spare the kids the details, but it hadn't been necessary as Leon promptly forgot all about it. He still had moments when he called out to her by the back door, forgetting she'd even gone missing in the first place. And he would call out to Lawrence too, waving enthusiastically whenever he saw him, forgetting he'd ever had a cross word with him as well. If it hadn't been so tragic, it would have been funny.

We'd had no more strangers at school.

No more dark-coloured saloon cars in the street.

But I didn't relax and assume that we were safe. That we could get on with the business of living. I kept alert, stayed watchful, whilst trying to get on with shepherding the children to school, making meals, teaching classes, cleaning the house, helping Leon learn how to live in the world once again. Ledecky had got nowhere with Ryan Toonen and the whole thing was taking its toll. I was jumpy and anxious, my body had become thin and angular, and I was now medicating with alcohol just to get a rest. I needed an out. I needed Leon's attackers to be caught so that I could feel safe, but with every day that passed, the possibility of that seemed more and more remote.

Eden remained an asset, a good distraction for Leon. I'd come to rely on him to the point that I couldn't imagine how we'd get through the week without him. Eden's natural geniality seemed to be somehow washing off on Leon, and since he'd been with us Leon had not had one violent episode.

When I'd left them this morning, for instance, Eden had been holding up a series of pictures of people and objects that he'd cut out from the Sunday supplements for Leon to identify.

'Britney Spears?' ventured Leon.

'Close,' replied Eden. 'So close, Uncle Leon. You're almost there. Try again.'

Leon had squeezed his eyes tightly shut as he tried to recall the name. 'Nicole Kidman?'

Eden snorted. 'No, man,' he said. 'But so close. Let's try another.'

Eden thought this would be a good way to work on improving Leon's short-term memory. Yesterday they'd started with four images: the Alps, a Stilton and broccoli quiche, Cambridge University, and a picture of a performance car from the Motoring section. Today the blonde in the picture that Leon was having trouble recollecting was Ellen DeGeneres.

I was pretty sure the game was having a negligible effect on Leon's memory, but I could hear Leon laughing uproariously from time to time, which would make me stop in my tracks and smile. Eden said they would move on to word recall soon, which he thought might be useful for him too as Eden's spelling was, 'As we all know, Auntie Jane, absolute shit.'

Back from my class at Wavertree Library now, I mounted the stairs and called out Eden's name.

'In the shower!'

'Where's Leon?'

'Attic,' Eden said. 'He asked for privacy.' When I didn't respond, wondering what Leon could be doing up there, Eden added, 'That's OK, isn't it, Auntie Jane?' with worry in his voice. 'I'm not supposed to be on, like, suicide watch or anything?'

'It's fine, Eden.'

I climbed the second set of stairs and found Leon lying on the sofa, his eyes closed. He was too big to fit into the thing comfortably and so lay with his lower legs hanging over the edge. I got the sense he was resting rather than actually sleeping.

'Hey,' I said softly and he roused, opened his eyes and turned his head my way.

'Hey.'

'Why don't you go to bed if you're tired? You'd be more comfortable. You could stretch out.'

'I like it here. How was your class?'

'You remembered,' I said, surprised.

And he flashed me his palm. On it, he'd written: 'Class'.

'Do you remember what the class was?' I asked.

He shook his head.

'Creative writing.'

He sat up. 'Oh yeah,' he said, suddenly enthusiastic, 'you want to be a writer. You want to be a writer like me.' He clapped his hands together, pleased with himself, and I didn't have the heart to tell him I was in charge of the class rather than attending as a student. 'You want to be a writer like me,' he said again and he looked around the room: took in the shelves containing his books, his foreign editions, his audio books that I'd moved up here for him to listen to if he wanted.

He gazed at the computer and the desk where the magic happened; on it was the paperweight I'd given him, the fountain pen that he liked to use to write his outlines. He shifted his gaze to the shelves and he took in the Gold Dagger, awarded to him by the Crime Writers' Association for the best crime novel of 2014. 'I'm a writer,' he said softly.

'That's right.'

'What sort of books do *you* write?' he asked.

'Not very good ones.'

He smiled. Waited for me to answer properly.

'I write about family. That kind of thing. Family drama, I suppose you'd call it.'

'Is there a market for that?'

'It's not as popular as crime. Crime's what's selling.'

'Ever written about me?'

I shook my head. 'Sorry, Leon, but to use one of your own sayings, real people are just not all that interesting. Maybe I will now though. Maybe, you know, after all that's happened recently, I might finally be able to put you into a book. Maybe this will be the one that gets published.'

Leon looked at me, alarmed. 'Don't write about me like this,' he said, gesturing to his temple. 'Not while I'm still like this.'

'I'm kidding, you idiot.'

'Oh.'

I moved towards him. Suddenly he seemed very sad and I sat down beside him and rested my head on his shoulder.

'What is it, Leon?'

'I can't do it any more.'

I lifted my head. 'Can't do what?' I said, mildly panicked. Did he want to leave? 'What can't you do any more?'

'I can't write.'

'Oh,' I said, letting out a breath. 'I thought you meant . . . Doesn't matter what I thought you meant. *Of course* you'll be able to write.'

He shook his head. 'I can't even read, Jane.'

'Yes, you can. Look at your hand. See? You wrote that. "Class". Right there. And you can read that, so there you go. You can read *and* write.'

'No . . . I asked Eden to look up what it takes to be a writer. Authors' top tips, stuff like that. I thought it might spark something. I thought there might be a secret that I'd forgotten and I could maybe remember what I needed to do.'

'What did they say?' I asked cautiously.

'Mostly you need to read a lot and you need to write a lot, and I can do neither. I tried reading one of my books and I couldn't get past the first paragraph. I kept forgetting what I'd already read. I'm not going to be able to do it.'

'You're not going to be able to do it *yet*. Focus on the "yet". That's what you used to say to me when I'd be moaning that I hadn't been published and I wasn't good enough. You'd say, "You're not a good enough writer *yet*. But you will be, Jane." That's what you used to say.'

He took my hand. 'You're kind,' he said.

'One of the reasons you married me.'

'What were the other reasons?' he said earnestly.

'Charm, wit, my good looks. And I was a better cook than Gina. Or at least that's what you told me. I imagine now though that that was bollocks, to be honest. You just hated cooking yourself, so you thought you'd better flatter me into it.'

He smiled. 'I need help, Jane.'

'You're doing so well! You don't need help; you just need time.'

'No. *We* need help. Eden says we have no money. That the money you're making is not even covering the basics and—'

'How would Eden know that?'

'I think my sister told him. Or else he overheard. Anyway, I made him tell me what the score was.'

'Leon, it's not your job to worry about this. What you need to focus on right now is—'

'Jane, stop.'

I stopped.

'Write the end of my book,' he said.

'What do you mean?'

'Eden says there's a book. A book I didn't finish, and we can't get paid for it until it's done.'

I turned to face him. 'Leon,' I said, 'I can't write that book.'

He paused. Regarded me. 'You *have* to write it.'

'No, you don't understand. I would if I could. I'd love to write it. But you and I don't write in the same way. Our styles are very, very different. You write short punchy sentences; you write about death and gore and mystery. I wouldn't know where to start with all that. It would be like me trying to write science fiction. Or a misery memoir. Or a clogs and shawls saga.'

He went to interrupt me, but I cut him off.

'Honestly, I have thought about it, Leon. Fantasized about it, actually, because, yes, it would mean the end of our financial problems . . . but I know I'm just not capable.'

'So,' he said simply, 'find someone who can.'

35

We met in the Cavern of all places. Don't judge, but after spending my entire adult life in Liverpool, I'd never actually been inside the place. Sacrilegious, the Beatles being our major export and all.

Frankie said it was one of the best places to watch life go by. One of his favourite places in the city. 'You get a crazy cross section of people in there,' he said.

On Mathew Street there was the usual low level of chaos as people hovered between the Cavern Club and the Cavern Pub opposite. A couple of ladies in their early seventies from the North East were taking pictures of one another outside the club and I asked if they would like one of them both together. I was a little early and Frankie was often late, so I thought I'd kill a few minutes. It was only as I was holding down the button of their digital camera – which seemed ancient, antiquated now – and they were fixing their scarves, their hair, their smiles, that it occurred to me that this was perhaps a seminal moment for them. Sure, everyone thought they owned the Beatles. That the Beatles belonged to them. But these women had actually *lived* through it. They had probably screamed at their radios until they hyperventilated and passed out.

'Who was your favourite?' I asked the woman on the left as I handed back her camera.

'Oh, Paul,' she said firmly. And then a wistful look came over her. 'I always thought I'd marry him . . . though I don't think I could've become a vegetarian,' she added quickly. 'But then again, maybe I could. I suppose you can suffer anything if you want someone bad enough.'

I addressed the other lady. 'What about you?'

'I'm not a vegetarian,' she said.

'I meant which Beatle did you like.'

'Ringo.'

Her friend gave me a withering look. 'She's always been a bit strange. Haven't you, Sheila?' and Sheila nodded, agreeing that she had.

I looked both ways up and down the street for any sign of Frankie but there was none, so I descended the stairs to the Cavern. I lost track of how many flights there were, but it was a *long* way down, further than I'd imagined, and I didn't like the fire risk. Add to that I'd always heard the Cavern was a bit of a shithole and I was not exactly looking forward to this meeting. Typical of Frankie to want to meet somewhere inappropriate. Somewhere only he found cool – but in an ironic way. I had asked if I could pop round to his house. Told him I had something I wanted to discuss, but he'd insisted upon meeting 'Anywhere except home' and I suspected things were still not good with Oona.

After the final set of stairs, I emerged into an intimate, agreeable, underground space, *where it all began*, so to speak, and I was pleasantly surprised.

'Well, isn't this nice,' I said aloud, and found myself drawn to the black and white photographs mounted on the walls, to the artfully lit alcoves in the brickwork displaying Beatles memorabilia. I was wending my way between tables when I heard 'Jane!' and looked to my right to see Frankie. He was sitting at a high table next to the small stage, on which there was a drum kit, various guitars, and a couple of large amps.

'Quaint,' I said to Frankie as I approached.

'Isn't it?'

He had a bottle of red on the go and as he went to pour, I said I didn't want one. 'I don't drink during the day, Frankie,' I explained, but he said, 'Nonsense,' and completely ignored my protestations.

'Honestly, I—'

'It's one of the joys of not having a proper job, Jane,' he said. 'If you can't indulge when all those poor sods are stuck doing nine-to-five, then what's the point? I mean, if you think about it, you *owe* it to them to be enjoying yourself.'

I took the glass.

'Now,' he said, 'what did you want to talk about? I sensed from your call that you require my services. Hope it's not babysitting.'

'It's not babysitting.'

'Then glad to help. Fire away.'

'It's Leon's book.'

Frankie put down his drink and sighed heavily. 'Aw, Jane,' he said, 'not this business again. I'm sorry but I really think you need to drop the whole Alistair Armitage thing and just put it behind you. There's little point raking over old coals when—'

'Not that book. I don't mean that book. And besides, Alistair Armitage won't speak to me.'

'You've phoned him?'

'Emailed. But I'd really like to meet in person. Anyway, that's not why I'm here. It's Leon's book. His latest book . . . The unfinished book.'

'Oh,' Frankie said, brightening. 'What about it?'

'It needs finishing so we can earn some money.'

'Oh,' he said again, though not quite so enthusiastically.

Frankie took a swallow of wine. He looked past my shoulder towards the entrance to the club. Then he fiddled with the inside pocket of his jacket.

The silence was uncomfortable, so I said, 'Leon's asked me to find a way of completing it.'

'And how are you going to go about that?' he said carefully.

'I thought you might have a suggestion.'

'Me?' and he laughed a little.

'Why's that funny?'

'Jane, you don't honestly think I could do it, do you?'

I paused before answering. It was such a loaded question.

Yes, I did think Frankie was capable of finishing Leon's book. I'd read most of his work, and to be honest, their styles were not all that different. The only difference was the subject matter. Frankie tackled what were considered more literary themes: modern man's place in the world; the emasculation of modern man in the family setting; modern man's inability to grow up until he reached the age of forty; modern man's relationship with his ailing, beginning-to-dement father.

Frankie's books were given serious consideration by serious journalists in serious newspapers. They were marketed to the thinking man. To book groups. To people who didn't read shitty genre fiction. But the truth of the matter was that if they'd been written by a woman, about women, they would have been immediately fitted with candy-pink jackets, and the author's name would have been changed to something like Amethyst Buntin or Sparkle McPhee. The books would not have been given serious consideration, by serious journalists, in serious newspapers, because they would have been regarded as chick-lit, or women's fiction. Tosh, basically.

'I thought you might know of someone who'd be willing to help,' I said to Frankie.

'Ah.' Frankie was instantly relieved. 'Ah, right, yes of course,' he said, 'because for a second there I thought you were suggesting that *I* should be the one to finish writing *Dead . . .*' Frankie paused. '*Dead . . .*' he said again, this time his eyes cast skywards, searching around for the word. 'What's the bloody book called?' he said, frustrated. '*Dead* something?'

'*Red City*.'

Frankie poured more wine and this time I did put my hand over the top of my glass and managed to stop him. He shot me a look that was supposed to mean I was being a killjoy. 'The kids, Frankie,' I said. 'They need a mother when they get home.'

'Yes, yes,' he said. 'Gotcha.'

He swallowed half a glass and then, after a moment, surveyed me with what was supposed to be a puzzled look, but the edge of his mouth was lifted slightly. A half-smile.

'What?' I said.

'Just thinking.'

'About?'

'About you . . . I'm a little bit in awe of you actually, Jane.'

I didn't speak.

Frankie could be a charming bastard.

He sat back in his chair. He had his fingers laced behind his head and looked like a cool university professor. One who had, at any one time, a series of clear-skinned, nubile young students hanging on his arm, hanging on his every word, hanging off his—

'You've been so strong throughout all of this,' he said.

'Haven't exactly had a lot of choice. I did look at the option of falling apart but decided against it.'

'Jane, I'm serious.'

'You think I'm not?'

He leaned forward.

He touched my face.

'You're remarkable,' he whispered.

I didn't move.

I stayed where I was.

I stayed where I was as Frankie ran his fingertips from my temple all the way down to my collarbone.

Don't, I heard myself say, but not out loud; it was inside my own head.

I'd been starved of touch for so long that I couldn't bring myself to pull away. My hair being touched, my face, reminded me just how much I needed to be touched, how numb and unfeeling I'd become without it.

'Run away with me, Jane,' Frankie whispered. 'We could be so good together; you know we could. You know I've always been enamoured with y—'

I scraped my chair back and stood.

'Christ,' I said, putting my hands up to my face. Through my fingers I could see Frankie was looking at me dolefully. 'Don't say you want an affair, Frankie,' I said. 'I don't want a fucking affair. In fact, don't say anything. I don't want to know what this is. I don't want to know what's going through your head right now.'

'Please stop,' Frankie said.

'Stop what?'

'Stop hating yourself for needing this. You *do* need it. We all do. You're human, Jane, that's all.'

'Human? Is that your bloody answer for everything?' I leaned over, grabbing my bag from beneath the chair, but Frankie reached out and seized my hand.

'You're overreacting. Please. Sit back down and finish your drink. You're in no state to leave. I'm sorry. I shouldn't have done that; I misread the signals, that's all. You just seemed so . . . lonely.'

'I am lonely!'

I snatched my hand away and out of nowhere, I started to cry.

I *was* lonely. So lonely and always so bloody afraid all the time. I didn't know how to behave, didn't know how to react. I couldn't act like a normal person any more.

I searched my bag for a tissue, couldn't find one, and Frankie set off for the bar, returning with a red napkin.

'This do?'

I wiped my face, blew my nose. 'How do I look?' I asked sarcastically.

'Pretty,' he said, and he gave me a sad smile.

I rolled my eyes. 'Please don't flatter me. I don't want to be this person, Frankie . . . I don't want to sit in a place like this and have you touch me like you just did. It's not who I am. It's not who I am and Leon . . .' I paused, unable to say his name without my voice faltering. 'Leon doesn't . . .' I couldn't finish the sentence.

'Leon doesn't deserve this?' he said.

I nodded numbly.

'No, he doesn't, but then neither do you. You don't deserve to find yourself where you are right now. Alone. Scared. Trying to cope with all that's happened to you. Life's fucking cruel, Jane.'

I was nodding. Blowing my nose and nodding at the same time. 'Sometimes I think it would be easier if I knew *why* this happened to us. It goes round and round in my head all the time, driving me insane. Why did it happen? Why us? And how do I make it stop?'

Frankie's face was full of concern and now I felt bad for shouting at him. He was just a man after all. A man with an inflated sense of his own importance, faced with a vulnerable woman. He had limited resources to make things better, and had probably gone with the first thing that came into his head.

Then a thought struck.

I wavered for a second, undecided if I should take the risk. Then I sat back down again and intimated Frankie should do the same.

Leaning across the table, I whispered, 'I have the name of someone.'

Frankie looked blank.

'The name of someone involved.' I swallowed before continuing, checking over my shoulder to ensure we were not being overheard. 'When I was at Walton Gaol there was an incident. I was threatened.'

Frankie widened his eyes.

'It's OK. I was shaken up, but I wasn't hurt. But I was

warned to stay away from asking questions. I was told by a prisoner that if I continued to ask questions about Leon's attack they would come after me and the children.'

'Jesus, Jane, did you tell the police?'

I shook my head. 'Not at the time. I was too scared, and I didn't want to risk it. But you still have contacts, right? You still drink with that group of scallies, those ex-cons you get your material from?'

'Not so much any more; I've moved on to other themes in my work. But I'm sure I could ask around. I'm sure if you know something then I could find out if there's any weight to it. What do you know?'

'Not what,' I said. 'Who. The prisoner's name is Ryan Toonen. But, Frankie, you have to be discreet. If you sense anything, anything at all, then you have to back off. These people are dangerous. Ryan's a nasty little scrote of a man, and he's connected. He promised his friends on the outside would be very pissed off if I continued trying to find out who hurt Leon . . . But I think there's got to be a link. You know, someone who's linked to both Leon and Ryan Toonen? Someone who *knew* both of them? That's what I need to know. That's what I need you to find out.'

Frankie didn't hesitate. He told me he'd do it.

He reckoned he could do so without raising questions. He trusted those men; he'd known them for years. Most had been in prison, but there was one in particular, one who still had friends in Walton. He seemed to make it his business to keep abreast of what was going on inside, Frankie said, and Frankie assured me he knew how to be discreet.

He told me we'd meet again soon. And I felt something release within me. Something begin to uncoil that had been holding me rigid for months. This was the answer and I cursed myself for not thinking of it sooner. Frankie could find out who had done this to Leon. And it would all be over.

He hugged me goodbye. Apologized again, for misreading the signals, and told me he'd give it his best.

And then, just before he left, he said this: 'You know what the sensible answer is to your financial predicament, Jane?'

And I told him I didn't.

'You need to finish the book yourself.'

'But I *can't* finish the book,' I said.

'You can. Publishers wet themselves over stories like this. *Bestselling author has head injury and dictates novels to his wife.*'

'Leon can't dictate his novels, you know that.'

'Yes, but *they* don't know that, do they? Pretend he can. Pretend Leon's guiding you and telling you what to write . . . The press will lap it up and the story'll go global. Far better than some ghostwriter doing it anonymously, and no one knowing a thing about it. You do it, Jane. You're more than capable . . . To be honest,' he said, shrugging on his overcoat, 'I think you'd do a rather excellent job. Do it. Why the hell not?'

36

So I did. I wrote the novel.

Frankie had a meeting with his criminal associates, who assured him they'd find out what they could on Ryan Toonen, while I set to, rereading Leon's manuscript, gathering his handwritten notes, and I made a start on finishing the thing. I read it twice, a red pen in my hand, making notes in the margins, and tried to come to some understanding as to why he was having such difficulty getting to the end. It was the same format, the same basic idea, every single time. Someone was doing something bad and DS Clement had to stop them. But the baddie was *no idiot* and he would plant lots of obstacles in DS Clement's way. Not exactly rocket science.

And yet, remarkably hard to pull off if you didn't know what you were doing.

But Leon *did* know what he was doing. That was what didn't add up here. He would outline each novel meticulously, so he didn't reach the end of a manuscript and not know how to finish it. He lived in fear of not knowing what to write, so he planned his novels until he knew exactly what to write at every turn.

Question was: Why hadn't it worked for him this time?

I went over his outline. The story was clear. Easy to

understand. It worked just fine. The ending came to a surprising and inevitable conclusion, just as Aristotle said it should. *What made you stop, Leon? What made this process so impossible for you that you got us into debt?*

'I honestly don't remember, Jane,' he answered, when I asked him about it.

I'd reached a point of agitation. Where nothing I was looking at made any sense and so I went to him. 'What was going on in your head when you were writing this?' But he had absolutely no recollection.

I told him not to stress about it. That I'd find a way forward. 'I thought perhaps there might be something in there . . .' and I tapped his forehead gently. 'I thought you might be able to show me a way to get started. I don't want to run into the same problems you did.'

Leon stared at his outline. 'It's like a foreign language.' He handed it back to me. 'I don't remember who I was, Jane.'

'I know.'

He gazed at me for an extended moment and his face was unreadable. I wondered if he was weighing up if he actually *wanted* to know who he was before this happened to him.

He took a step towards me. 'Can I hold you?' he asked quietly.

I was taken aback, but I nodded.

'Is this OK?' he said, cocooning me with his arms.

And I told him it was.

He brushed his lips against my cheek.

'Is this OK too?' he asked.

And I told him that was OK too.

*

Christmas was approaching, but over the next few days every spare moment I had was spent in the attic. And, slowly, slowly I was beginning to make headway. I explained to Leon I thought I might have a real shot at this working, that the more I wrote, the closer I got to the end, the more I could see the manuscript coming together. He listened to me reading aloud from my work and began willing me to succeed. He brought me tea and hot buttered toast and told me I could do it. And as each day went by, I started to really believe it.

A few times, I considered getting in touch with Leon's editor: telling her what I was doing, asking for feedback along the way, but I was too terrified.

What if she rejected the plan?

I had no writing credits to my name and as far as she knew I was a housewife who liked to dabble in some women's fiction. What if she told me to step away from Leon's manuscript? That I had no business interfering with his work?

I would just have to present it to her when it was done, when it was as good as I could make it. And I would present it with only Leon's name on the front. (Although Frankie Ridonikis correctly pointed out that if two names went on there, we'd get double the tax allowance.)

Of course, there was another option.

I could choose to *never* tell.

To never come clean.

Sometimes, I found myself fantasizing about writing Leon's novels for years to come, no one ever knowing that I was the brains behind the whole operation.

But I was getting carried away.

I needed to focus on the novel in front of me. Even if it

wasn't exactly up to par, his publishers were still contractually obliged to pay the next part of the advance upon delivery. Which for Leon's books usually meant an instalment of around thirty thousand pounds. Something we really needed. If things worked out the way I hoped, I could clear the debt we owed to Charlie instead of just the nominal interest I was covering right now.

It started to rain and I checked my word count. I'd set myself the target of one thousand words per day. Today's target was short by 260; I couldn't seem to get the last few words out. I began scrolling through the *Mail Online*. I was procrastinating. A soap actress had lost seventy pounds in weight and was promoting her new exercise DVD; another actress had been left with huge bald patches after her hair was torn away from her head by the weight of her hair extensions; the bookies had now slashed the odds on a white Christmas, as we were in for a sustained blast of Arctic air.

I scrolled down further and that's when I saw it.

'AUTHOR FOUND DEAD NAMED'.

I clicked on the story and moved closer to the screen.

> Alistair Armitage (53), pictured left, has been named as the man found dead at the base of an apartment building in MediaCity, Salford, yesterday. Mr Armitage was the author of two novels and lived with his mother, Shelly Armitage, in the waterfront flat. It is believed that Mrs Armitage was not home at the time and Greater Manchester Police are appealing for witnesses. Neighbours claim Mr Armitage was a quiet man who kept himself to himself and are shocked by the news. Touching tributes have been left for Mr Armitage on Facebook, and on the author's blog page.

My heart began to pound.

I scanned the rest of the story looking for those telltale words: *the police are not looking for anyone else in connection with the death*, meaning Alistair Armitage had taken his own life.

Those words weren't there.

Which meant Alistair had been thrown to his death.

Which meant he had been murdered.

37

Alistair had told me not to contact him again. He'd said he feared for his safety and I'd dismissed him as being paranoid. I scanned his Facebook page. There were reams of messages from readers. His blog, too, was full of messages of condolence. People were beginning to speculate about why someone would want to kill this gentle soul, who'd brought so much reading pleasure to many.

I stared at the screen. The words blurred.

My hands shook.

Had Alistair died because of something I'd done?

I didn't know what to do.

I felt unsafe.

I scrolled through the *Daily Mail* article again. Alistair's apartment was on the sixth floor. The report was worded in such a way as to avoid saying he fell to his death, intimating it had been no accident, that he'd been pushed. I imagined Alistair's fear in that moment. Imagined what went through his head as he was forced on to his balcony.

At the end of the article was a number. 'Did you know Alistair Armitage? Do you have information? Call our team in confidence.'

My hand hovered over the phone.

Did I owe it to Alistair Armitage to disclose what I knew?

No. These were just scandal-hungry journalists. What good would it do? It was too late for Alistair now anyway. Whoever he was living in fear of had already got to him.

I turned the phone over in my hand. But perhaps I could find out more about what *had* happened to him.

I could always hang up at any time.

I typed the number in and it rang twice before being answered. 'Rhoda Farley,' said the voice at the other end. There was background noise, street traffic.

'Yes,' I stammered, 'I'm calling to talk to someone about a story in today's *Mail*?'

'Can I take your name?'

'Jane Campbell. It's about the man who fell from his apartment building?'

'Mr Armitage, yes. You're through to the right person. You can talk to me. Hold on a sec though while I get off the road. I can barely hear you.'

I heard her footsteps quicken and then the loud whoosh-whoosh of an automatic door opening and then closing.

'That's better,' she said. 'Sorry about that. I was between buildings. Were you a friend of Mr Armitage's?'

'Yes,' I said quickly. And then: 'Actually, no. No, I wasn't.'

'OK.'

She didn't sound put off by my indecisiveness.

'He wasn't a friend,' I said, 'but I'd corresponded with him recently. Really, I'm calling because . . .' I exhaled, pausing for a moment to organize my thoughts. 'To be honest, I don't really know why I'm calling.'

'Why don't you begin by telling me how you knew Alistair?'

I hesitated.

'My husband is an author and he knew Alistair.'

'So *they* were friends?'

'Not exactly.'

This wasn't going as I'd hoped. I was backing myself into a corner.

'I'm covering the story,' she said, 'but it seems Alistair was rather a private individual and it's proving difficult to find out much about him. What can you tell me? What kind of person was he? Would your husband be available for an interview? I could travel to—'

'No,' I said quickly. 'No, that won't be possible.'

I cursed myself for calling. What had I been hoping to achieve? Did I really think they were going to tell *me* anything? That's not how these things worked. Rhoda Farley would be skilled in the art of information retrieval; she would not be spilling her guts on what she knew about Alistair's death.

I'd been stupid.

'I'm sorry,' I said to her, 'I really don't know anything. I shouldn't have called.'

'Mrs Campbell,' she said.

'Yes.'

'You said your husband is an author. Would that be Leon Campbell? The crime author?'

I didn't answer.

She took my silence as an affirmation. 'You're probably going to want to speak to an ex-colleague of mine,' she said. 'Giles Beatty over at the *Guardian* . . . I know he tried to contact your husband many times. I think it would really be in your interest to speak to him. You're on a mobile right now, yes?'

I told her I was.

'Well, I've got your number stored. I'll text you Giles's information in the next couple of minutes. Do call him, Mrs Campbell. It's important.'

And she hung up.

I knew who Giles Beatty was. We bought the *Guardian* each Saturday, so I was familiar with his work. He was one of those exposé types who dealt with weird goings-on on the fringes of society – a lesser-known Louis Theroux or Jon Ronson.

What did he want with Leon?

I looked at my phone. Two minutes had passed since Rhoda Farley had ended the call. Still no message. She said Giles Beatty had tried to contact Leon. Many times. But Leon had never mentioned it. And I'd not been aware of Giles Beatty attempting to make contact *since* Leon's brain injury – when I'd been managing his inbox.

I logged on to Leon's Microsoft account and typed Giles Beatty's name in the search section of his email.

Nothing.

So I typed in 'the Guardian'.

Same. Nothing.

I got up. Stuck my head out of the room, and shouted, 'Eden?' down the stairs. 'Eden, are you busy?'

Eden appeared, looking at me quizzically.

'I'm trying to retrieve some old emails,' I said to him, 'but I don't know how to go about it.'

'Have you tried in the search box?'

'Done that.'

'Have they been deleted?'

'I think so.'

Eden moved towards the computer and sat down. 'You use Microsoft, don't you?'

I nodded.

He opened up a new window. Into Google he typed: 'How to retrieve deleted emails on Outlook'.

And an information box popped up with: 'Here's how to recover items from the Recoverable Items folder'.

'As easy as that?' I said to Eden and he smiled.

'Get with the times, Auntie Jane . . . So, just follow the instructions and you should get them back easily enough. Or do you want me to do it for you?'

'Can you do it? I'm looking for some messages from a guy called Giles Beatty.'

Eden typed like he was playing keyboard in a rock band. Hard and fast. Seconds later I had eighteen emails. The last of which was sent just before Leon's attack. It was labelled: 'URGENT. DO NOT IGNORE.'

I waited until Eden was downstairs and I clicked on it.

Dear Leon

I must urge you to respond to my messages. As you're aware, I've made repeated attempts since May of last year to get your side of the story and I'm afraid time is running out. Here is my mobile number again, if you would prefer to do this over the phone: 07898 143679.

All I'm trying to do is present a balanced view of events, but I can't guarantee how you'll come out of this career-wise if you continue to stay silent on the matter.

Giles Beatty

I stared at the message.

What had Leon done that was so bad Giles Beatty wanted to write a story about him?

There could only be one thing.

I called the number.

38

'Sock puppetry,' said Giles Beatty, as if this explained everything.

I adjusted the phone at my ear. 'Sock puppetry?' I replied, wrong-footed, confused. 'As in—'

'As in Leon was sabotaging a rival author's career,' he said. 'As in he was leaving fake reviews on sites such as Amazon, Goodreads, Waterstones, etc., so that his rival's sales took a hit, whereas his own sales increased because of the number of positive reviews he'd been leaving for himself.'

I'd heard the term before. Sock puppetry was mentioned often amongst the writing community with utter disdain. They hated anyone who didn't play fair.

'You're telling me Leon was actually doing this?' I said. 'Leon was leaving bad reviews for other authors and positive reviews for himself?' It seemed very far-fetched.

'I'm telling you exactly that, yes,' he replied.

'But what's the point of it all?' I asked, still not getting the full relevance.

Giles Beatty sighed. 'The point, Mrs Campbell, is that sock puppetry really does affect sales in a big way. Take Amazon for example: their algorithms are linked to review activity. So, the more good reviews a book gets, the more exposure Amazon will *give* that book, and as a result, the sales go up . . . It's *anything* but a pointless activity.'

I was trying to take this in.

Leon had manipulated reviews to increase his own sales, and tried to reduce the sales of others. Had this been why Alistair Armitage had heckled Leon at events? Had Leon not only stolen his manuscript, but been wrecking his book sales as well?

I'd heard about desperate authors *buying* reviews before. Apparently, you could buy a bundle of five-star reviews for a few quid. But this was more personal. This was—

'Hang on,' I said, 'wouldn't it be obvious that the bad reviews were all coming from the same person? I mean, if Leon really had been sabotaging someone else's books, then wouldn't it be obvious that all the bad reviews were from him?'

'Not at all. Authors who partake in this kind of sabotage set up many accounts. They go at it with real tenacity. They have numerous aliases and can really affect how well a book does . . . If a book had over fifty single-star reviews would you buy it?'

'Depends on how many five-star reviews it had.'

'Let's say ten.'

'Well, no, probably not.'

'And let's say a book you were not so excited about had dozens of glowing five-star reviews, comments along the lines of: "An instant bestseller!" "A classic!" "Leon Campbell has created a masterpiece this time!" Would you buy that book?'

I went cold.

'Did Leon actually write those things?' I asked quietly.

'Yes, Leon actually wrote those things . . . and many more. I'm happy to show you all of this if you would be willing to meet. I can come north. I can get to Liverpool in say, two hours . . . two and a half?'

'Around that,' I said reluctantly.

'The evidence is more than compelling, Mrs Campbell. Particularly now that we have the websites too.'

'What websites?'

'The ones Leon created devoted entirely to the denigration of another author.' Giles Beatty was about to go on, but he paused. 'You really never knew about any of this?'

'No.'

'He never talked of it? Mentioned it? I only ask because your husband went kind of rogue on this, Mrs Campbell. He went to extraordinary lengths, and it would have been all-consuming, I expect.'

I thought about all the hours Leon had spent alone in the attic. Not working. Blocked. I thought about the loan he'd taken out just to cover the month-to-month household expenses because he'd not been able to write.

'He never mentioned it,' I said.

'Well, I am surprised because—'

'Look, until you show me proof,' I cut in, 'I'm not going to make the assumption that these things *were* created by Leon. It's totally crazy. What if it was done by someone wanting to sabotage Leon's work instead?'

Giles Beatty took a weary breath. 'We've had a very skilled set of technicians working on this story for over a year, Mrs Campbell. I assure you I would not be going ahead with the article unless I was absolutely certain of my facts.'

I closed my eyes.

I thought about the folder entitled 'Bad Reviews' I'd found on Leon's computer, and realized, with sickening clarity, that it was unlikely those reviews were ever received by Leon himself. They were his bank of judgements for others. He fished them out when he needed them and posted them on online forums.

'OK, I'll meet you,' I said.

I waited in the Adelphi Hotel bar, next to Lime Street Station.

When he arrived, I asked Giles Beatty if he wanted something to eat but he told me he'd had a full English on the train. 'Virgin do a half-decent fry-up,' he said, impressed, as if dealing with bacon and eggs required real skill.

He wore a clean shirt, dirty spectacles, and carried an extra twenty pounds around his middle. I surveyed him as he took his seat, emptying his bag of his laptop, phone, and an envelope folder that had once been used for a purpose other than 'Leon Campbell' – lettering which was now printed above a scored-out name.

I tried to discern his intentions. He wanted something. Didn't everyone? He wouldn't be making the trip north for no reason.

So what *did* he want?

'I thought Leon might be joining us,' he said hopefully.

'Leon's in no position to talk to you. Perhaps I should have made that clearer.'

'How's his recovery?'

I shrugged, reluctant to give this man any more information than was necessary. 'It's been a process. Challenging's the word I might use.'

'Is he working right now?'

'Not exactly.'

'Is he writing anything?'

I didn't answer.

'Do you think he'll be well enough to tackle something eventually? Another book?' he asked.

I held his gaze. 'Would you like to know what it is that we're tackling right now, Mr Beatty?'

He nodded, not sure where I was going with this on account of my barbed tone.

'Right now, every time Leon makes toast he almost burns the house down. He can't remember that setting the timer to maximum keeps the toast in there longer. He thinks maximum means *intensity*. So every day he whacks the thing up to the highest setting, thinking it will toast his bread faster, and every day it catches fire. Even though I've attached a note to the toaster telling him not to use it. He sees the note and thinks I'm trying to control him. So that's where we're at. And you see why your timing with this article is less than ideal.'

He nodded, acknowledging my words, but decided to continue to probe nonetheless. 'Have the doctors given you any clue as to his long-term prognosis?' he asked. 'Any idea how it might be with regards to working again?'

'We try not to think about it.'

'But what did the doctors say?'

'We really don't know at this point.'

'But if you had to call it?'

'Then you'd be the last person I'd tell.'

He smiled.

'Most brain-injured patients never return to the work they did before, Mr Beatty,' I said.

'Giles, please.'

'Their brains simply can't cope with the amount of information necessary, and so they often end up in minimum-wage employment.'

'That's very sad.'

'Isn't it,' I said flatly.

I took a sip of my drink. I'd ordered a San Pellegrino and could feel the cold liquid streaming behind my sternum. 'We're relying on the money from the sales of his backlist right now,' I said. 'It's not a lot, but we're relying on it. And if you write this article, and it has a deleterious effect on Leon's image, then I'm not sure what we'll do . . .' I let the words hang.

Giles didn't respond.

'What exactly is it that you want from us?' I asked.

'I just want to talk to you and get your side of the—'

I held up my palm. I enunciated slowly. 'What. Do. You. Want? I have very little time available to me right now. I've called in sick this morning to meet with you, so I suggest you say whatever it is you came here to say.'

He sat back in his chair with an air of resignation. 'I was hoping to interview Leon,' he admitted, and when I went to argue the case against that ever happening, he talked over me. 'I see now that was presumptuous. I really didn't know what . . . what the full extent of Leon's limitations were. I just sort of assumed he'd lost his memory. I apologize. That was insensitive. But look,' he said, leaning forward again, 'I know for certain Leon carried out this sustained attack on another author. Others know he did it too. Leon was clever, but he was also pretty stupid at the same time. I'm not so interested in getting you to believe me; I have all the proof I need. What I'm really interested in is the *why*.'

'*The why*,' I mirrored back.

'That's what I need to tie this story together. As it stands, all we have is professional jealousy as a motivator, but I can't help feeling that it goes deeper than that. Leon's demonstrated a level of hatred that is completely unprecedented, and I'd really like to know where that comes from.' He looked at me as if to say: *Any thoughts?*

'I can't help you.'

'Did you talk to him about my coming here?' he asked.

'He doesn't know.'

'I owe it to the author involved to proceed with this.'

'Even if it damages Leon?'

He looked away. 'Even if it damages Leon,' he said. 'Obviously, I didn't anticipate this set of circumstances when I began to cover this. I wanted to expose Leon for all the damage he'd done. I felt it was only fair on the person involved who's suffered humiliation, had their name smeared, watched helplessly as their book sales tumbled. I felt it was essential Leon be brought to task over his actions. I'll be completely honest with you, Jane – can I call you Jane? I wanted to publicly shame Leon.'

'Wanted to or want?'

For a moment he didn't answer.

Then he said, 'Wanted,' firmly.

Past tense.

'So what changed your mind?' I asked. 'Because I'm assuming that small sob story about his backlist and our financial situation wouldn't affect a hardened journalist such as yourself.'

Giles Beatty looked at me levelly. 'Frankie Ridonikis changed my mind.'

I frowned. 'Frankie?'

'He told me he wouldn't lend his name to the piece, wouldn't comment upon any of this, if I was to go ahead and shame Leon. Now that Leon was . . . well, now that Leon wasn't the person he used to be any more. He didn't think it was fair.'

'I don't understand,' I said. 'What's Frankie Ridonikis got to do with any of this?'

Giles Beatty's eyes went wide. 'Everything,' he said. 'Absolutely everything. Frankie Ridonikis is the author Leon tried to destroy. Has *completely* destroyed, in fact. I'm not sure he's got much of a career left.'

I swallowed. 'Frankie Ridonikis,' I said. 'You're quite sure?'

Giles Beatty nodded. 'Of course.'

'You're sure you don't mean Alistair Armitage?'

'Who?'

'Alistair Armitage.'

'Never heard of him.'

39

The event was being held in the Arts Theatre, inside the Victoria Gallery and Museum. Parked near the entrance was a black saloon. A black Volvo S90. Frankie's car.

Now I knew it was the car that had appeared in Leon's video footage of the street, the car that had tried to frighten me, scare me away from digging amongst Leon's personal files, and finding out the truth about what happened between Frankie and Leon.

Ledecky had said dark-coloured saloon cars like that were remarkably common. Perhaps if I'd caught sight of the registration plate I'd have put two and two together earlier.

Perhaps.

The place was full on account of Frankie being paired with Liverpool screenwriter Jimmy McGovern. They were here to discuss how the city informed their writing, and how the people of Liverpool themselves featured in their work.

I'd watched Frankie speak to readers several times before, but never alongside someone of Jimmy McGovern's calibre. Another type of crowd had been drawn today. There were students from the university, English professors, as well as Liverpool's well-heeled. Frankie's literary events were usually populated with a different demographic: readers between the ages of fifty-five and seventy, mostly women, with the occasional man who came along, I suspected, so his wife wouldn't have to park the car.

I sat in the back row; Frankie didn't know I was here. I had the folder and the book resting on my lap, and as the event came to a close, the last questions taken from the audience, I began to shift restlessly in my seat. A film and literature student, who'd announced herself as such, asked Jimmy McGovern what kept him continuing to write after all these years, and he laughed uproariously, before his clip-on microphone fell from his collar to the floor, and there followed a small moment of chaos as he was reattached.

Then that was the end.

The sponsors announced that sadly there would be no more time for questions, but that Frankie would be signing books in the foyer, and Jimmy was happy to stay behind for photographs.

I rose from my seat.

I made my way forward into Frankie's line of vision.

Gripping the folder and the book in one hand, I waved my other around to attract Frankie's attention. He shaded his eyes from the bright overhead lights and his face darkened with concern as soon as he saw my expression. 'Can I speak to you?' I mouthed. 'Urgently.'

Frankie quickly made his apologies to the host and followed me, taking the steps two at a time, out of the theatre to the lobby area outside.

'Jane,' he said, running to catch up. 'What's wrong? Has something happened to Leon?'

He was panting a little. His shirt was crumpled as if he'd slept in it and his breath was as it always tended to be these days: sour and pungent from last night's booze.

'You could say that,' I said.

I handed him the folder. Inside was the manuscript. Alistair Armitage's manuscript.

He took the folder, but he didn't open it. Instead, his eyes rested on the hardback I was holding. It was Frankie's debut novel. A signed first edition. Probably worth something now.

His mouth dropped open ever so slightly.

'Look in the folder, Frankie.'

He held my gaze. He wouldn't do it. But at least he now knew why I was here.

'Jane,' he said, 'I don't know what this is. I don't know what you're doing, but I've got people in there waiting for me.'

'They'll wait. Look in the folder.'

He opened it and flicked through the pages. I saw him swallow. Saw his jaw tighten.

'I don't know what this is.'

'Sure you do.'

He exhaled long and hard. Pulled his hand through his hair.

I reached forward, and I touched his cheek. '*Run away with me, Jane,*' I whispered, mimicking him. 'Remember saying that? Remember saying that to me? How very desperate you were, Frankie, to keep me away from this.'

I smiled at him.

'Remember taking somebody else's novel too, Frankie? Remember passing it off as your own?'

He handed the folder back. 'This is worthless.'

'Is it,' I said flatly. 'See, I don't think it is. The first time I read Alistair's manuscript I'd assumed Leon had stolen it for himself. I couldn't really think which one of Leon's novels it became though. So when I read it again yesterday, and then I read your debut novel all over again – *Nightwatch* – I was kind of stunned to see so many similarities. In fact, this is such an odd thing, but they're almost identical plot-wise. You see, I was so focused on Leon's annotations, I didn't realize he'd made those notes for you to use, Frankie.'

I waited for him to say something. He shifted his weight to his other foot.

'Alistair Armitage wasn't threatening *Leon* with plagiarism, was he?' I said. 'He was pissed off at him for giving the manuscript to you. For handing it over to you, and then not saying anything when you got your first deal by reproducing it in your own words . . . How many countries did that book go on to sell in again? I can't quite remember.'

'Twenty-seven.'

'Bravo.'

'I don't know what you think you're—'

'How did Leon come by Alistair's novel in the first place? That's what I can't work out.'

'They were in a writing group together, not that it's relevant; they critiqued each other's work. Leon was helping him make it a better novel when he gave it to me. He thought I could learn from it . . . to use it as a work-in-progress study.'

'Why didn't Alistair go to your publishers? Why not tell them you'd stolen it?'

'He couldn't prove anything. What exactly do you *want*, Jane?'

'Why, have I got you nervous?'

He looked away. 'What do you want?' he repeated. 'Spit it out, or I'll—'

'What?' I snapped. 'What will you do? Try and kill me as well? I know what you did, Frankie. I know what you did to Leon. And I know what you did to Alistair, the poor sod. Did you really have to kill him? He would've kept his mouth shut. Couldn't you have just threatened him?'

Frankie looked around, over his shoulder, to check if anyone could hear what I was saying. The foyer was empty.

'I know you didn't want this information to go public,' I went on. 'And I know that every time you thought I was getting too near to it, every time I was on the verge of discovering, you tried to frighten me. You made sure I backed off.'

'Jane, I'm going to have to ask you to leave. Leave now, and I'll spare you the embarrassment of calling security.'

I laughed in his face. 'I'm not leaving, you idiot. Do you think I came here looking for clarification? Do you think I want an *apology*? I'm not here to hear you say the words "I did it . . . I shot Leon." I don't care about that.'

'Then what do you want?'

'I want what's mine.'

'Yours?'

I nodded. 'I'm not going to be greedy, Frankie,' I said, 'but I want the money Leon lost. I want the money he lost while he was blocked, while he wasn't writing . . . while you two were too busy sabotaging each other's careers to write, while you were trying to destroy each other with all the negative reviews, the negative press . . . I want the money I owe to Charlie, and I want a little bit more as well to tide me over.'

'How much?'

'Thirty thousand.'

He laughed. 'I don't have thirty thousand.'

'Course you do.'

Frankie rubbed his face with his hands.

After a moment he said, 'Thirty thousand, and then that's it? That's the end of this? You'll never go to the police? You'll leave me alone?'

'You have my word.'

A door opened behind Frankie and a woman in an orange blouse started to walk towards us. 'Mr Ridonikis—'

Frankie held his hand up. 'Just a minute.'

'Mr Ridonikis, I really must ask you to—'

'Just a *minute*, I said. I'll be back in there in a minute. Please show some courtesy.' He turned back towards me. 'Thirty grand and you assure me this is over?'

'You'll never see me again. I've signed a long-term lease on a house on the south coast and we're all leaving on Saturday. You can transfer the money to . . .' I reached into my pocket and withdrew a piece of paper with a sort code and account number on it. 'You can transfer it into this. The names of the account holders are Mr and Mrs Campbell. Do it and you'll never hear from me again.'

Frankie took the paper and stuffed it into his jacket pocket. 'I can maybe have it to you by Thursday.'

'Thursday works.'

'And you won't be back for more?'

'No,' I said, and I paused. 'Why?' I asked. 'Is that what Leon did? Did Leon come back for more?'

'Your husband never wanted money from me, Jane.'

'So what did he want?'

'He wanted recognition. Prestige. He wanted what I

just got on the stage in there.' He motioned to the theatre behind him. 'He couldn't bear to see me getting the kind of adulation he so coveted, and so he had to destroy my career.'

'You don't think he got sick of you getting all this adulation when he knew you'd lied your way in? When he knew your career was a lie?'

Frankie didn't answer.

'Did he threaten to expose you?' I asked.

'Yes!' he shouted angrily. 'Yes, he threatened to expose me! What? You think I'd do something like that over nothing? You think I'd shoot him in the head over *nothing*? Jesus Christ, Jane, I'm not an animal.'

Frankie was breathing hard and a fine layer of sweat had now appeared on his upper lip.

'You were waiting for him,' I said. 'Leon didn't stand a chance, did he?'

'I wasn't waiting for him,' he replied. 'I came around that day to sort things out. I wanted to be reasonable. I was sick of all the online shit and wanted to hear what Leon had to say. But when I got there he was all riled up after arguing with that old guy opposite and he basically laughed in my face. He told me if I didn't come clean and admit to plagiarizing the manuscript then he'd do it for me. He refused to discuss it.'

'And so you shot him.'

'Yes, Jane, I shot him. I hadn't planned for this to turn violent though, whatever you might think. But Leon was laughing at me . . . and then the nail gun was right there, and before I knew it I had it in my hand and . . .' Frankie shrugged, as if really it was all out of his control.

'What about Alistair?'

'What about him? You told me yourself you were going to speak with him. Then you would've known, Jane. You would've known all of it.'

'But did he really have to die? I can't believe he actually let you in to his apartment.'

'I told the stupid fuck I'd come to apologize.'

I smiled.

'What's so amusing?' he said, as I continued to smile, but he didn't wait for an answer. 'Look, I'm going to need that file from you,' he said. 'And any other copies you have of Alistair Armitage's novel. I want your assurance that you're not storing this thing anywhere, that all the copies have been destroyed.'

I pointed to the microphone attached to his collar.

'You're still transmitting inside the auditorium, you dickhead.'

And Frankie frowned in confusion.

He looked from me to the theatre and back to me again.

Then the theatre doors opened and Hazel Ledecky was standing there, flanked by two detectives. She nodded once in my direction.

'Good luck, Frankie,' I said, and he seemed really quite bewildered.

I turned, started to make my way towards the exit.

Behind me, I could hear Ledecky explaining to Frankie his rights, asking if he understood. 'Do you understand what I'm saying to you, Mr Ridonikis? Do you understand, or do you want me to repeat it to you?'

40

When the story broke it went global.

Even though Frankie could never have claimed to have celebrity author status, he sold enough books, in enough different countries, for there to be worldwide interest. Frankie was charged with the murder of Alistair Armitage, and for the attack on Leon – grievous bodily harm. The trial was scheduled for the summer. And Frankie had been remanded in custody until then.

There was huge speculation around what length of sentence Frankie would receive. Long, was all I was hoping for. A reporter was filmed asking Frankie what he would do with his time inside, should he be convicted, and Frankie answered, 'Write my masterpiece.'

He even had a smile on his face as he said it.

That was until the reporter informed him that any monies earned from such a book, while he was detained by Her Majesty, would probably not be his to keep. Jeffrey Archer, the reporter said, had had to give all of his royalties away to charity when incarcerated for perjury because there was such an uproar. And Frankie's smile faded rather quickly after that.

I wondered if he'd end up in Walton Gaol. With Ryan

Toonen. It sickened me every time I thought about it – that Frankie had set that up.

After the dinner party during which Frankie had been so supportive, so supposedly stunned to find out we were struggling financially, he'd made sure, through his circle of ex-cons, that Toonen was paid to threaten me in Walton. This was in response to Oona's suggestion that I should snoop through Leon's computer. Frankie was shit-scared of what I might find so he organized Toonen to attack me to make sure I stayed away.

I hoped he suffered inside. I hoped, after taking away Leon's brilliant mind, after taking away the lives we had before, after sending some bastard to scare Jack in the playground, to scare my darling boy, I hoped Frankie Ridonikis really suffered. I hoped he found prison life unbearable.

We had endured enough and now it was his turn. But we would get through it. We would keep getting better.

The media circus lasted close to a week, during which there were reporters camped outside my door day and night, camera operators pointing zoom lenses through my windows. Boom poles and microphones were held aloft by tired-looking assistants. And then, as tends to be the way with these things, they got bored and moved on to something more interesting, to the next story, and we tried to get back to our lives again.

Eden stayed on to help us, and Leon continued to improve, but more often than not it was three steps forwards, two steps back. I resumed work on Leon's novel again. I worked at it every day, every spare moment I had, and eventually, in the early spring, I sent it off to his publishers.

I waited in anticipation, checking my emails daily, *hourly*, trying to remain busy, my mind occupied, but it wasn't always easy.

And then, ten days later, I received a response.

They wanted a meeting in London.

They wanted a meeting in London with me.

I had submitted the manuscript with Leon's name on the front but with a note attached explaining that because Leon was unable to type, he had dictated the rest of *Red City*, and I had transcribed his words. I was hoping that the editor would find a certain romance to the situation and, as Frankie had suggested when he told me to complete Leon's novel, that it might be used to market the thing. This was an outright lie, I knew, but I figured we were entitled to be a little sketchy with the truth after what we'd been through.

At the end of March, I stood on the platform at Lime Street Station in my best coat and boots, receiving the kind of send-off one usually gets before embarking on a one-way trip. My mother was there, as well as Gloria, Leon, Eden, Jack and Martha, and there was a frisson of excitement amongst the group, but underlying it all I could feel the weight of expectation: *Everything depends on this*, I could feel them thinking. *Everything.*

I just hoped I didn't screw it up.

With the train ready to board, my mother held my face in her hands, last night's vodka on her breath, saying, 'You deserve this. You've worked so hard, you're brighter than you give yourself credit for, and nobody deserves a shot at this more than you. Make sure they understand what they're getting. Make sure they know how much you've put into it.'

I didn't have the heart to tell her it didn't really work like that.

Writing's like sport, in that if you're good enough, you get to play. (And, also like sport, if they think they can make money out of you, then you get to play too.)

The kids clung to my legs and I lifted each one of them in turn.

'Give Mummy a good-luck kiss.'

Martha planted a kiss on the end of my nose and asked when I would be back.

'Tonight. But you'll be tucked up in bed, so I'll creep in when you're asleep. Be a good girl for Daddy.'

She assured me she would, and it occurred to me as I said those words that we had reached a kind of milestone. This would be the first time I would go away and leave Leon in charge of the children. Sure, Eden would be there too, though Eden was still classed as a minor. But as I looked around at my hotchpotch family, I realized that we were all doing a pretty good job of taking care of each other now. We relied on each other. We were there for each other. We were doing OK.

Leon stepped forward. He took Martha from my arms and placed her on his hip. Still tired from such an early start, Martha rested her head against Leon's chest and stuck her thumb in her mouth.

'This is a done deal, baby,' he said to me. 'Don't be nervous. They'll want the book. I promise.'

I wanted him to be right. I so hoped he was right.

I leaned in for a kiss and then boarded the train.

It pulled away from the platform and I waved to them from my seat next to the window. The back of my shirt was wringing with sweat and I was grateful the adjacent seat was vacant as my hands were shaking. I had to tuck them under my thighs just to get them to still.

I kept rehearsing what I was going to say. Kept running through the various responses to the question I was dreading: 'Is this really Leon's work? Did Leon actually dictate this novel?'

I still hadn't decided which way I was going to play it. Erica had said: *Deny everything*, but I wasn't sure I had it in me to pull it off.

Ten minutes outside Euston and the train slowed. Passengers began putting on coats, collecting briefcases from the overhead shelves, making their way to the end of the carriage, ready for a swift disembarkation. I stayed seated and let them go first. I didn't want to be rushed. I glanced at my watch. I'd allowed ninety minutes to get to HarperCollins.

I queued for a black cab behind a mother and daughter who were beyond excited to be seeing *42nd Street* that evening, the daughter tapping out rhythms with her feet on the concrete. I tried to settle myself. My cab driver was from Kosovo. He talked for the entire journey, which I found reduced my nerves, so I encouraged him by asking the odd question here and there. He'd been a lecturer in economics in his home country and told me that he missed his mother, but not the rest of his family, or the people of his village for that matter, who were all, according to him, 'jealous shits'. He deposited me at the front of HarperCollins with forty minutes to spare and I made my way in trying to look as if I belonged there.

I was given a visitor's pass and asked to wait in the lobby. Ruth Pumford, Leon's editor, would be down to collect me shortly.

Within minutes, I heard the whoosh of a door opening, the sound of footsteps, and 'Jane!' as Ruth exclaimed my name, warmly, upon entering. 'So good of you to make the trip south.' We'd never met but she greeted me as if we were long-time buddies. 'How was it? Not too awful, I hope?'

I blustered out a reply, said something meaningless about a woman conducting business calls in the quiet carriage, and Ruth agreed it was the height of bad manners. Once in her office, she asked her assistant if she wouldn't mind getting us drinks. 'Coffee? Tea?' Ruth asked. 'I think we have some redbush, Jane, if you're off caffeine.'

'Coffee's fine.'

Ruth's office was big. She was a senior commissioning editor and had been at HarperCollins 'half my life – I should really think about a change of scenery,' she confided, 'but I'd just hate to lose my authors! They're like family. How is Leon, by the way?'

'Doing better, thank you.'

She was a diminutive woman, tiny in frame, who wore the loose, flowing clothes of a committed yogi. There were pictures of her children in graduation robes on the desk and a couple of manuscripts held together with bulldog clips.

Red City was not among them, I noticed.

'Well,' she said and fixed me with a big bright smile, 'we should really get to it, shouldn't we? Now that we've dragged you all the way here.'

I sat up, readying myself in anticipation.

'I'm afraid it's going to be a "no" with regards to *Red City*, Jane.' And she smiled regretfully. 'I'm so terribly sorry.'

I swallowed.

I didn't know what to say.

Really?

I looked out of the window. A bus was stationary at the kerb and the occupants of the top deck were staring. A small child with a fur-trimmed hood waved my way.

'Could I have some water, please?' I managed to murmur.

Ruth jumped up. 'Of course.' She seemed relieved to get out of the room.

No.

They didn't want it. They didn't want Leon's novel.

How could they not want it? After everything we'd been through? After all I'd put into it?

Ruth returned and handed me a glass. 'Here you go.'

I gulped down two big mouthfuls. I tried to think of something to say to fill the silence, but I had nothing to say. There *was* nothing to say.

'I know this is not the news you were expecting,' she said carefully. 'And I assure you we haven't taken this decision lightly. The team was split . . . if that makes it any easier. I really wanted to take it on. I really liked it.'

'Can I ask why the others didn't?'

'The style, ultimately. It just didn't correspond to the rest of Leon's work. His readers are such a loyal bunch,' she explained. 'They want Leon. They don't want . . . if I may be presumptuous here . . . they don't want *you*, Jane.'

She watched me carefully and waited for me to take in what she was saying.

She knew.

'Was it you who wrote the book?' she asked. 'I know Leon had done a chunk of it, but are those your words in the last hundred pages?'

I thought about denying it. Thought about being outraged. But what was the point? She knew. They all knew.

'I wrote the last part.'

I tried to hold it together. I felt so bloody pathetic, but I had so much invested in this. We all had. This was our lifeline. We had pinned everything on this. What were we going to do now?

'I can't believe it's not going to happen,' I said weakly.

'I am truly sorry . . .

'You did an admirable job, Jane,' she said after a time. 'It can't have been easy, what with caring for Leon and the children too. I know how much you've tried to make this work. I know how hard it must have been.'

So why did you drag me down here full of false hope? I wanted to scream at her.

But I didn't. Because this was publishing. Publishing people were polite.

'And you're probably wondering why I dragged you all the way down here, if we're not going to go ahead with it.'

I lifted my head and feigned surprise, as if that hadn't crossed my mind at all.

'Well, we have a proposition for you,' she said. 'It's something you'll need to think long and hard about, because this wouldn't be easy. And I appreciate you have a lot of commitments, a lot of responsibilities, right now. But we saw something in your writing. You've written novels before, is that right?'

I told her I had.

'What genre?'

'Women's fiction. Family drama. Nothing's been good enough to be published though,' I said.

She nodded. 'Well, while your style was not suited to

the kind of gritty crime that Leon writes so well, we did feel it might be suited to the domestic thriller genre. *Gone Girl* and the like. The genre's showing no sign of cooling off, quite the contrary actually, and we're always on the lookout for something fresh. We think you could be it. Do you read much domestic noir?'

'A little.'

'And do you think you might be able to come up with a story, something set in the home, something with a woman as the main character? We want a normal woman, someone a bit like yourself perhaps. Do you think you might be able to create something thrilling, something that puts the main character in all kinds of jeopardy?'

41

Well, did I?

I told her I'd do my best.

I told her I'd go away and put an outline together and get back to her as fast as I could, because, frankly, we needed the money. We needed money fast.

As a gesture of goodwill, she said that if I could come up with something really exemplary, then she might be able to swing an advance my way on receipt of the synopsis. 'It would have to be bloody good though,' she warned.

In the end, I didn't get the advance.

My synopsis was a bit all over the place. Outlining has never been my strong point.

But eighteen months after my trip to London, I was sitting in the lounge, listening to Leon read aloud from one of his novels. After a slow start, he was now working his way through each of his books, and he was growing in confidence. He wanted to read to everyone. Anyone who'd listen. And his mother now came over twice a week, bringing her own reading material. It was kind of fun to hear him tackling Joanna Trollope, Jodi Picoult, Diane Chamberlain, while Gloria dozed quietly in the armchair beside him.

While we sat in the lounge, the doorbell sounded. Leon

paused in his reading, and went to answer. He returned with a package, which he'd had to sign for, addressed to me, and all at once he looked very nervous and twitchy.

'You open it,' I said.

He did, and he placed the new book in my hands, carefully, reverentially, and then he handed me the note that had been inside.

Dearest Jane,

Please find enclosed the finished copy of your debut novel OPEN YOUR EYES.

Isn't she beautiful????

I'm immensely proud to have worked on this with you and can't wait to see it in the shops. Let's hope it flies off the shelves and into the hands of your new readers!

Much love,
Ruth

I opened the book and flicked through the pages. Sure, the names were different, and I'd given the children slightly different ages, but other than that, everything was the same.

I looked up and Leon was smiling proudly.

'Well done, baby,' he said.

Leon's story had made it into print.

It's the book you're holding in your hands right now.

Acknowledgements

The author would like to thank the following people:

Frankie Gray, Jane Gregory, Stephanie Glencross, Corinna Barsan, Becky Short, Debbie Leatherbarrow, Zoe Lea and Lucy Hay.

Paula Daly is the critically acclaimed author of five novels. Her books have been sold in fifteen countries, shortlisted for the CWA Gold Dagger for Crime Novel of the Year award, and are currently being developed for television. She was born in Lancashire and lives in the Lake District with her husband, three children and whippet Skippy.

Just What Kind of Mother Are You?

Paula Daly

No family is as perfect as they seem.

A husband, three children and a full-time job, so many plates to keep spinning.

No wonder you forgot to pick up your friend's daughter.

No one's seen her since yesterday.

She's not the first to go missing from your small town.

Who's hiding something?

'Fiendishly addictive'
GUARDIAN

'The very definition of a page-turner'
ELIZABETH HAYNES

Keep Your Friends Close

Paula Daly

Your best friend isn't who you think she is.

You've been friends since university, when you became the people you are today.

You don't see each other enough but when you do it's as if you've never been apart.

She's one of the family. You would trust her with your life, your children, your husband.

And when your daughter is rushed to hospital, you're grateful that she's stepping in at home, looking after things.

But your best friend isn't who you think she is. You're about to find out just how wrong you were.

'Utterly gripping, fast paced, and scarily believable'
LESLEY PEARSE

'Deliciously dark and addictive. I defy anyone who starts it not to race through the pages until they reach the final, brilliant twist'
COLETTE MCBETH

The Mistake I Made

Paula Daly

We all think we know who we are. What we're capable of.

Roz is a single mother, a physiotherapist, a sister, a friend. She's also desperate.

Her business has gone under, she's crippled by debt and she's just had to explain to her son why someone's taken all their furniture away.

But now a stranger has made her an offer. For one night with her, he'll pay enough to bring her back from the edge.

Roz has a choice to make.

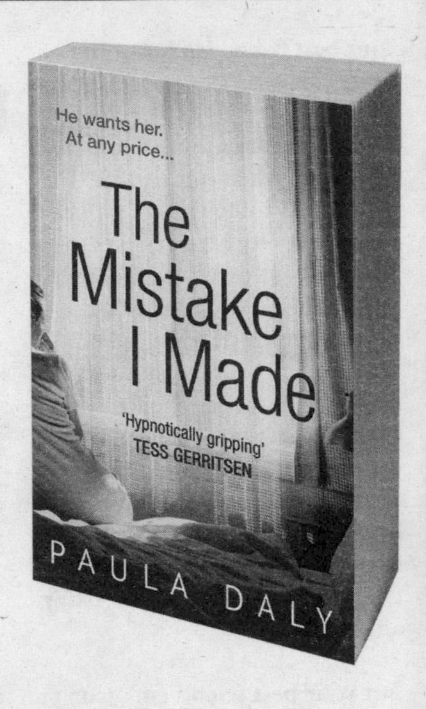

'A page-turning thriller with heart'
RENÉE KNIGHT

'A big-hearted, empathetic novel about ordinary lives and the tremors that can rock them'
GUARDIAN